THE GILDED SANCTUM

Keith Veverka

For Traci

PROLOGUE

Washington, D.C.
Present Day

Ryan Walker glanced one final time at the photograph on his smartphone as he entered the local mini-mart and heard the cowbell clang behind him. He busied himself at an aisle end cap displaying individually wrapped pastries and feigned interest in the nutritional information while watching a haggard man approach the counter. This man had attempted to run, attempted to hide, and attempted to escape from the inevitable, but now that Walker had found him, death was certain to follow.

Edward Collins. Accountant. Formerly of Hellerman & Associates in downtown D.C., one of the more prominent accounting firms on the East Coast. The photo on Walker's phone was a standard portrait from H&A — similar to any you'd find in the corporate world — with the subject neatly dressed in a suit and tie against a light blue background. With his perfectly sculpted hair and a matching smile, Collins appeared to be a rising star.

The early middle-aged man was now a shadow of his former self. He was disheveled, his blonde hair tousled, and he moved at an awkward pace as he peeked around nervously like his head was on a swivel. The smile from the photo was gone, replaced by a sour tension that wrinkled his freshly-worn face.

He wore expensive shoes and a fancy wool coat — a status symbol from another time — but inappropriate for the beautiful summer day, almost as if he was trying to disappear inside the oversized jacket. But there was no escaping from this. Collins had made a terrible mistake, and Walker was here to deliver the sentence.

Because of the warm coat and the weighty burden of fear, sweat cascaded from Collin's forehead, forcing him to push his wire-rim glasses back up onto his face, while struggling to carry the grocery bag in his arms as he exited the store and returned to his temporary home across the street. The dilapidated motel — built in the shape of a U around its parking lot — hadn't been cared for in years, and the weeds growing out of the parking lot's broken asphalt formed a root structure that snaked its way along the cracked and worn streets of this northern D.C. neighborhood. Urban renewal had yet to find its way to this section of the city, and it clearly wasn't a place for designer shoes. Collins obviously didn't belong here.

It was indeed a long way from his upscale condominium in Tysons Corner, but once Collins came to the conclusion that his lies had been discovered and his life was in danger, this was his only choice. With one last nervous glance, he quickly opened the burnt orange-colored door and hurried into the motel room. Walker stared at the aging building from the opposite sidewalk, picturing the frightened man immediately dead-bolting the flimsy door, believing he was somewhat protected from the evils of the outside world, safe in his temporary sanctuary. Nothing could be further from the truth.

Collins had succumbed to a typical human weakness and made the grave mistake of trading time for money. Many had done it before him with surprisingly similar results. Collins had forgotten that time was the one priceless commodity none of us could do without. He was blinded by a short-term investment, intrigued by the possibility of unimaginable wealth, but as people never quite seemed to understand in that moment of weakness, he wouldn't be taking his money with him.

Edward Collins had been a very good accountant, had worked for one of the most prestigious accounting firms in the country, and had enjoyed the opulent social class it provided.

He gave everything to his company in those early years, working the insane hours required for a young executive to climb the corporate ladder, stepping off on the thirtieth floor into a corner office. Life had been good. For a time. When the Great Recession hit and the economy tanked, his firm made cutbacks, and he was one of them.

However, Collins still had a family to care for, a wife accustomed to an affluent lifestyle. No one was hiring while the economy slowly recovered, so he entered into the employment of a very unsavory character: Lorenzo Arcuri. But Collins should have known better. Years earlier, his younger brother had worked for Arcuri as well, and after one of those jobs went bad, the younger Collins had been fished out of the Potomac with his throat slashed. Never able to hold down a steady job and in and out of Virginia's state prison system, Collins's brother had learned the hard way the downside of working for a criminal, especially one as relentless as Arcuri.

Lorenzo Arcuri was the head of an organized crime family, tethered in Washington D.C., but with tentacles throughout the country. By any standard, not just criminal, Arcuri was ruthless and cunning — the latest in a long line of such leaders for this family, a vast extension of the Italian mafia. Known for his bold moves against his enemies and even bolder taunts against law enforcement, he was a force to be reckoned with. His criminal activities touched on so many industries, it was difficult to keep track — even for the FBI — and his business interests were as diversified as any legitimate or criminal enterprise could hope to be.

Therefore, Arcuri needed accountants who could track, bury, and clean all of the money which flowed from his criminal empire into his legal front businesses. The lines had always been blurred, and so a skilled mathematician was very useful at making the operations look legit and keeping law enforcement at arm's length. Collins was well paid for his services, and in a short time was making more money than he had ever imagined, but he had also lost his perspective, forgotten about his dead brother, and gotten greedy.

Impressed by the grotesque amount of money being laundered by his own hand, he felt as though he rightly deserved a piece of it, and so he started to skim a little off the top for himself. With each transaction, a little more went into his pocket, and because he was good at what he did, the ruse lasted much longer than he expected. Although the amounts were insignificant to the overall haul being funneled into the Arcuri family fortune, it was still stealing. And in the eyes of Lorenzo Arcuri, stealing was unforgivable. No one made a selfish decision like that in Arcuri's empire.

So now, Edward Collins was on a list; a list from which you were only removed when you were dead. Most of the people on the list knew they were targets — knew they had made a mistake — so attempted all the usual methods of escape. But the family never forgets, and Arcuri hired Walker to track down these traitors and check them off the list.

Walker considered the grim nature of his work as he lumbered into his unwashed car parked on the street and threw his cell phone on the passenger seat. He glanced in the rearview mirror and the reflection of three-day-old stubble that covered his solidly framed cheeks and chin and his lengthening brown hair was much different than the close-cropped, clean-shaven look of his former life. His gray-colored eyes were sunken and bloodshot, and his lips were chapped. He hadn't slept well last night. Never slept well.

Walker knew that because he was the one who located these people, he was complicit in the judgment that had been issued. *Were these people guilty? Perhaps. Did it matter? No.* His only task was to find them. Thankfully, Walker didn't do the actual killing; he was not the executioner. But once a target had been found and the call had been made, the sentence was officially handed down. So in essence, he did kill them, just from a distance.

There was some relief in that not all of his assignments were like this; he didn't only work for Arcuri. Walker's other clients were mostly criminals, too, but Arcuri usually paid the most. It seemed like the personal cost of each case was commensurate with the salary, each successive job tearing away another piece of his soul. Following a cheating spouse or tracking down a runaway child was standard fare until Arcuri offered him the chance to be the hunter.

Walker called himself a private investigator, but he didn't have an office or a business card. He only learned of new clients through word of mouth, and he only worked for certain types of people. The criminal underworld was surprisingly well-connected in that respect. Without much deviation, his clients were wealthy and powerful, probably through illegal means, and so if they called upon Walker, his investigations needed to be discreet. His was not a 'shingle above the door' kind of operation, and in most cases, the people he tracked down ended up dead.

This was in stark contrast to his former life: a special agent with the FBI. Assigned to the Violent Crime Division after graduating from the Academy, his focus had been on kidnapping and child disappearance, a notoriously difficult area with its tragedies usually outweighing its successes, but he was determined to make a difference. After fifteen years stationed at the fast-paced FBI Field Office in Northwest Washington, covering the District of Columbia and several counties in northern Virginia, Walker had gained a wealth of experience and was highly respected for his work in the division

But that was before the mistake. The mistake that still haunted him. The alcohol dulled the screams, but only slightly. They were always there, just a little quieter sometimes — the whispers of the guilt he carried with him. He could not escape the eternal condemnation, even after all these years and in the company of these vile human beings. It was his personal Hell, and he was their fallen angel. Walker had honed his skills in the best law enforcement agency in the world, and now was merely a disgraced former agent with a much-needed skillset. He was their kind of guy, an investigator for hire who could find the people that could not be found by traditional means or under normal circumstances. This was his penance.

Walker looked down at the scattering of post-it notes and other documents — an investigator's jumbled collection of clues pieced together during his search for the subject — on the passenger seat. Staring back at him was a close-up photograph of Collins taken the day before, reminding Walker of himself. It showed Collin's left hand, devoid of any jewelry, only the circular band of untanned skin on the finger where his wedding ring had been. His mistake had already cost him dearly, his family obviously destroyed in the process, and Collins was now going to die alone and afraid. Walker wondered if he was eventually destined for the same fate.

He stared at the smartphone. *Was he going to make the call and send this man to his death? Was he ready to issue his death sentence?* Walker picked up the phone and paused. *What if he didn't make the call? Would they ever know? Probably not.* He could just pull away. *Sorry, I can't find him.*

Walker's head started to ache as the morning dullness was wearing off. He grabbed a nearly empty bottle from under his seat and took a long drink. The liquid was hot on his throat, but the pain quickly subsided as a wave of relief washed over him, quelling the tension in his temples. Walker debated his options as the headache was slowly numbed by the hard liquor. He tapped at the phone, inputting the address and room number. He hesitated again, glancing back at the crumbling structure across the street, but finally pushed 'send'. The ding of the sent text message rang in his ears.

Walker sighed heavily. *Too bad*, he thought. *But everyone makes choices. Collins simply made the wrong ones.* Walker understood terrible choices all too well. *We all have to live with the consequences. Sorry, Collins.* After several minutes, he put the vehicle in drive and pulled away.

CHAPTER 1

Potomac, Maryland
Two Months Later

Walker had been summoned by Lorenzo Arcuri to his sprawling family estate, situated on a series of lush green bluffs overlooking the Potomac River. He had only met the crime lord once — about nine months earlier — when his father had passed away suddenly and the forty-two-year-old inherited the family business. It was Lorenzo's father who had originally hired Walker many years before, and so the brief meeting in an abandoned warehouse outside of D.C. was simply to size up Walker and ensure his father had made the right choice.

Being the new head of the Arcuri crime family brought with it many responsibilities, and Lorenzo had to know that all in his employment could be trusted. To his credit, Walker had always delivered, and in the months since meeting Lorenzo, he continued his stellar record of success.

However, this wasn't the way it usually worked for new assignments. Three weeks had passed since his latest job — locating a corrupt banker in New York City — had ended. It was about right in terms of the timing, but new assignments had always come by way of one of Arcuri's lieutenants, never by Arcuri himself, and always in some obscure location, never at his estate. Until now. Walker was unsure of what to expect.

The Arcuri family estate was a collection of buildings, pools, and courts — both tennis and basketball — surrounded by a six-feet-high continuous white plaster wall. The ten-acre compound was undoubtedly the most noticeable structure on this section of the Potomac, yet few had ever been inside its walls. It was a highly-protected, highly-secure piece of property, so not just anyone could gain entry. The bulletproof Mercedes sedans and SUVs — the typical vehicles to enter and exit the compound — told much of the story.

The security wall had only one entrance, down a long drive, where a decorative black gate completed the perimeter. As the gates slowly opened, Walker was waved through by the unarmed guard who was stationed there. The tall gate and polite guard were the public's only view of the estate, but once inside the walls of the compound, Walker was quickly greeted by two men with weapons at their sides.

Like all of the security personnel stationed on the compound, they were well-dressed in expensive suits, well-armed with semi-automatic rifles, and well-fashioned with dark sunglasses, reminding Walker of the Secret Service. All of the men were former law enforcement or military who were fully licensed and capable of utilizing the weapons they brandished. Any assault on this compound by a rival crime lord or law enforcement agency would be met with stiff resistance. It was a tremendous show of force, certainly in line with Arcuri's reckless style, but perfectly legal under Maryland law.

The first security guard raised his hand, so Walker immediately stopped the car as the guard approached the driver's side window. The other guard circled around the right side of the car — assault weapon outstretched — looking around and underneath the car. Walker had already told the unarmed guard at the front gate his name, and that he was being expected, so these men were simply ensuring he was alone in the car and no kind of explosive device was immediately visible. For the man they were protecting, they could never be too careful.

The security guard made a quick glance at his partner, who nodded his approval, having made it to the rear of the car and completed his visual inspection. The guard brought his hand to his face, which held a tiny microphone and said something that was inaudible to Walker, who noticed the earpiece in the guard's right ear. After listening for a moment and acknowledging with a slight nod, he waved for Walker to proceed.

Walker nodded as he pulled through the checkpoint onto the main driveway toward the mansion, a structure near the center of the estate just shy of 10,000 square feet, built in a contemporary style with plenty of bedrooms, bathrooms, and natural light. The paved driveway continued to the front of the mansion, where it made a circle around a decorative collection of weeping willows, their branches nearly touching the ground. The evening sun cast a long shadow across the driveway as the final days of summer had given way to fall and the coolness in the air bristled through the trees. As he exited the vehicle, Walker admired the enormity of the mansion, but was still taken aback by the excess — the gaudiness of it all — although he assumed when you had that much money, you simply had to figure out ways to spend it.

Greeted at the front door by another security guard in a suit and sunglasses, he was immediately patted down. Walker knew to leave his handgun in the car as the unarmed guard had informed him that no weapons were allowed in the house. His .40 caliber Glock, the FBI's standard-issue firearm, was safely tucked away in the glovebox. Although no longer with the Bureau, Walker still believed it was the best choice of firearm, and quite honestly, the weapon reminded him of that life. The guard led him down a long hallway until he reached a curved entryway off to the left. Standing on the other side of the entrance, the guard gestured for Walker to enter, so he turned and found himself in what appeared to be the study.

It was a massive room, surrounded by large windows and custom, built-in bookshelves, alternating as they encircled the room. A broad wooden desk sat at the forefront of the room, in front of the main window, while two brown leather couches faced one another in the center of the room, a glass coffee table between them. A multistory pool and tennis court were visible outside the window, as well as several more armed guards scattered throughout the perfectly manicured grounds of the estate.

Being Walker's first time in this room and only the second time he had met Arcuri, he wondered why Arcuri would meet him in what appeared to be a formal gathering space. Walker glanced at the seating arrangement and thought, *What kinds of conversations took place there?* He imagined they were probably about life and death. *Why so formal, Lorenzo?*

Lorenzo Arcuri made his entrance through a door on the opposite side of the study, wearing a dark polo shirt and khaki pants that fit perfectly over his slender, athletic build. He held a drink in one hand and removed his Ray-Ban sunglasses with the other. The six-feet-tall Arcuri tossed the sunglasses onto a nearby table and ran his fingers through his distinguished head of slightly graying hair. Walker smiled to himself. Arcuri was one of the deadliest men in the entire country, but he played the role of dapper young playboy better than anyone.

Arcuri stopped and stood behind the sofa closest to him. He smiled and raised the glass. "Mr. Walker, welcome. I hear your last assignment was a success. Another traitor discovered."

"Yes, sir."

"Please, call me Lorenzo. I would say we're on a first-name basis by now, yes? You've done more for me than I could possibly thank you. I trust my payments are thanks enough." Arcuri gestured to the couch. "Please sit down."

"Yes. Very generous," Walker said as he cautiously settled into the leather couch.

Arcuri sipped his drink. "Can I offer you a drink, Ryan? Some brandy perhaps?" Arcuri pointed to a liquor counter in the corner of the room next to one of the tall bookshelves. Walker had noticed it when he first entered the room, and it appeared to be a great collection.

"No. Thank you," Walker responded.

"Are you sure? I have some twelve-year-old California over there. Very smooth."

Walker glanced again at the cabinet and smiled. "Thank you again, but no."

"Probably best." Arcuri nodded, as he sat down across from Walker.

Walker ignored the comment. *Was it that obvious? Probably. How much did Arcuri know about his drinking? His past? It didn't matter.* Walker didn't much care what Arcuri thought of him.

Changing the subject, Walker asked, "What can I do for you, Lorenzo?"

Arcuri settled back into the opposite couch, crossing his legs, and resting the glass on his knee. Walker could hear the ice cubes gently clink against the crystal, and then settle once again in the brown liquid. Arcuri sat still for several moments, choosing his words carefully. "You do incredible work, Ryan. Not everyone can do what you do. Perhaps not anyone."

"I wouldn't go that far. It's a lot of luck really. Just knowing when to follow the right lead."

"Instinct?" Arcuri mused.

"I suppose you could say that. But it's probably more experience than anything else."

Arcuri nodded in agreement. "Yes, experience. You certainly can't teach that. Or is it natural ability?"

Walker shrugged, unsure of the answer.

Arcuri suddenly got up from the couch and approached the desk. He stood for several moments in front of the desk with his back to Walker. Finally, he put down his drink, turned, and leaned on the desk with both hands.

"I need your experience right now, Ryan. Perhaps more than ever. This time it's personal." Arcuri paused for a moment, considering his next statement. "I'll pay you a great deal for this one. I would hate to lose you, but this could be enough for you to retire from this nasty business. It could all be over for you."

Walker leaned forward, intrigued by Arcuri's introduction to this new job.

"It's my daughter," Arcuri said, the emotion draining the

color from his face. "I haven't actually seen her in years. Her mother takes care of her, keeps her away from me, and I don't blame her. This is no place for a young girl. A young woman now, I suppose. I do send them money and keep tabs on them of course, but being far away from all of this is the best I can hope for. I have many enemies, and the less my enemies know about my family, the better. I'm sure you understand."

Walker nodded in agreement, surprised by Arcuri's acknowledgment of the danger inherent in this line of work, both for criminals and law enforcement. Although no one liked to admit the mortality of what they did, everyone knew full well that any day could be their last. Even scarier was the thought of their families being targeted and forced to pay with their lives for the wicked sins of the father.

It was an unthinkable scenario, but too often families became the collateral damage for poor decisions and unforgivable mistakes. Walker knew this all too well, keenly aware of the guilt he felt for not seeing his own daughter in years. Not by choice, but by circumstance. Just like Arcuri, it was better this way. But in Walker's case, it wasn't the dangers of a criminal enterprise or the many enemies at the gates. He was his own worst enemy, and for her own good, his daughter needed to be far away from him.

"She attends Washington Academy in Loudoun County," Arcuri said proudly.

"I know WA. Might just be the best private school in the country."

"Indeed, it is."

"What do you need, sir?"

"She disappeared. Two nights ago. From the school grounds. I was notified the next morning. The school has already done a full investigation. But nothing. Not a trace. She's simply vanished."

Walker sat upright. "Have you contacted the police?"

Arcuri crossed his arms. "No. I contacted you."

"Lorenzo, with all due respect, I don't think I can be of

any help to you. If I'm remembering Washington Academy correctly, they have a state-of-the-art security system, a full-time campus police staff, and a security chief. If they don't know what happened, there's really nothing I can offer you."

Arcuri, as if anticipating the hesitation, moved quickly toward Walker, and sat down again. "You're right about WA. It is state-of-the-art. The kids who attend Washington are, shall we say, the top one percent. Their families are enormously wealthy or powerful, or both. You have politicians, CEOs, and other business owners," he said with a slight grin, referring to himself. "They are very discreet and very protective, which is why we all send our kids there. And you're right, if there was something to be found, they would have found it."

Walker listened intently and nodded in agreement.

Arcuri leaned forward to make direct eye contact with Walker. "But that's why you're here. You're the best. You can track down people that others can't. You have a gift."

Walker shook his head, "Lorenzo, you don't understand. The people I find for you are trying to disappear, you see? They're trying to get off the grid, but in most cases, they're not career criminals. They have no tradecraft, so they make mistakes, lots of mistakes, and they're easy to track. I just follow the errors."

Arcuri attempted to speak, but Walker continued. "But a disappearance, or a kidnapping, I would need the resources of the local or state police or the FBI, access to records, entry to locations. I simply don't have the support. I'm no longer..."

Arcuri stopped him by raising his hand in the air. "Ryan, that's exactly why I need you." He spoke slowly. "You have the instincts. You'll be able to see what others don't. And you're not law enforcement anymore, so that protective shield that the people at Washington Academy pride themselves on might bend a little, maybe to the point where they actually put their guard down and give you more than they were ever willing to give. They won't fear you. Do you understand? You may be the only one who is able to get past their walls...literally and figuratively."

Walker pondered the thought for a moment, staring at the floor. *Arcuri could be right*. Washington Academy was indeed famous for its academic program, but also notorious for its relatively closed society — an exclusive club to which few could enter. WA did pride itself on its secretiveness, which is why the rich and powerful sent their kids there, but perhaps they *would* let their guard down with him, knowing they had nothing to fear from a washed-up former agent. *And did they have anything to fear? Probably not*. Walker looked up and shook his head again. "I don't know."

Rising from his seat and walking over to his desk again, Arcuri said, "I'm actually acquainted with the dean of the school, Robert Ellis. He and my father did business together, and you would not believe the amount of money I give to that school each year beyond the tuition. I think they may have named a building or two after me by now. I do all of this for a reason of course. Because I know that one day I may need something from them. And this is one of those times."

"You've already spoken with him?" Walker asked.

"Yes," said Arcuri, with a smirk. "I've already arranged for you to visit the campus and start your own investigation into my daughter's disappearance. The dean has agreed for you to stay on campus for three days and conduct your inquiry. He's promised full cooperation from himself, his security team, and any students or faculty you deem of interest.

Arcuri moved toward Walker to close the deal. "I need you, Ryan. I need you to find my little girl. I need you to bring her back to me."

Walker sighed. "Lorenzo, I've done this for a long time. You need to contact the police or bring in the FBI. That's the only way you're going to get your daughter back. I'm sure you know the odds. The first couple of hours are crucial. It's been two days. Any trail that might have been there has gone cold by now. If I am able to find her, I'm afraid it's not going to be good news."

Arcuri sat down again, still leaning forward. "I understand. I truly do. I know the statistics. But as you and I both know, Washington Academy is its own little world, so the idea of some lunatic or pedophile from the outside entering the campus and abducting my daughter is very unlikely. I can assure you that nothing happens at WA without those in charge knowing about it. That's why I've instructed them to not contact the police or FBI. I need this to be low-profile. I know the answers are there, somewhere on that campus. I just need someone to find them."

"But the police can bring so much more manpower to bear, Lorenzo."

Arcuri leaned back. "Think about what you just said. How many officers would be involved? How many news outlets would be notified? I don't want a gaggle of volunteers traipsing through the woods calling out her name. If word of this gets out, I could have enemies at my doorstep, trying to exploit me while I'm vulnerable, pretending they have my daughter to exact some revenge." He paused, pondering the unthinkable. "But if one of my enemies does actually have her, and I'm about to receive a ransom demand or an ultimatum, I need to be in a position of power. I need to be informed, so I can put my apparatus to work. You need to either bring me back my daughter, or help me to understand what happened, so I can better fight whatever enemy this might be." Walker listened intently as Arcuri made his final offer. "Again, my payout will only be exceeded by my gratitude, and if you want to retire from this life, that will finally be available to you."

Thoughts were racing through Walker's mind so quickly he could barely keep up. To any objective observer, his life was in shambles, and he would probably be dead from his own self-destructive behavior or an executioner's bullet before long anyway. *Was this his way out? A way back?* But everything he just told Arcuri was also true. He had no resources, no support, and no ability to solve a missing persons case in three days. *Would he be the newest addition to Arcuri's list if he failed? Fine by me. That was also a way out.*

Walker stared at Arcuri, could see the sadness in his eyes, the determination in his brow. Aside from all the havoc this crime lord had wrought upon the world, Arcuri was still a father, and Walker could relate. Although he hadn't seen his own daughter in years, if he was in the same situation, he would move heaven and earth to find her. This must have been unbearably frustrating for Arcuri. An entire empire at his disposal, which he could mobilize at a moment's notice or take action on a whim, but he was completely helpless to find his own daughter. Walker was his only chance.

But he had learned some sad truths in the FBI, had attempted to console too many grieving parents. Mothers and fathers weren't supposed to lose their children. At the very least, all they could ask for — all they craved — was some kind of explanation, something which brought a small semblance of sanity back to their lives. Parents needed to know the reason why their child was no longer with them. The most Walker could hope for was that he could give Lorenzo Arcuri a reason why his daughter was gone. Give him some closure. It was the least he could do for this father.

After several moments of silence, while he struggled with his shifting thoughts, Walker reached out his hand to shake Arcuri's. "I'll do what I can, Lorenzo, I promise you."

Lorenzo was seemingly surprised by Walker's sudden reversal, but more than happy to return the gesture, pleased with his private investigator's tacit agreement. Arcuri grabbed his hand and shook it tightly. "Thank you, Ryan. I know you will."

CHAPTER 2

Washington, D.C.
Six Years Earlier

FBI Special Agent Ryan Walker smiled at the applause. He peered out into the crowded auditorium, locating his wife and daughter seated in a row near the front. Walker sat on a small folding chair on the stage as the FBI Director recounted the great investigative work and unparalleled courage of Agent Walker.

It was a special day for the FBI, and the main auditorium at the J. Edgar Hoover Building in NW Washington was packed with audience members. The countless television and flashing hand-held cameras in the back of the hall captured the historic moment. The sound of the clicking cameras was only overpowered by the Director's voice, echoing through the auditorium's speakers, as he spoke from the center of the stage at a podium emblazoned with the FBI seal.

"Awarded for extraordinary and exceptional achievements in connection with criminal or national security cases," the Director stated, "the FBI Medal for Meritorious Achievement is being presented today to Special Agent Ryan Walker of the Washington Field Office. As you might remember, this case did not have a high probability of success, but because of the actions of Agent Walker, we returned a child to his family."

The Director recounted the thrilling story for the audience, while Walker was deep in thought, remembering the ebb and flow of the case that had grabbed international headlines and captivated the country for a week. A congressman's ten-year-old son had been abducted by a disgruntled former aide who had been fired for inappropriate behavior. Seeking revenge, the mentally unstable aide kidnapped the Congressman's son on his way to school and demanded a $3 million ransom and safe passage out of the country, or he would kill the boy.

The kidnapping fell under the purview of the Washington Field Office, and Walker was assigned the case. Relying on his many years of experience and some painstaking investigative techniques, he was able to track the assailant and his victim to a small hunting cabin in the Shenandoah Valley. Walker brought in the field office's SWAT team to surround the location while they started their negotiations. After several hours of fruitless progress, the negotiations started to break down and the assailant became extremely agitated. Walker made the fateful decision for the SWAT team to breach the cabin, and in a matter of moments, they had killed the kidnapper and rescued the child.

It was an unprecedented public success for the Bureau, which so often did its best work behind the scenes and was usually unable to tout its wins to the general public. Since Walker was instrumental in that success and with the nation's attention still captivated by the positive outcome, the FBI wanted to bask in the glory, bringing the entire episode to a dramatic close by presenting the medal to Walker in the packed auditorium.

As the Director finished his remarks and presented the honorary medal to Walker, the room was illuminated by camera flashes and deafened by a cacophony of camera shutters. This continued for several minutes as Walker, wearing his medal proudly, made his way to the podium for a brief speech. He relished the moment. Although never required, his many years of hard work were being rewarded, and he now felt as though he was a symbol of sorts for all the men and women who worked tirelessly every day in the Department of Justice. Walker wisely knew it would be a fleeting moment, but he would enjoy it nonetheless.

While speaking from the podium, Walker thanked everyone involved with the case, and specifically commended the bravery and courage of his field office's SWAT team. As he spoke, he reflected on how much the SWAT team had impressed him with their professionalism, precision, and perfect composure under stress. In his years as an agent, he had certainly interacted with the SWAT team, but he had never depended on them so completely as he had for the favorable outcome at the hunting cabin. He knew the agents, worked alongside them, but never realized the extent to which they went beyond the call of duty.

Each of the FBI's fifty-six field offices across the county maintained their own SWAT teams. These teams weren't quite as prestigious as the FBI Hostage Rescue Team, the full-time SWAT team based in Quantico, Virginia, but they were as good a special weapons and tactics force as you would find anywhere in the world. These SWAT teams were composed of agents from each respective field office, who did this on a part-time basis in addition to their regular duties and would be called upon for high-risk events such as hostage rescues or barricade situations.

As Walker looked out into the audience, finding his wife and daughter again, he was proud of what he had accomplished in his fifteen years as an agent but decided it was time for a new challenge, a way to give back to the agency that had given him so much. He was excited about what was to come, not only to increase his own law enforcement experience but also to undertake something he felt could make a real difference. And so, as Ryan Walker stood at that podium, thankful for what he was a part of, he decided to join the FBI's SWAT team.

***

Special Agent Walker, his wife Nicole, and seven-year-old daughter, Elise, crossed the plush interior courtyard of the Hoover building, making their exit from FBI Headquarters. After shaking lots of hands and posing for multiple pictures, the Walker family had finally gotten to leave the auditorium. The three walked together, Nicole holding Elise's hand as they descended the steps. In her other hand, Elise swung the medal in circles by its patriotic-colored lanyard.

"Be careful with your dad's medal, sweetheart," Nicole said. "He worked really hard for that."

Walker smiled at Nicole as he watched his daughter swing the precious piece of medal in circles. "No worries. I think I can order a replacement if it gets broken."

Nicole nudged her husband and smiled back. "Stop it. This is not just a piece of jewelry, honey. You did something very special. You brought that child back to his parents. You should be very proud of yourself. I'm very proud of you."

Walker grinned and winked at his wife. "Thanks, babe. I know it's important. We do good work here. People don't always realize it, but we do really good work."

Nicole stared at her husband for a moment and then looked forward. "I know. I never thought I would be married to a man in law enforcement. Too many sleepless nights. Waiting for that knock at the door." Nicole shuddered. "But I always had faith in you. Faith that you would always do the right thing. Do your duty. No matter what."

"You know I will."

"Just please promise me something," she said with pleading eyes. "Please be careful. Please don't ever take unnecessary risks." Nicole looked away again and glanced at the swinging medal. "I don't ever want to be given a medal because you're not there to receive it."

Walker put his arm around his wife and pulled her closer to him. "You know I'm always careful. I'll always be there for you. I promise." Walker decided he would not mention the SWAT team decision now. He would save that for another time. It would certainly cause some tension between them, but it would ultimately be a good thing, he reasoned to himself.

Nicole looked at her husband with a mixture of fear and relief in her eyes. She scanned his face to ensure he was telling her the truth. "I know. I love you."

"I love you," he said, suddenly reaching down and picking up Elise, who in her surprise, dropped the medal. Walker caught it by the lanyard and placed it around her neck, while still carrying her. "And I love you," he said, as he planted a kiss on her cheek. "Thanks for carrying dad's medal, sweetheart. It looks great on you."

Elise wrapped her arms around her father's neck and squeezed. "You're my hero, daddy, and you always will be."

CHAPTER 3

Walker glanced at the worn medal in the center console. *A lifetime ago.* He hadn't touched it in years, just left it in the car's console as a reminder of what life had once been. It had actually saved his life many times since then when he felt like using the Glock in his glove box on himself. Looking at the medal always brought him back to the positive memories of the FBI and the happy moments with his family.

Elise was thirteen now, and he hadn't spoken to her in four years but convinced himself it was for the best. He wouldn't know the first thing to say, and he wondered if she would even recognize him in his current state of deterioration. Although he had shaved this morning and dressed in a freshly-pressed button-down and khakis to give his audience a serious first impression, deep down it was all a facade. He wasn't the same man he was when that medal was presented to him. So much had changed. So much had been lost. It was simply better that his daughter didn't know him like this.

Turning off the highway onto a long, winding road, Walker's vehicle crested a slight hill, and the private school campus came into view. It was just past dawn, so the warm sunrise cast a golden hue on the ornate iron archway, emblazoned with a decorative crest and the words 'Washington Academy', which connected two red brick pillars, forming the main entrance. It was a stunning sight, fitting for an institution with this kind of storied and distinguished past.

Washington Academy was founded in 1805, one of the

earliest private academies in Virginia, started by an endowment from the Becker family, originally from the Tidewater region of the state. Tracing its roots to the original settlers to the New World, the Becker family had made its fortune in tobacco and cotton, a family business passed down through generations. The most recent patriarch of the family in the early 1800s was Augustus Becker, a budding entrepreneur and politician from Richmond, constantly looking for new opportunities in either business or politics.

He found both with the establishment of Washington, D.C. and the growing federal government taking shape there in 1800. Augustus imagined that many politicians and businessmen would soon be relocating to the District of Columbia, with the hopes of sending their children to an esteemed preparatory school. Always the prescient, Augustus was correct, and Washington Academy was born. Named after the new capital city, with its burgeoning supply of sons and daughters from the wealthiest and most powerful families in the nation, Washington Academy quickly became home to the rising young class of America's elite.

One of the oldest continually operating private schools in the country, Washington Academy still enjoyed the largest endowments of any private institution in America and remained an independent, non-denominational school since its inception. Catering to the highest social class in the country, Washington quickly garnered a reputation for its superior academic program as well as its penchant for secrecy.

The yearly tuition, far beyond the reach of most average American families, was paying for both. And the results were impeccable. Nearly all attendees to WA, so long as they followed the rigid guidelines set forth by the Board of Trustees and remained with the program all four years, attended Ivy League schools, and the cycle of wealth and power continued.

Washington's current enrollment in grades 9-12 was just over 700 students. The bucolic campus covered over 100 wooded acres, with the student dormitories and academic buildings spread artistically throughout the grounds. The nine-teenth-century restored structures combined with the modern facilities gave the campus a traditional yet modern feel, which easily rivaled the nearby college campuses. Expansive athletic fields, a three-story library, and an original Virginia mansion completed the picture of one of the most prestigious, expensive, and successful schools in the country.

Becker had originally purchased the land on which Washington Academy was located, a hillside hamlet just northwest of Washington, D.C. in Loudoun County, Virginia, for mere pennies on the dollar. The sleepy suburb with its rolling hills, horse farms, and rich agriculture was known as a breadbasket during the American Revolution and home to John Mosby's partisan raiders during the American Civil War. It remained a quiet and rural stretch of land until the early 1960s when the construction of Dulles Airport in Sterling, Virginia led to rapid development and a population boom, literally transforming Loudoun County into a bedroom community overnight. And through it all, Washington Academy had remained a fixture in the county.

Walker pulled up to the front gate and was greeted by one of the security personnel for the campus, an embroidered crest underscored with the words 'Campus Security' located above his pocket and on his sleeve. He smiled at Washington Academy's similarities to the Arcuri estate, just across the Potomac River.

"Ryan Walker," he said as the guard leaned down to the open driver's side window.

The officer glanced down at his clipboard. "Yes, sir. I have you right here. Welcome to Washington Academy."

"Thank you," he said but wasn't so sure.

The guard handed him an orange visitor tag for his rear-view mirror. "Here is your visitor tag, Mr. Walker. It's good until the 28th." *Three days.* "Dr. Ellis is awaiting your arrival. His office is in the administration building, just go straight ahead on Main and take your first right on Locust. I will call ahead and let him know you've arrived."

Walker thanked him again, and the campus security officer slipped back into a small, brick enclosure, which matched the brick façade of the front gate, and placed a call to the administration building. Walker drove under the opulent archway and entered the private school campus.

The short drive to the administration building was breathtaking. Beautifully sculptured walkways meandered through a sea of trees, winding their way across the decorated grounds of the campus. The leaves on the deciduous trees had just started to change color with the early onset of fall, so soft shades of red, orange, and yellow added an additional glow to the already sparkling sheen of the campus. Students glided along the pathways, carrying their backpacks, talking with friends, ensconced by the beauty of academia. It seemed like the ideal location. *How could this place be the scene of a crime?* Walker thought.

He parked his car in a small lot directly in front of an impressive three-story, nineteenth-century building that had been beautifully restored. The red brick mansion was encircled by a white wraparound porch, with a large set of concrete steps leading up to the entrance. A sign in the ground, just to the right of the building, was engraved with the words 'Augustus Hall – Administration Building' just above the Washington Academy crest.

Walker admired the building as he made his way to the front entrance, complete with a huge wooden door and traditional door handles. He glanced at a golden plaque just to the side of the entrance which read '1805' and thought this was perhaps the first building on the campus. The school had certainly grown a lot since then and was modern in every way, but here on this wraparound porch with the splintered wooden door, he felt like he had stepped back into history.

Washington Academy, it seemed to Walker, was about as far removed from the fast-paced and crowded streets of D.C. as you could get, and it was as stunning as anything he had ever seen. *No wonder it was closed off from the rest of the world.* Here, it was its own little utopia, a perfect society unto itself. But Walker had read enough dystopian novels to know that if something appears too good to be true, it usually is. And he was sure Washington Academy, amidst all of its splendor, also had its share of secrets.

CHAPTER 4

Walker peered at the building directory — a tiny rectangular board with a gray background and white magnetic letters — as he entered Augustus Hall and found the Dean's Office located on the third floor: Suite 301. There was an elevator to his left, but he decided to take the stairs instead. Upon reaching the third floor and opening the heavy wooden door to Suite 301, he entered a smaller room than he expected, which had been converted into a lobby.

A Persian rug covered the hardwood floors and historic prints in thick frames decorated the walls. Off to his right was a wooden desk with a pretty, young receptionist, and to his left were four high-backed chairs, which appeared to be authentic pieces from the same time period as the building. He gave the receptionist his name and settled into the closest chair to the only other door in the room, which bore a nameplate engraved with the name and title: Dr. Robert Ellis, Washington Academy Dean.

Two of the paintings in the room immediately caught Walker's eye. The first was a large portrait of Augustus Becker, which hung next to the dean's office door, and the second was a Civil War print of John Singleton Mosby, serious and straight-faced, hanging above the receptionist. He stared at the Mosby painting for a few moments, and the receptionist gave him a stern look, probably thinking he was looking at her. He smiled back.

Living and working in Virginia, a state rich in history,

Walker was a weekend history buff, traveling to battlefields and historical sites as often as he could. He immediately recognized Mosby, who had always been popular in this area of the state. Also known as the Gray Ghost, Mosby was a Confederate cavalry commander who operated his partisan ranger unit out of Northern Virginia. During the war, Mosby's Rangers, as they had come to be known, conducted highly successful raids against the Union Army, disrupting communication and supply lines with near impunity.

When the conflict finally ended and the onset of guerilla warfare was a likely scenario, Mosby was one of the last Confederate officers convinced to surrender. Today there were as many as thirty-five monuments and markers in Northern Virginia dedicated to the actions of his rangers. This area of Virginia, in fact, was still known as Mosby's Confederacy. Even the Loudoun County High School mascot in Leesburg, Virginia was the *raider*. Walker chuckled to himself as he realized these two paintings represented Loudoun County's prodigal sons.

The far door suddenly swung open, and Dr. Ellis entered the lobby. The dean of Washington Academy was only about 5'8", but his presence was looming. By exuding incredibly calming confidence combined with a rational, learned demeanor, Ellis simply commanded a room. He was dressed in a perfectly tailored three-piece suit, capped off by his full head of white hair, expertly styled, without a strand out of place. There was no mistake; when you were in the presence of Richard Ellis, he was in charge.

"Mr. Walker." He said loudly as he stretched out his hand.

Walker leaped from the low seat and shook the hand while still in a crouching stance. "Dr. Ellis. Glad to meet you."

"And a pleasure to meet you, sir," Ellis said, looking directly into Walker's eyes as he finally stood upright, although Walker was now three inches taller.

Ellis turned on his back foot and motioned with his left hand toward his office. "Please, come inside."

Walker entered the spacious office, a room much larger

than the lobby, adorned with a masterfully restored mahogany desk, tall bookshelves, and large bay windows that overlooked the campus. The space took Walker's breath away for a moment.

Two brown leather chairs — similar to the ones in the lobby but smaller — sat in front of the desk, the one on the left already taken by a Hispanic gentleman, who was well over six feet, with his arm and chest muscles bulging through his tight polo shirt. His black hair was slicked back and his goatee was neatly trimmed. He immediately rose from his seat with an outstretched hand.

Ellis, entering behind Walker, put his arms on the newcomer's shoulders and said, "This is Joaquin Castillo, Washington Academy's Security Chief. I've asked him to join us because of the circumstances, of course. He's a former CID agent."

Walker was familiar with the United States Army Criminal Investigation Command, usually abbreviated as just CID, which harkened back to the original Criminal Investigation Division that was formed during World War I. USACIDC was headquartered at the Marine Corps Base in Quantico, Virginia, just minutes from the FBI Academy.

CID special agents, who actually did their training at the Academy, investigated felony crimes and any serious violations of military law within the United States Army. However, jurisdiction over certain national security crimes — such as espionage, treason, or terrorism — resided with U.S. Army Counterintelligence and the FBI, so joint investigations between the two happened frequently.

Walker shook hands with Castillo, who did not say a word. It was a tight grip and went on for several seconds. The eye contact with his deep brown eyes was penetrating. *A head of security with a military investigative background? You can't do much better than that,* Walker thought to himself.

Dean Ellis moved behind his desk, and all three gentlemen sat in the comfortable chairs simultaneously.

"I must say, Mr. Walker," Ellis began, looking directly at him. "Your reputation precedes you. The young man you found,

Billy Suffolk, a few years ago. He was actually a former student here. A very good student as I recall. Quite a happy ending. Very admirable."

Walker acknowledged the compliment, picturing the medal in his car. "Thank you, sir. It was a long time ago."

Ellis nodded. "Indeed."

A few moments of silence lingered until Walker broke it. "I want to thank you for allowing me a few days to investigate the disappearance of Mr. Arcuri's daughter. He very much appreciates your willingness to open your doors for me."

Ellis leaned back in the chair, comfortable with his position. "Absolutely. Anything for Lorenzo. His father and I had been friends for many years. I was so sad to hear of his passing."

"Of course," Walker agreed.

Ellis retained his solemn expression as he pointed to Castillo. "Joaquin and I are as mystified as anyone as to Miss Amanda Bryson's whereabouts. As you know, we take security very seriously here, and for one of our students to disappear from our own campus, it's simply unfathomable."

Realizing that Amanda used her mother's maiden name as her last name, Walker wondered how many faculty and students actually even knew who her father was. "I know. Disappearances are very difficult for all involved."

Ellis peered at Walker, seeming to try and decide what he could and should say, choosing his words carefully. "We've kept this disappearance very quiet thus far, but I'm not sure how much longer that will last. We pride ourselves on our privacy here. It's one of the reasons parents decide to send their children to us, so no information has been released to the media as of yet. We prefer to keep it that way. We are a very close-knit community, Mr. Walker, so we see no need why the general public needs to be informed of this disappearance. I'm sure you understand."

Walker nodded.

"However," Ellis continued, "our faculty is very much on edge. We've tried to keep them as informed as possible, but unfortunately, we simply don't know enough. As for the students, we've been trying to keep them calm as well, even fabricated a story about Amanda going home to visit her parents to quell some of the questions, but the rumors are starting to swirl and the tension on campus is definitely palpable."

"I see," Walker stated flatly.

Ellis turned to Castillo, who hadn't yet spoken a word. "I've had Joaquin prepare a case file for you on Miss Bryson. Everything we have from our own investigation. Perhaps with your keen eye, you can discover something that has eluded us."

"Yes, that's good. Thank you," Walker said, giving a nod to Castillo, who remained expressionless.

"It appears you have a multitude of cameras on campus," Walker said, gesturing out the window behind Ellis. "I will need to have a look at that footage."

"Of course," Ellis announced. "Joaquin will give you a complete tour of our security center and provide you with all of the relevant camera footage of Miss Bryson." Ellis paused for a moment and then continued, "In fact, we've decided to give you complete access to the entire campus — save for our security center which only Mr. Castillo and our technicians have access to — for the duration of your three days with us. Joaquin will provide you with a keycard."

Walker was surprised by the generous offer of a keycard that worked for every building on campus, so he nodded his head in immediate agreement.

"We've also arranged for you to stay in one of our residential housing units for these couple days," Ellis said. "Some of our full-time faculty live in these units, which increases their presence on the campus. Once Joaquin has shown you our security apparatus, I will arrange for a student ambassador to show you to your housing unit. I trust the accommodations will be satisfactory to you."

Walker nodded again. "That sounds wonderful. Thank you, Dr. Ellis." Arcuri had told Walker he would be staying on campus for several days, which made sense to Walker as it would allow him more time to be close to the case. He had packed a small suitcase with a change of clothes and some toiletries and was somewhat looking forward to the slight reprieve from his lonely, dark apartment for a few days.

Ellis stood, and Walker and Castillo quickly followed. Ellis extended his hand to Walker. "Whatever you need, Mr. Walker, please don't hesitate to ask. We desperately want to find Amanda and put an end to this nightmare that has overshadowed our school. We truly hope you can help us."

They shook hands. "I'll do what I can, sir. Thank you."

Walker turned and suddenly noticed that Castillo had already walked to the back of the room and was holding the office door open for him. Walker made his way to the exit, and as he passed Castillo, the security chief finally spoke with a slight smile, "Now you're entering my world."

CHAPTER 5

Just across the lobby from the Dean's office was an elevator. Both Castillo and Walker entered, and Castillo pushed the button for the basement. *A subterranean level security center?* Walker thought sarcastically. *Perfect.*

No words were exchanged between the two former law enforcement officers on the brief elevator ride to the lower level of the administrative building. The doors hadn't opened yet, but Walker imagined this was going to be quite an operation. He had heard the rumors, knew the reputation, but now that he had met Castillo, the architect behind this security apparatus, he understood. Former military police. *Made perfect sense.*

The elevator doors swung open to a long hallway with nineteenth-century paneling on the walls and a decorative carpet lining the walkway, remnants of the original building. However, at the end of the hallway was a bright pane of translucent glass, clearly a twenty-first-century addition to the historic structure. It covered the entire end of the hallway with a barely visible outline of a door in the center, almost as if it had been precisely cut out of the cloudy glass. Next to the outline of the door was a single black keypad.

As the two made their way toward the glowing light, Castillo removed a keycard from his pocket. Walker glanced from side to side, noticing several doors along the way. They were the traditional wooden doors like he had seen in the rest of the building, but these handles had been replaced with black keypads, similar to the one up ahead on the gray glass. He figured only Castillo's keycard worked for these doors as well.

Having reached the pane of translucent glass at the end of the hallway, Castillo waved his keycard in front of the keypad, and the door slid open with a *whoosh*. Cold air rushed from behind the glass, nudging Walker back slightly. Castillo stretched out his arm, welcoming Walker to enter the enclosure. Walker stepped across the threshold and was amazed at what he saw.

Three successive counters, cluttered with computers and monitors, formed a semicircle toward the front of the room, which was dominated by four large screens, projecting the Washington Academy campus in real-time and living color. With this vast collection of surveillance equipment, this room could easily be mistaken for the security center of a small city. Although there was space for more, only two men and one woman worked at the monitors, clicking at their keyboards, and did not make eye contact with Walker or even acknowledge his presence. *Well-trained soldiers*, he thought.

According to the monitors and screens, the campus was alive with activity. Walker was so preoccupied with the colorful screens, he did not even notice Castillo enter the room behind him and the door automatically close. "You may want to wear a coat down here from now on," Castillo said with a chuckle as he moved past Walker. "We have to keep the temperature low for all of this equipment." Walker noticed Castillo, in his collared polo, was not even bothered by the cold.

Walker suddenly felt the chill, penetrating between his button-down and undershirt. The sweat from the dean's office started to freeze on his skin, and he shivered. He quickly snapped out of the trance, rubbed his arms through the long sleeves, and turned to follow his tour guide. Castillo went to the back of the room and sat in an executive leather chair located in a small cubicle in the far right corner of the space. There was a smaller seat nearby, so Walker rolled it over and sat, now having a complete view of the entire room and all its visual candy.

"Quite an operation," Walker stated, obviously impressed.

"Yes, it is," Castillo responded, smiling. "Cutting edge. Completely digital. Motion sensors. Face-recognition software. We see everything."

Castillo pulled a drawer from a filing cabinet built into the cubicle and removed a file. He flipped it open in front of Walker and pushed it toward him. Inside was a stack of papers, stapled together, with what appeared to be a small rectangular keycard on top. Castillo removed the access card, revealing Amanda Bryson's senior portrait, which was paper clipped to the first page of the file. She was an attractive young woman. Her milky white skin, outlined by her shoulder-length dark hair, was flawless, and her high cheekbones resembled those of her father's. Amanda's piercing green eyes stared back at Walker as if beckoning him to find her.

"Here is our case file for Amanda Bryson," Castillo said. "Everything we have from our investigation. Schedules, demographics, personal information." He paused for a moment, then continued. "Confidential personal information."

Walker looked inquisitively at the file and started to flip through its pages.

"We can gather a lot of personal data about our students through our surveillance, keycard, and computer systems, Mr. Walker, but under no circumstances is this information to be shared with anyone. Is that understood?" Castillo said.

Walker nodded in agreement, not looking at Castillo, still engrossed in the content of the file. "This information is only used for situations like these," Castillo said flatly. "I know what you're thinking, but don't. If it helps us find Amanda, you'll be glad we had it."

Walker nodded again. He understood that most of this information was probably collected illegally and would not have been agreed to as part of any application or security form. But Castillo was right, it might be the only thing that enabled Walker to find Amanda, and he was no longer with law enforcement, so for now, he was just fine with it.

As Walker acquiesced to the benefits of his surveillance system, Castillo smiled, settled back in his chair, and twisted the keycard in his hand. "So, based on our video feeds, the last known location of Miss Bryson was just outside of Mavis Hall, the girls' dormitory, at approximately 7:13 PM, just over sixty hours ago."

Walker looked up from the file and refocused on a digital monitor in the cubicle, where Castillo projected the last known images of Amanda. The video image was captured from in front of the girl's dorm by a camera that appeared to be about twenty feet from the entrance. Everything appeared to be normal — girls entering and leaving the building — business as usual. Then, from the left corner of the screen, Amanda Bryson entered the frame.

"There." Castillo gestured.

Walker stared at the screen as Amanda came into full view. He easily recognized her from the picture. She was moving at a leisurely pace, wearing a long pink sweater over tight black pants. On her shoulder was a backpack with red and gray stripes, and she was texting on her iPhone as she walked. Making her way across the walkway, she used her keycard to open the main doors, and entered Mavis Hall. Castillo paused the feed, and the time stamp on the still image of Amanda entering the dorm read 19:13. *Military time.*

He stared at the young girl entering the dormitory as nonchalantly as any student returning home after a day of classes. She appeared calm and everything around her seemed perfectly normal. Nothing was out of the ordinary. Castillo let the video run for a few more seconds to drive home the point that nothing suspicious was happening at the time. It was obvious that Amanda was not in distress — she was not moving in a hurried fashion, she was not being chased, she was not looking around nervously. Her entrance into the dormitory was normal in every way.

"So that's the last we see of her? There's no footage of her leaving the dorm?" Walker asked.

"No," Castillo said quickly, still staring at the screen.

"Could she have avoided the cameras?"

"Possibly"

"How possible?"

"Not likely."

"Did anyone see her?"

"Yes. Her roommate, Heather Yates, says she left the dorm around 9 PM, but we have no footage of her exiting the building at that time or any other time."

"Where was she going?"

"Roommate says she was going to see her boyfriend, but he claims he never saw her that night. He wasn't supposed to either."

"Who's the boyfriend?"

"Josh Easterly. We'll talk with him later."

"Both their stories check out?"

"As far as we can tell, everything checks out."

Castillo tapped on the keyboard in front of him and a map of the campus projected on the monitor screen. It was not an aerial photo, but rather a white and gray map of small blocks, surrounded by large areas of green, obviously created by the marketing department as a user-friendly map of the campus, which probably appeared on signs throughout the campus.

He pointed to a quad area, surrounded on three sides by a building, on the northern edge of the map. "This is Mavis Hall — her dorm," he said and then moved his finger about two hundred yards to the south, according to the map's key, to a similar quad, "and this is the boys' dorm. Ninety percent of the students who attend Washington Academy board on campus, so these two residence halls house most of our students. We've checked the video footage for this entire route multiple times, but again, nothing."

Walker gave an incredulous look at Castillo. "That's it? That's all you have? Two million dollars in security cameras, and that's all you have? A girl walking into her dorm in broad daylight. I thought you said you see everything." Walker said, sarcastically.

Castillo looked perturbed. "Two and a half million dollars actually. And you're right, we do see everything. But just having the cameras doesn't guarantee it's catching everything. Anyone that has spent a few hours on campus knows where we have our cameras and knows what they can see. Avoiding our camera system, Mr. Walker, although difficult, isn't impossible."

"You think someone knew what the cameras wouldn't be able to see?"

"That's one theory."

Walker sighed and looked back at the monitor, still paused on the entrance to the residence hall.

"And you checked all of your footage after this?"

"Indeed. Everything. We used our face recognition software first, and when that didn't turn up anything, we went through all of it by hand. Painstaking. Thorough. But still nothing."

Walker wished there was more. Something to go on. He was ready to ask more questions when his phone vibrated, indicating a voicemail had been left. It probably hadn't rung because he was below ground, but the notification had somehow gotten through. He pulled the phone from his pocket and immediately recognized the contact. Unfortunately, he wouldn't be able to listen to the voicemail until he was above ground, but it was obviously important.

Walker replaced the phone in his pocket, closed the case file, and lied. "I'd like to review the case file before we tour the campus and talk to any witnesses if that's okay?"

Castillo stared back at Walker as though he doubted the excuse for the delay, but agreed anyway. "Of course. How's 1 PM?"

Walker glanced at his watch. "Perfect."

"Good. I'll meet you outside the administration building at one o'clock and escort you to the girls' residence hall. I'll also arrange for you to interview both the roommate and boyfriend."

"Great. I'll see you then."

"Wait. Don't forget this." Castillo reached out and handed Walker the keycard. "Gives you access to the entire campus. Please don't abuse it."

Walker hesitated for a moment and then grabbed the card. "Thank you."

He was escorted out of the security center and back to the first floor by a security officer. As soon as he exited the building, he played the voicemail and immediately recognized the voice.

"Ryan, it's Mark. Something has come up. It's urgent. I need to see you right away. Please meet me at the waterfront in Leesburg in one hour. Thanks."

Walker looked at his watch again. Leesburg was about thirty minutes away. Plenty of time to get to the city, but it sounded urgent. Knowing his former partner from the FBI, Mark Lewis would be there early, Walker hurried to his car.

CHAPTER 6

"Why are you choosing to take these risks?" Nicole shouted at her husband.

Walker responded. "The SWAT team is no more dangerous than what I've already been doing. My life is at risk every day. Just because we know we're walking into a high-risk environment doesn't make it any more dangerous. It's the ones you don't know are high risk that turn out to be the dangerous ones."

Nicole stepped back into the kitchen counter and slapped the dishrag on the counter. She lowered her head and rubbed her forehead, frustrated by her husband's decision to join the field office SWAT team. "I can't believe you did this behind my back," she said, still looking down, tears falling from her face.

"Behind your back? We talked about this!" he retorted.

She glared at him with scorn. "Talked about this? Yes, we've talked about this, but that's all we've done. Actually, all we've done is argue about it ever since you first mentioned it."

"I thought we agreed."

"Agreed? Agreed on what? That you were going to join the SWAT team and put yourself in more danger every day? For what?"

Walker sighed and leaned on a kitchen chair. He let out a long breath. "You knew this about me when you signed up for this. You knew I was in law enforcement. You knew I was in the FBI. We chase down the worst criminals out there. The worst. You don't think I could be killed at any time?"

"Damn you!" she shouted, then immediately lowered her voice, realizing their daughter's bedroom was just above the kitchen, and hopefully Elise was sleeping soundly. "Yes, I knew you were in law enforcement, but that doesn't mean you have the right to invite even more uncertainty into our lives. Being an agent is stressful enough. Do you know that my heart stops every time the phone rings? Every time!" Nicole paused and then pointed to Elise's bedroom. "We have a little girl up there. She worships you. What would she do without you?"

"Stop it!"

Nicole recoiled, embarrassed by what she had just said. She lowered her head and rephrased, "What would I do without you?"

Her sobbing continued as Walker walked over to his wife and put his arms around her. At first, she resisted, did not look up, did not return the embrace, but eventually, she relented and accepted his gesture half-heartedly. She wanted to return the embrace, put her arms around him and squeeze tightly, but she wasn't ready yet. Perhaps soon, but not yet.

"I need to do this," he whispered.

Silence.

"You know I need to do this," he repeated.

"I know." Nicole finally answered under her breath.

A long pause lingered between them before Walker finally spoke. "I'll never leave you and Elise. I won't get hurt. I swear."

Nicole did not respond, just pulled a little tighter into the embrace, not wanting to let go.

CHAPTER 7

Like most of Loudoun County during the latter half of the twentieth century, Leesburg, Virginia had grown as well. Located just thirty miles from Washington, D.C., bordered by the Catoctin Mountains to the north and the Potomac River to the east, the historic town had experienced a boom in tourism. To cater to this new influx of visitors, Leesburg decided to take advantage of its Potomac River real estate by revitalizing its historic waterfront and built a large community park along its shoreline. Buffeted by appealing restaurants and boutique shopping, the park soon became a mecca for visitors as well as the locals, who appreciated the refurbished look and enjoyed the frequent occurrence of festivals and special events.

As Walker approached the riverfront, making his way through the park on the neatly-designed paver walkways, he noticed several metal benches positioned on the edge of the water. Mark Lewis was seated alone, staring forward, on one of those benches. Walker took notice of the three other FBI agents trying to blend into the surroundings but without much success. He smiled, surmising that Mark had brought the cavalry with him just in case he did something stupid. *Too late.*

He had known Mark Lewis since the FBI Academy, where they were recruits together. Walker had joined the FBI right after completing his Juris Doctorate degree from Penn Law in Philadelphia at the age of twenty-three. Lewis was already thirty, having worked in a county prosecutor's office in Ohio for several years before applying to the FBI. Only acquaintances during their time at the academy, both much more focused on passing the rigorous training program, they became friends when they were both assigned to the same field office in the Crime division. Lewis also worked in the Missing Persons section, so he and Walker had frequently worked cases together.

The two had become friends outside of the office as well, both buying houses in Arlington, Virginia, and entertaining each other's families on a regular basis. Lewis and his wife, Amy, had three kids, their youngest the same age as Elise, so playdates were common between the two young families. Nicole had even reached out to Mark to talk her husband out of joining the SWAT team, and although he argued on her behalf unsuccessfully, he understood and respected the decision. They were closer then.

They didn't talk much anymore. Everything had changed after the accident. The divorce, the selling of the house, the drinking — it all happened so fast. Mark had tried to help his friend through the worst of it, but Walker just pushed him away. The few times they did see each other, Walker could feel the judgment in his eyes, the pity for what he had sacrificed. And of course, there was Walker's jealousy.

Walker was envious that Mark was still working for the FBI, still solving crimes. He would read about him every once in a while in the newspaper. In recent years, in no small reaction to the public's increased interest in missing persons cases, the FBI had updated its response protocol for missing children. Today, Lewis was part of the FBI's Child Abduction Rapid Deployment (CARD) Team, which brought together federal, state, and local authorities for the quickest possible response to a child's disappearance.

These teams also coordinated with the National Center for Missing and Exploited Children, which assisted the FBI with over 20,000 cases of missing children each year, most of those endangered runaways. NCMEC's nationwide database was adrift with missing kids — disappearances never solved, children never found. Over 450,000 children were reported missing every year in the United States.

It was a grim statistic, but the vast majority of those were family-related abductions or runaways. Only about 100 were referred to as *stranger abductions*, meaning a child had been taken by an unknown person. It was a small percentage, but just half of those were ever returned alive, so the odds of success were literally fifty-fifty. However, with the increasing ubiquity of cell phones and easy access to social media, today's children were much more susceptible to predators. It was no longer just a stranger grabbing a child from a neighborhood street or waterfront park. Today's world was much more dangerous.

Walker approached the bench where Lewis was sitting. Mark Lewis, a black man, was in his mid-50's now, but still looked good for his age. Always working out to maintain his athletic build, his chest was well-toned and his abdomen, even while sitting, was flat. His collared shirt revealed arms taut with muscles, and his closely trimmed black hair matched his dark sunglasses. He stared out at the water.

"Great day to be in the park," Walker chuckled.

Lewis turned and smiled. "Indeed."

"So what brings you here...just wanted to be out of the office on this beautiful day?" Walker asked jokingly.

"How's Nicole?" Lewis asked, ignoring Walker's question.

Walker sat down next to Lewis and looked straight ahead toward the Potomac River, boats meandering through the calm waters. "You know. Same. Haven't actually spoken with her in a few weeks."

Lewis turned to his friend. "I'm sorry."

Walker shook his head. "Don't be. It is what it is."

"Yeah, I guess it is."

"So what brings you here, Mark?" Walker inquired again of his friend.

Lewis let out a long sigh. "What are you doing, Ryan?"

"What do you mean?"

"What are you doing at Washington Academy?"

"How did you know?" Walker asked, surprised.

"Long story"

"I have time."

Lewis chuckled and looked back toward the water. "I'm serious. Why are you there?"

Walker took a long pause, considering his response. "Just some investigation for a client."

"Lorenzo Arcuri? His missing daughter?"

Walker shook his head in disgust. He could feel the anger swelling up inside of him, so he took a deep breath and let it out slowly. *How did Lewis know so much?* He didn't care to hear the answer.

"I really gotta hand it to you guys. The FBI is relentless." Walker took another deep breath, and then asked, "What do you need from me? You said it was urgent."

"I brought you here to warn you."

"Warn me? Of what?"

"To stay as far away as you can from Washington Academy."

"What?"

"You have no idea what you're getting yourself into here, buddy. No idea."

"Listen, my friend, I do appreciate the concern, but I can take care of myself." Walker started to rise from the bench to leave.

Lewis reached out and grabbed Walker by the arm. "They call it the gilded sanctum. Did you know that?"

Walker paused, looking down at Lewis holding his arm. He pulled away, cocked his head, and smirked. "What?"

"That's what we call Washington Academy...the gilded sanctum."

"Catchy."

"It's not catchy. It's true. You just need to get underneath that thin layer of brilliance to see the truth."

"Scratch away the gold plating to reveal its secrets, huh?"

"You're a history buff, right? You remember the Gilded Age at the turn of the twentieth century? To the outside world,

America looked phenomenal — industries were booming, factories were churning, and money was being made by the truckload — but beneath that glossy exterior was another world — one of greed and poverty and corruption."

"You know your history, Lewis."

"Just doing my research," Lewis smirked, staring back out at the water. "But that's Washington Academy, Ryan. That's what you're dealing with here. Beneath that shiny veneer is something very sinister."

Walker stared at Lewis for several beats before responding. "Well I have to say, for the FBI, that's a pretty bold statement. Do you have any proof of that?"

Lewis turned his body to face Walker, and Walker returned the gesture by tilting his head to listen. "All I can say is that Washington Academy has been the subject of an open inquiry for the past two years."

"On what grounds?"

"You name it. White-collar crime, racketeering, public corruption, organized crime; the list goes on and on. You have no idea what we suspect them of being capable of. You really think you could be intimately involved with the elites of this country, both legal and illegal, and not try to pull some favor, make some deal, or have some hidden agenda? If you think about it, it's actually the perfect cover — a private school for kids, with its hands in the pockets of the top one percent of this country."

"Interesting play. You can't get anyone to talk to you? Anyone on the inside?"

"Believe me, we've tried." Lewis shrugged. "We've talked to every one of the security personnel multiple times over several years. They've been well-trained. Standard responses. Nothing more. I'm sure the weak ones are weeded out quickly, and they wouldn't know anything anyway. You obviously have to prove yourself before you're given any important information. It's like a military operation in there."

"Yeah, I've seen it first—hand."

"You've been to their underground bunker?"

"Good name for it. That's where I was when you called."

Lewis leaned in. "Then you know what I mean. That academy has more cameras than most small cities. With that kind of security apparatus, nothing happens there without them knowing about it. Someone knows what happened to Arcuri's daughter, just not the faculty or students."

"Why don't you get a warrant — seize the footage?"

"No probable cause. No reason to believe they're hiding something. And it wouldn't matter anyway — it's all digital, so whatever was on there can be altered or erased with no record. They're all professionals in there. They can cover their tracks better than we can find it. A lot of former law enforcement in there. Castillo is former CID."

"I learned that today."

"Then you also know that he can do whatever he wants with that footage. We'd have more luck identifying the second gunman on the grassy knoll than finding any images Castillo didn't want us to see. He could even make it look like you took Arcuri's daughter."

"That's not funny."

"I wasn't trying to be funny. I'm serious. That's why you need to be careful. As I said, someone on that campus knows exactly what happened, but they can make it look like whatever they want."

"I don't believe the FBI can't do *anything*!" Walker was incredulous.

Lewis chuckled. "That academy's been a fixture in Washington, D.C. for 200 years. Do you know how many of our CEOs and politicians went to school there? Do you know how many of their kids go to school there now? Lots of well-connected families. No judge is willing to pull the trigger because if we're wrong, there will be hell to pay. We need something more, something concrete, but we haven't found it. Yet."

Walker hesitated. "You need someone on the inside."

Lewis smiled. "You could say that."

"They've given me complete access to the entire campus for three days."

"Complete access? Three days? Are you kidding me?"

"I know," Walker smiled back. "Special invitation. Arcuri must have given a shitload of money to that school."

Lewis crossed his arms. "I'm sure."

Walker carefully considered his next move for a long moment before his unusual request. "I need to see the case file on the academy. Everything you have."

"You know I can't do that, Ryan. That's my job we're talking about."

"You have to give me something. Anything. I need to know what you guys have, so I know where to look. I'm your man on the ground, your eyes and ears inside those walls."

Lewis sat up and looked around, making visual contact with the other FBI agents still lurking in the background. "I'll see what I can do, but no guarantees."

"That's all I'm asking for. I know how the system works."

"You're asking for a lot, my friend. But you're right, we need to get inside, and right now, you're our only link."

Walker agreed. "So, what's your theory?"

"Excuse me?"

"What's your theory?"

"We have no theory, "Lewis said with resignation as he settled back on the bench again.

"Come on, Mark, I know you guys better than that. Remember, I *was* one of you guys. You have to have a theory, at least a working one."

Lewis was silent.

"You think she found out something? Discovered the corruption?"

"Perhaps," Lewis said after a long pause.

"You think it goes all the way to the top."

"Without a doubt."

"Okay, what's the theory?"

Lewis was silent again, staring forward, until finally, he

said, "Trafficking"

"Sex trafficking?" Walker asked.

"Yes. Think about it. Beautiful girl. No evidence that she ran away, was abducted or killed. Private school is covering up the disappearance with some altered video footage and a pre-determined storyline. Girl's father is head of one of the largest criminal syndicates in the country. Do you think he wants the extra attention from the cops? No, he prefers it stays quiet, and the school is more than happy to oblige. No publicity. No AMBER Alerts. No community searches. Just a former FBI agent with a troubled past."

Walker lowered his head.

"I'm sorry," Lewis said. "I didn't mean it like that."
"It's alright. But it does make sense."

"I know. And it makes you wonder if there have been others. More girls. How many over the years that have never been reported to us? How many that have simply disappeared?" Walker asked, "Any evidence of this?"

"No, as I said, that school is a fortress, and we can't yet convince a judge for a warrant to search records or the like without some kind of probable cause. We simply don't have enough for a warrant." A slight pause. "But he did give us surveillance," Lewis added, with a smile.

"Surveillance?" Walker laughed. "Outside of the campus only, I imagine? Watch who's coming and going?"

Lewis returned the smile. "Yes."

"That's how you knew I was there?" Walker realized.

"Yes."

"Wow. I really hate you guys," Walker said, shaking his head.

Lewis placed his hand on Walker's arm again and leaned in closer. "Seriously, my friend, we haven't built enough of a case to do anything just yet, but something strange is happening in there. This school deals with all kinds of criminals, and it wouldn't surprise me at all if they had their own illegal enterprise running like clockwork underneath that gilded exterior."

Walker placed his hand atop Lewis's. "Understood." And rose from the bench.

"Be careful, my friend," Lewis pleaded.

Walker nodded and walked away.

CHAPTER 8

The FBI case file on Washington Academy was laying neatly on the passenger seat when Walker returned to his vehicle. He stared at it for several moments, admiring the FBI seal, the red lines which outlined the otherwise ordinary manila folder, and the word 'confidential' stamped on the cover. It was about an inch thick.

Son of a bitch, he thought. Lewis came through, after all, having one of the agents put the file on his seat while the two talked. Those agents weren't concerned about Lewis's safety after all; they were there to protect them. Neither he nor Lewis would put anything past Castillo, so his long-time partner obviously wasn't going to let anything happen to the only break he had in years. He now had an agent — albeit a former one — on the inside, and his quick glance to the other agents in the park, Walker now realized, had signaled to them that he was indeed going to help them.

He assumed Lewis wasn't thrilled about depending on Walker to provide the break in an investigation that had spanned several years, but it was obviously his only shot, so Lewis was going to take it. Also, he was positive that Lewis hadn't consulted his superiors about the unorthodox suggestion of enlisting the assistance of a former agent, especially this one, because they would have torpedoed the idea immediately. To anyone still at the Bureau, Walker was damaged goods. Whatever the circumstances, it really didn't matter to Walker. He needed a break — just like Lewis — and if the FBI provided it, so be it.

Walker glanced at his watch. He was scheduled to meet Castillo in an hour for the tour of the residence hall where Amanda lived as well as interviews with the roommate and boyfriend. It was clear from his initial glance at Castillo's case file on Amanda that she had lots of friends and was very popular on campus, but although many people had seen her that day, the roommate and boyfriend were the *last* ones to see her, which catapulted them to the top of the interview list. The dormitory room was also Amanda's last known location, so it was the natural place to start their investigation.

He now had the FBI's case file for WA in addition to Castillo's file, so he would try and review both before meeting with Castillo, giving him a slight advantage over the security chief. Walker currently had no reason to trust Castillo, and so corroborating what he provided in his file on Amanda with any intelligence contained in the FBI folder would be crucial to staying one step ahead of him. Being able to essentially control the flow of pertinent information, Castillo could give Walker only what he wanted when he wanted, seriously hampering his investigation. Based on what he could glean from the FBI's file, Walker would now have a slight edge. *Thanks, Lewis.*

Walker also wasn't sure if Castillo would have actually put something of value in that file. He and Ellis had two days to figure out how to approach this situation, determine how to best handle Arcuri's request for a private investigator. Based on what Walker knew about the former CID agent so far, he exuded thoroughness, so he doubted Castillo didn't at least have an idea of what had happened. Or how to handle any potential outside interference. *Was Castillo covering for Ellis? Or were they both involved in some way?*

Perhaps this was all just a charade, their plan all along to simply placate Arcuri, play Walker, and pretend they had done all they could to assist the investigation. But in reality, Castillo would simply keep a close eye on Walker for the three days, ensuring that he came up empty-handed, so they could all go back behind the walls of their gilded sanctum and hide the real truths beyond those thick, opaque doors.

It made sense. Walker mused about Castillo's likely reaction when Ellis had told him they were hosting a private investigator. The security chief was probably mad as hell that someone was going to be investigating him and his operation. Castillo obviously didn't appreciate the extra set of eyes on his campus. *He — and his camera system — were the only sets of eyes that were needed on this campus,* Walker was sure he had told Ellis.

But now, Walker could match wits with Castillo. Keep him off balance. Go in his own direction and not be guided by a person with a vested interest in maintaining the veil of privacy that had been stretched over the campus. Perhaps Castillo would make a mistake or tip his hand, but Walker simply couldn't allow him to get in the way. Missing person cases were difficult enough without any additional, man-made obstacles placed in your way.

Based on law enforcement protocols, missing person cases were divided into several categories, based on the circumstances surrounding the disappearance. The first category was known as *catastrophic missing* in which a person was the supposed victim of a natural disaster or another type of catastrophe. Unless there had been a hurricane or earthquake Walker didn't know about, that obviously wasn't the case here.

Lost was the second type of missing person in which a child had wandered away and his or her whereabouts were unknown. In this scenario, Amanda may have gotten lost or confused, was high on drugs or alcohol, or had stumbled down a rocky hillside or fallen into a river. Any of those situations were possible here, and only an investigation would uncover the truth. Video evidence would probably exist for one of these outcomes, but Walker doubted he could trust Castillo to turn over any related footage, so of course, this was a huge impediment to his entire inquiry.

The third kind of missing person was an *abduction*, including a parent or family member, which happened extremely frequently and probably accounted for the vast majority of all missing child cases. Stranger abductions were far less frequent, yet typically garnered much more media attention because of the fear factor for parents and the rating spike for news outlets.

Abduction was indeed possible, but not likely. Amanda's mother would have no reason to abduct her own daughter, especially since Arcuri did not appear to be a direct threat to them and actually supported them both financially. Arcuri wanted his daughter as invisible as possible already, so a co-parent abducting her to escape from the father simply didn't seem plausible. A stranger abduction was possible, but as Arcuri had said, someone from the outside penetrating the security apparatus of WA, without at least some video footage, was also unlikely.

A *runaway* was the next type, but these kids typically had some reason for going missing — a fight or confrontation which proceeded the disappearance or evidence of a bus or plane ticket. *Missing under suspicious circumstances* was based on evidence of foul play, such as getting into the car with a stranger or a witness seeing something unusual, but that did not appear to be the case here, or at least, there was no evidence to suggest that. It may very well have happened, but as far as Walker knew, no one on campus had witnessed a crime.

The final category of missing persons was *unknown*, which meant that there were insufficient facts to determine the circumstances of the disappearance. To any investigator, that's exactly where Walker was with Amanda Bryson. He simply did not have enough facts nor evidence to support any kind of conclusion. And that was baffling.

Every missing persons investigator always hoped for at least something to go on — a train ticket receipt, a fight between lovers, a suspicious occurrence — something that would lead you down a certain path. There was no obvious path here, and for an experienced FBI agent who specialized in missing persons, that was odd. But *odd* wasn't a technical term. It usually meant that there was a certain degree of premeditation involved and that someone had gone to great lengths to cover their tracks. *But who? And why?* Walker wasn't sure he wanted to know the answer.

CHAPTER 9

Walker arrived back to the administrative building a few minutes before he was scheduled to meet Castillo, so he took both files and made himself comfortable on a wooden bench beneath a small copse of trees, providing some shade as a gentle breeze rustled through the campus. He opened Castillo's file first, the pages fluttering from the soft wind as he flipped through the collection of documents. He had grabbed some fast food on his way back to campus, so he chomped on chicken nuggets and fries while perusing the file.

Amanda's picture was still paper-clipped to the front of the report — her eyes staring back at him again — so Walker gingerly lifted the photo from the page to read the text. His delicate handling of the photograph was a typical subconscious reaction to the missing person as if any mishandling of it would somehow lead to more suffering. Walker had worked enough of these cases to know the horrors she might have endured, and so he had to be careful to control his tortured imagination at this point to not be distracted from the contents of the documents.

The first page of the report listed a physical description of Amanda. Five feet, eight inches tall, approximately 125 pounds, black hair, green eyes, seventeen years old. A senior. Walker remembered the large color image of Amanda on the screen in the security bunker.

The following pages revealed her demographic and academic data: parents, teachers, friends, grades, college applications, etc. Walker skimmed through this section, forming an overall profile of Amanda Bryson in his mind. Smart girl. Popular student. Excellent grades. Involved in several student organizations and sports. Student Council President. Great soccer player. She even worked a part-time job on campus at the Tuition/Student Aid Office. Walker found that interesting and made a mental note to himself to remember to visit it.

Each subsequent page contained multiple reports related to the school's investigation. Walker was surprised by the level of detail that had been provided to him. It appeared these documents were copies of the original reports written by the officers who investigated, all supervised and approved by Castillo. Nothing had been redacted.

Walker was impressed by the adroit investigation. In his experience, it was superb. Castillo was CID, so he should have expected nothing less. According to the reports, all evidence had been collected, all witnesses had been questioned, and all leads had been followed. It was an exceptional investigation. There was only one problem...there was no evidence, there were no witnesses, and far as Walker could discern, there were no credible leads. Based on the preliminary findings of the school's investigation, Amanda had simply vanished.

He continued reading. No video evidence of an abduction, no eyewitnesses to an abduction, no forensic evidence of a crime, and Amanda's personal belongings, including her cell phone, laptop, and backpack had not yet been recovered. This was unfortunate as any one of these items could provide an investigator with immediate clues as to the person's whereabouts. But those did not exist. *Did she take them with her when she ran away, or was abducted, or fell into a river?* Any number of scenarios were possible, but without those personal belongings to provide some clues, it was simply a stab in the dark.

A sweep of the local cell towers revealed some innocuous text and phone messages, but nothing sent after she was reported missing. And a scan of the school's email server located a few old emails, but nothing was out of the ordinary — no red flags — just typical, routine stuff. Her social media accounts were overwhelmingly benign, and there was no indication whatsoever that Amanda was in trouble or had made a nefarious connection via digital media. Even if she was a runaway, there would have been some video footage of her leaving the campus in a car or walking out the front entrance, anything to indicate she was alive and well when she left Washington Academy. And what exactly was she running away from? A free ride to an elite private school, money in her pocket every week, a dad that kept his distance, but still paid the bills and sent the checks. Not likely.

Walker wondered if Amanda may have committed suicide. There was no direct evidence to support this, but the academic and social pressures inherent for a popular young adult at a private school were enough to at least warrant it as a possibility. There would probably have been some warning signs, some kind of red flags to indicate she was unhappy or wanted to end her own life, but the mere absence of those behaviors did not automatically dismiss the potential. Today's teenagers had gotten very good at hiding their true feelings or expressing them only online, parents woefully unaware of what their children were thinking. Although the absentee father lent credence to the possibility, the warning signs were simply not there, so for now, Walker left that theory alone.

The next few pages of the report listed a timeline, based on the limited information available. Amanda had disappeared on September 23rd. According to the surveillance footage, she had entered her dormitory at 7:13 PM. The roommate recalled her leaving their room at approximately 9 PM, but there was no video evidence to support this. The roommate claimed she did not know where Amanda was going, but according to surveillance, she never left the residence hall. The roommate also had gone out that night, leaving the dormitory at 9:38 PM and returning back home at approximately 11 PM, all verified by the surveillance footage. Discovering that Amanda has not yet returned home and after several unanswered calls and texts, the roommate called Campus Police at 11:31 PM, according to the police log.

Campus police arrived and conducted a cursory search in the vicinity of the dormitory, and Mr. Castillo personally interviewed the roommate. One of his students had just disappeared, so Walker did not think it was unusual for him to interview all involved. The roommate's texts and phone records — in addition to the surveillance footage — corroborated her story.

The boyfriend's text messages backed up his story as well. He claimed to have fought with Amanda earlier in the day but didn't see her that night, and his texts from that evening went unanswered. A check of his phone showed that any return texts had not been deleted, so at least for that part of the story, he was telling the truth.

Both witnesses had willingly turned over their phones, so in that respect, they were fully cooperating with the campus authorities, which made them persons of interest and not necessarily suspects. Yet. Perhaps she was already dead, and they both knew it, so the unanswered texts were simply for show. People watched enough cop shows on television to know that trying to create an alibi after the fact was typical of first-time offenders. But it usually got messy after that — suspects' stories shifting, conflicting evidence coming to light — so if that was the situation here, his interviews with the two would most likely have revealed some inconsistencies.

Walker flipped to the last section of the report which contained Castillo's witness interviews, including the roommate and boyfriend. He didn't read the interview notes, didn't want to prejudice his impression of his two most important witnesses before he had a chance to speak with them. All interviews followed a certain format, but the interviewee's answers could certainly steer the conversation in a certain direction, and those directions — depending on the interviewer — could be highly divergent. Therefore, separate interviews conducted with the same person could actually yield very different results. Finally, the nonverbal cues or specific way of answering a question could also take the interview on starkly different pathways.

He didn't want to know the pathway Castillo had taken or see where it had gone, which might color his thinking and dissuade him from asking certain questions, ultimately excluding important details. No. He was going to conduct the interviews himself and simply see where they led, where the non-verbal communication and answers took them.

As Walker reached the end of the report, multiple questions still nagged at him: Did Amanda know about the cameras? Was there another way out of the dorm? Did she knowingly evade the cameras or was Castillo hiding some footage? Was this about a student with an elaborate plan to circumvent campus security, an accidental homicide by two students trying to cover up their tracks, or a classic cover-up by the men in charge because Amanda had witnessed something she shouldn't have? Whatever the reason, this was a very dangerous game.

Castillo suddenly exited the front doors of the administrative building, emerging from his underground war room, wearing a dark green windbreaker with WA emblazoned on the pocket. He pulled it closer as the breeze met him at the door. Walker quickly closed up the documents to ensure Castillo did not see the FBI file and placed the two folders in his worn cloth briefcase as he stood to greet the security chief.

CHAPTER 10

The two men walked with purpose toward the female dormitory along the meticulously designed brick pathways through the campus, passing eager students on their way to and from class. The student body was remarkably diverse, but the Washington Academy uniforms — green blazers or blouses with khaki pants or skirts — cast an impression that was unsettling to Walker, as if any clues that laid just below the surface could be easily drowned out by the sea of uniformity. The sweet smell of autumn hung in the air.

It was a short walk, and after several minutes of silence, they reached a small decorative plaza of rounded walkways and flower beds, intersecting each other in a beautiful array laid out directly in front of the entrance to the dormitory.

Castillo spoke first again. "This residence hall is for females only. We don't have strict guidelines about males in the dorm, but rooms are assigned to females only."

"So males are allowed to enter and exit the dorm?"

"Yes, as long as they are escorted by a female resident, but everyone has to be back to their respective dorm by 11 PM."

"Do most kids follow the rules?"

Castillo smiled. "For the most part. We have our frequent offenders of course, but most follow the protocol."

Walker wanted to push. "A safe campus, huh?"

Castillo glared. "Yes, Mr. Walker, a very safe campus." Castillo paused. "Look around at all of these cameras, all of this surveillance." Castillo gestured to the cameras attached to the light poles along the paths. "This allows us to see what is happening, see what rules are not being followed, allows us to keep this campus safe."

Walker nodded at the cameras. "I'm still amazed that you didn't capture any images of Amanda after 7 PM that night?"

"I am as well," said Castillo, in a smooth, matter-of-fact tone. "Like I said, if someone wanted to avoid the cameras, they can do it."

"You think Amanda tried to avoid the cameras?" Walker asked, pointedly.

Castillo shook his head. "I don't know, but it's the only way I can account for the lack of video footage. If she didn't make the effort to avoid detection, I'm confident we would have her on the video feed."

Walker pushed again. "All your footage is digital, right?"

"Yes."

"So someone with the proper expertise could alter those images?"

Castillo halted.

Walker took a few more steps and turned to Castillo. Castillo approached slowly until he was only a few inches from Walker. Both men made eye contact and kept it.
"What are you saying, Mr. Walker?"

"I'm simply saying that someone with the technical expertise could alter that video footage."

Castillo breathed and spoke slowly. "Yes, someone could. But why would someone do that?" he retorted.

Walker looked Castillo directly in the eyes, "We all have secrets. And most of us want to keep it that way."

With that, Walker turned and continued along the pathway to the front of the hall. Castillo huffed and followed him, pulling out his keycard to open the door. Walker suddenly moved away from the entrance around to the corner of the building.

"Where are you going?" Castillo yelled.

"I want to have a look around," Walker said, not turning

around.

Castillo followed, visibly exasperated.

The edge of the dormitory building was overcrowded with small trees and shrubs. Walker climbed into the waist-high mesh of twigs and leaves, chopping his way through the vegetation with his legs to make his way around the building. Castillo looked at his fancy shoes and nice pants as he entered the web of dagger-like shrubbery and muttered under his breath.

Walker spoke as he trudged through the bushes, "The dorm was searched?"

"Yes," Castillo responded. "Under the guise of a canine search, my campus security officers did a complete search of the entire dormitory. All rooms and closets as well as the basement and any ancillary spaces."

"Anything?"

"No."

Walker pushed through the last row of bushes, stepping down slightly from the elevated bed of mulch onto the flat ground at the rear of the dorm. He entered into a small clearing, which hadn't been mowed in years and was overgrown with tall grass and brush. The clearing butted up against a tree line, which looked like an interwoven tapestry of thick trees, patchwork branches, and lush vegetation which encircled the space behind the residence hall. It was simply one section of the many acres of wooded land that surrounded the campus.

Walking along the rear wall of the dorm, Walker eyed a series of old windows near the base of the structure, surrounded by small metal enclosures, buried in the ground. Walker selected one of the first windows, knelt down, and peered through its grime-laced glass. It led into a basement laundry room, but the rusted, dirty window appeared to be sealed shut and hadn't been opened in years. He continued to the next one and knelt down again. The small grassy area just outside the metal enclosure appeared to be flattened and thin scuffs of dirt in the soft earth were visible throughout the immediate space. Walker picked up a handful of dirt and let it sift through his fingers.

Castillo stood over him, still perturbed at having walked through the razor-sharp shrubbery to this desolate spot. "Tracking something? Are you planning to taste the dirt?"

Walker smiled. "I might."

Walker wiped his hands together as the last bit of dirt fell from them, and still crouched, peered at the beaten-down grass and disheveled brush. He reached for the window and grabbed the small handle on the bottom edge of the pane. A quick pull and the window opened effortlessly. Walker stood up and looked down again at the small area of rustled earth beneath his feet and the metal enclosure which encased the window. The small space was easily accessible from the window, large enough to fit a person, and best of all, far away from the ever-watchful eyes of Castillo's cameras. *Escape hatch.*

Walker turned and tilted his head for a better angle with the ground. Seeing it immediately, he followed a foot-worn path in the grass from the rear of the building to the tree line where the brush had also been trampled down. After a short distance through an easily navigable barrier of trees, the path emptied into another clearing. The edge of campus. Walker noticed several more grass-beaten paths leading off in various directions. He surmised that if one were to reach this point, he or she could either escape the campus or enter it again at any one of a dozen other entry points along the wood line.

Castillo walked up beside Walker and squinted angrily at the multiple footpaths peeling off from the clearing.

"Looks like we may have found how Amanda left the dorm undetected," Walker said.

He watched as Castillo shook his head, a light shade of embarrassment moving from his neck to his face. So enamored was Castillo with his omniscient security system and the blanket of protection he thought it provided, he was oblivious to its flaws, the chinks in the supposedly impenetrable armor of any video monitoring system. The blind spots. And they had just discovered one.

CHAPTER 11

Amanda's dormitory room was typical of any student residence one would find on a private school or college campus. It measured 20x20 feet with a large, two-section window at the opposite end from the door. If a straight line was drawn from the window to the door, each side of the room was nearly a mirror image of the other. Matching closets and clothes drawers were located on either side of the entryway, followed by two twin beds — neatly made — and finally, identical wooden desks built into the wall symmetrical to the window. Shelves were also attached to the walls above the desks, and the entire space was painted in a drab green color.

Walker entered the room and glanced at the eclectic array of posters that clung to the empty space on the walls, including inspirational quotes, band posters, and faux famous paintings. He grinned at the collection. *If you've seen one dorm room, you've seen them all*, he thought to himself. What irked Walker most of all, however, was the fact that nothing was out of the ordinary. It was familiar in every sense of the word. And for that reason, it would provide no additional clues to him.

The left side of the room appeared to have a current occupant, evidenced by a scattering of books on the desk and clothes on the floor, whereas the other side seemed empty and sterile. Amanda's side. He rotated to the closet door and opened it. Her clothes all hung neatly — separated by type and color — and an impressive collection of shoes neatly lined the floor.

Walker turned and walked toward the desk at the far end

of the room, brushing up against Amanda's bed and running his finger along the edge of the linens. Upon reaching the desk, he scanned the shelves above, looking for any clue as to Amanda's state of mind. It was your standard collection of textbooks, teacher-made packets, and the latest fiction novel, all stacked neatly on the wooden ledges. No self-help books, drawing pads, or journals — which would give Walker some insight into Amanda's psychological well-being — were present. Discouraged, he looked to the other side of the room, but aside from the slightly more chaotic appearance, it was the same story, and exceedingly normal in every possible way.

Because the most important items to this case — Amanda's backpack, laptop, and cellphone — were still missing, the dormitory room provided nothing of any real value to the investigation. Except for a roommate: Heather Yates.

CHAPTER 12

Just inside the entrance to the girls' dormitory, there was a large study room filled with circular tables and wooden chairs. Massive windows provided for an easy distraction, so in the back of the large space, there were also three private study rooms. The private rooms were minuscule, but that was good. It reminded Walker of an interrogation room — small and uncomfortable — which put the subject at an immediate disadvantage. He wanted the kids to feel somewhat claustrophobic and be looking for a way out. The truth will set you free, so to speak.

The only thing in the room was a square table with a chair on either side. A thin pane of glass was cut into the wooden door, but other than that, it was completely private. The doors did not lock. As Walker sat in the far chair, so he could see the students as they entered, he was sure many interesting things had probably happened in these mostly private rooms, but for right now, it was the location of his first interview in a case he desperately needed to solve.

Castillo led Heather Yates into the room, closed the door, and leaned against the wall, directly behind Walker. Studying Heather as she sauntered into the room and unwillingly took her seat across from him, Walker noticed that her body movements suggested a tough exterior, but most likely hid some vulnerabilities inside. Her shoulder-length, dirty blonde hair — streaked with pink — was pulled behind her ears, revealing several piercings, and her lipstick was bright red, in stark contrast to her otherwise light and clear complexion. Her expression was one of scorn and disinterest. It was obvious from her demeanor that this was the last place in the world she wanted to be.

Walker smiled. "Hi. My name's Ryan Walker. I'm a private investigator."

Heather simply huffed and glared at Castillo for bringing her into this situation. She was seemingly prepared for this encounter, so Walker decided to dispense with the pleasantries and launch right into the interview, knocking her off balance and perhaps triggering a reaction.

"Were you and Amanda friends?" He started.

"Roommates." She answered quickly.

"That's not what I asked," Walker quipped. "Were you friends?"

Heather flinched and gave Walker a puzzled look, seeming to realize that this interview would not be as simple as she had thought when she stepped into the small room. She paused for a moment, appearing to carefully consider her answer and struggling to determine who she was up against. "We were friendly if that's what you mean, but I guess not, no, we weren't friends."

Heather could have stopped there, but she didn't. Walker imagined he had riled her with his first question, and so she wanted to push back, telegraphing to him that she wouldn't simply cave under his applied pressure. Like a rebellious teenage daughter trying to aggravate her father, she added with a smirk, "I like to experiment a little more. Amanda was a goodie two shoes, so she didn't do that kind of thing."

Walker smiled on the inside. "Experiment?"

"Yeah, you know?"

"Can you explain?"

"Is this interview about me or Amanda?"

"You're right. I'm sorry."

Walker watched Heather relax, satisfied that she had put an end to his clever questioning with her colorful banter, so he continued to push. "I guess daddy never bought you that pony," he whispered, looking at his notes.

"What?" she snarled.

"Never mind."

Castillo laughed.

Walker could see the anger building in Heather, sure that these two over-the-hill men were making fun of her, so she decided to put them both on notice. "Listen. I don't want to be here, okay? I don't know where Amanda is. I really don't care, but I didn't have anything to do with it, okay?"

"We didn't say you did," Walker said calmly.

Heather huffed again, increasingly pissed off by the interaction.

Walker reclined in his chair. He had succeeded, had gotten Heather frustrated — perhaps not thinking clearly — so if she was going to make a mistake, now was the time. He decided to methodically retrace her steps the night of September 23rd to determine if she was indeed telling him the truth.

"So," he began, "let's talk about the night of Amanda's disappearance."

"Okay," she said with relief.

"When was the last time you saw Amanda?"

"About 9 PM that night."

"What happened at 9 PM?"

"She got a text and left the dorm."

"Where was she going?"

"I don't know. I think to see her boyfriend."

"Josh Easterly?"

"Yep."

"She didn't tell you?"

"Nope. She took all of her stuff with her, so I assumed she was going to see Josh."

"Her stuff?"

"You know, her backpack and stuff."

"Did she always take her *stuff* with her when she went to see Josh?"

"Yeah."

"And is that why you thought she was going to see Josh?"

"Yeah."

"But she never actually told you that?"

"Right."

"Where were you that night?"

"I was in my room."

"All night?"

"Most of it."

"What does that mean?"

"It means I didn't go out until later.

"I thought you liked to experiment?"

Heather shot him a glare and sighed. "I was going to go out later, but I had a chemistry exam the next day. I had to study for it. I'm not doing very well right now, and if I don't pass this semester, dad said he's going to pull me out."

"Dad?"

Heather grunted.

Castillo interjected, "Jonathan Yates. CEO of Organic Enterprises."

"Whoa," said Walker.

"Whatever," Heather said, scowling again. "Anyway, I have to do well, so I had to study. I went out about 9:30 and got back at 11. Amanda still wasn't back, so I got worried."

"Why were you worried?"

"She was usually back by then even if she went to Josh's place."

"Did she usually go over to Josh's?"

"Sure. Probably two or three times a week."

"So why were you worried?"

"She would always text me if she was going to be late. We kind of have this thing between us, you know, where we text each other just in case, so we can help each other out. A girl thing, you know?"

"That's good. And so, there was no text that evening?"

"No, so I texted her a couple of times, but nothing. That's when I called the campus police."

Walker already knew that Heather's cell phone corroborated the texts to Amanda as well as her lack of response. "And Mr. Castillo was notified?" pointing his thumb toward Castillo.

"Yes."

"Did you talk to Mr. Castillo that night?"

Heather shifted in her seat. "Yes."

"And what did you talk about?"

"He just asked me what had happened."

"Anything else?" Walker probed.

"No."

"You didn't see her at all while you were out?"

"No."

Walker, again already knowing the answer, turned to Castillo, "And you can corroborate Heather's story about going out between 9 to 11?" Castillo nodded, while Heather continued to glare, knowing full well that the cameras had captured her exploits that night.

"Do any drugs that night? Drink any alcohol?"

"No."

"Are you sure?"

"Yes, I'm sure. I was just hanging out with friends."

"So, no experimenting that night because you had a big test the next day?"

Heather paused for a long moment then deadpanned, "Where did they find you?"

Both Walker and Castillo laughed. Walker decided to change the subject. "What do you know about her boyfriend, Josh Easterly?"

"He's okay, I guess."

"Nice guy?"

"Maybe."

"You see him much?"

"No, I wasn't into that kind of guy. I'm more into jocks. He's a prep. Boring. And he's into all that secret society shit."

Walker's interest was piqued. "You think Josh is a member of a secret society?"

"Yeah, you know, the *Sons of Liberty*. At least that's what I've heard. He's weird like that, so probably."

"The *Sons of Liberty*?"

As Heather started to speak, Castillo interrupted, "It's nothing. An old story. It doesn't exist. Anyone the kids don't like is automatically in the *Sons of Liberty*. Isn't that right, Heather?"

She shrugged.

Walker looked at Castillo, who said, "I'll fill you in on the history later."

Turning back to Heather, Walker asked, "So how did Amanda get along with Josh?"

"Well, they had a huge fight that day if that's what you mean."

"They did?"

"Yeah, but it was like that every day with them. They were always fighting."

"You witness it?"

"Not that day, but yeah, a couple of times before."

"What did you think?"

"He was an asshole. Actually, they were both assholes. They bugged each other. Shouldn't have been together."

"Was she going to meet him to make up after the fight?"

"I don't know."

"And she didn't tell you where she was going?"

"I told you already. No."

"Did you think it was odd that she took her stuff with her and didn't tell you she was going to see Josh?"

Heather shifted again in her seat, appearing more uncomfortable. "She doesn't always tell me, she texts me. Like I said, we weren't friends. I didn't know where she was every second of the day. Maybe she was embarrassed because she had just fought with him like two hours earlier, said she was going to break up with him, and now she was crawling back to him."

"She said she was going to break up with him, that she didn't want to see him again?"

"Yes, but she always said that, and she always eventually went back with him. Or he would come crawling back to her. It was pathetic. They definitely weren't good for each other."

"Did you ever see Josh touch Amanda or see any physical violence between them?"

"Not that I remember. Honestly, I didn't pay much attention. They made me want to puke. They were all affectionate one minute and then screaming at each other the next. It was sick."

Walker circled back. "So you assumed she was going to meet her boyfriend because she took her stuff."

"Maybe."

"Maybe?"

"I said I didn't know where she was going, but sure, if she took her stuff, she was probably going to meet Josh."

Walker paused. "Were the two of you fighting that day be any chance?"

"No."

"Did the two of you ever fight?"

"Sure, but just dumb shit. You know, roommate stuff."

"Heather, did Amanda ever express any frustration with anything...with school, with life, wanting to get away from it all?"

"No. Never. Amanda loved it here." Heather said with a hint of scorn.

"Okay, last question. If Amanda was going to meet Josh, and you're assuming she was going to meet Josh because she took her stuff with her, she should have texted you if she was coming home late that night. Is that correct?"

"Yes. And that's why I called the campus police." Heather slumped, exhausted and overwhelmed by all of the questioning.

Walker nodded his head and realized the interview was over. Heather obviously knew more than she was willing to tell him, but there didn't appear to be anything suspicious about it. She just wanted to give as little information as possible to stay out of the crosshairs of law enforcement and avoid jeopardizing her current tenuous situation with school. "Okay, Heather, thank you so much for your time."

Heather looked relieved as she rose from her seat, did not say another word, and hurried from the makeshift interrogation room.

Walker leaned back in his chair and turned toward Castillo, "You believe her?"

"Hard not to," Castillo said as he made his way to Heather's seat across from Walker. "Her story checks out. Cameras and cell phone records confirm everything she's saying, at almost the exact times she said it."

Walker let out a long sigh.

Castillo continued, "We interviewed the friends she was with that night, and again, everything checks out. For once, I think they *were* just hanging out. We didn't find any evidence of drugs or alcohol, and all the alibis were clean. To be honest, I don't think she cares enough about Amanda to be that involved. She's obviously very detached."

Walker agreed. "Yeah, she wasn't really that broken up about it, was she?

"Nope."

Walker leaned forward and folded his hands. "Tell me about this secret society."

Castillo huffed. "Bullshit." He leaned back. "It started a few years ago. Some of the boys wanted to be like their college brethren, so they decided to start a secret society — a skull and bones club if you will. They called it the *Sons of Liberty*. I guess that's what you get from smart kids."

"Did it exist?"

"Yes, but we went after it pretty quickly. Threatened expulsion and the like for anyone associated with it. We came down hard, so it broke up."

"Or went further underground?"

"Maybe. But we kept a close eye on it ever since and we've never seen it reappear."

"Is Josh a part of this club?"

"I doubt it."

There was a knock at the door. Josh Easterly had arrived for his interview. Castillo looked over and smiled. "But I guess you can ask him."

CHAPTER 13

Heather had been right. Josh Easterly was the epitome of a preparatory school student. He was dressed in his Washington Academy blazer, emblazoned with the school's emblem on the pocket, and his khaki pants. His black hair was longer, yet styled atop his five feet, ten-inch slender body. Although not the toughest skinny kid Walker had ever seen, Josh seemed to be very sure of himself. Nervous but cocky.

Greetings were exchanged, and Walker decided to take the same approach to knock Josh off-kilter if that was possible. "Did you and Amanda have a fight the day she disappeared?"

Josh groaned, visibly angered by the question. "Are you saying I had something to do with her disappearance?"

Walker held up his hand to calm the tension, proud of his accomplishment but realizing it may have worked a little too well. This guy obviously had some anger issues, so he worked to calm him down. "Of course not, Josh. We've just heard that you had a fight with Amanda that day. Is that true?"

Josh settled back in his seat, making eye contact with both Walker and Castillo before answering, appearing to consider his options. "Yes."

"And did you fight often?" Walker followed up.

Josh again paused before answering. "Yes."

"What did you guys fight about?"

"Girlfriend and boyfriend stuff."

"What did you fight about that day?"

"I can't remember."

"Would you call it your worst fight?"

"No, we've had worse."

"Amanda's roommate tells us she wanted to break up with you?"

"I don't think so," Josh dismissed.

"You think Heather is lying?"

"No, she just doesn't know what she's talking about. She didn't know us. We couldn't stand her anyway, so we didn't spend much time there. Amanda was always at my place."

"She was at your place often?"

"Mostly. A couple of times a week."

"You have a roommate?"

"I live in a single"

"Where were you that night?"

"Out."

"Out where?"

"Hanging out with some buddies."

"You see either Amanda or Heather that night?"

"No"

"You sure?"

"I said no."

"What were you doing with your buddies?"

"Playstation."

Walker turned to Castillo, and he nodded. "His story checks out. He was in a friend's room at the boy's dorm. They were playing *Call of Duty*."

Walker turned back to Josh, who was smirking. "Did Amanda text you at all that night?"

"No."

"Was that odd for her to not text you?"

"Our fights sometimes lasted a few days, so no, I expected she wouldn't text for a while."

"Please tell us what you fought about that day."

The polite question seemed to calm Josh's combative stance and softened his tone somewhat. He looked embarrassed and lowered his head. "Because she was flirting with Ben Rhodes in class"

"Ben Rhodes?"

"Just a classmate. An old friend."

"And all of you had a class together?"

"Yeah. Chemistry. First period."

"And she was flirting with him?"

"Yeah, she was all over him, laughing and joking around."

"And this was during class?"

"Yeah, they were lab partners."

Walker sighed. "So, they were lab partners, but being a little too friendly that day?"

"Yeah."

"And that made you mad?"

"Yeah!" said Josh defiantly.

"So after class, you laid into her?"

"Yes, and she got pissed and said she was done with me."

"Done with you as in breaking up with you."

"No, just done with me for the day I thought."

"And you never saw her again after that?"

"No."

"And no texts, calls, or emails the rest of the day?"

"No."

"You ever touch Amanda or get physically violent with her?"

Josh was immediately incredulous. "Of course not! We would yell pretty loud, but I never hit her if that's what you're asking."

"Anything physical that day?"

"Absolutely not."

"Your insecurity from that morning didn't lead to any violence later in the day?"

"Jesus. No. I didn't do anything to her."

Castillo pounced. "Roommate says she met you that night."

Walker glanced at Castillo. *He knows what he's doing.* Heather never said that, but Castillo wanted to see Josh's reaction.

Josh pounded his fist on the table, "That's bullshit! I told you I didn't meet her that night," he yelled at Castillo.

Walker carefully watched Josh's facial expression. He had been telling half-truths the entire interview. Eye twitches, blinking, looking around — it was all a combination of fact and fiction — but this was the first truthful statement of the entire interview. Or at least Josh believed it to be true.

Not getting a reaction from Castillo, Josh turned to Walker, trying to find a friend in the room. "I didn't see her that night. You have to believe me. I didn't kill her!"

"Who said she was dead?" Walker asked.

Josh paused, gawked at Walker and Castillo as though he had just gone too far — said too much — then slowly slumped back in his seat with his head down. The room was silent for a long moment as Walker let that question hang in the air like the smell of a rotting carcass.

Then he went in for the kill. "We're just trying to find out the truth here, Josh. Are you telling us the truth?"

"Yes, of course," he said, exasperated and still looking down.

Walker paused for a moment. "Tell me about the *Sons of Liberty*?"

"What?" Josh looked up, surprised.

"The *Sons of Liberty*. Rumor is that you're a part of it."

Josh pushed back. "That's an old legend. Years ago. Before my time."

"Does it still exist?"

"I wouldn't know," Josh said, inadvertently twisting a ring on his right hand.

"What's it all about?" Walker asked, peering at the silver ring, a rendition of an owl carved into the thickened top, encircled by words he couldn't quite read.

"I wouldn't know." Still twisting the ring.

"What's with the ring?" Walker asked.

Josh suddenly realized he was touching the ring and immediately put his hands down. "Nothing. Just something a lot of the guys have. Sort of a symbol of Washington Academy. Kind of like a class ring, I guess. One of my friends...his father actually hand-carves them...so I've helped to sell a few them to other kids on campus.

"Just for guys, huh?

"Yeah."

"What does it say?"

"It's Latin — Numquid Avis Tincta."

"Which means?"

"Bird of Prey," Josh said with a long smile.

Walker stared at Josh for several seconds and then changed the subject again. "Were you sexually active with Amanda?"

His smile turned into a grin. "Yes."

"Any issues?"

"Any issues?" Josh clarified.

"Meaning, did you have any issues with your sex life? Were you trying to spice things up? Play any sex games perhaps?"

"No. Amanda liked it...traditional."

"Is that how you liked it?"

"That was fine with me."

"How about drugs?"

"Yeah, maybe."

"Pot, heroin, cocaine?"

"None of the hard stuff. Just pot occasionally."

"Were you smoking marijuana that night?"

"Maybe."

"Impair your judgment at all?"

"What?"

"Loss of memory, poor decision-making, anything like that?"

Josh was fed up. "No, man, I told you, I was hanging out with the guys that night. I didn't see Amanda at all. My judgment was not impaired. And I don't know what happened to her. Can I please go now?"

Walker looked at Castillo who shrugged and said, "Yeah, kid, you can go."

As Josh slammed the door on his way out, Castillo again sat in the seat across from Walker. "What do you think?" he asked.

Walker thought for a moment. "I don't think either one of them is telling us the whole truth, but obviously they're scared and don't want to get wrapped up in this. They both put up a nice front, but some cracks may start to emerge as we continue to turn up the heat."

"Agreed. I just hope they crack sooner rather than later," Castillo said, caution in his voice. "Amanda's life may be depending on it."

CHAPTER 14

Several more of Amanda's friends were interviewed over the next few hours, but nothing more about the night in question was learned from any of them. The interviews, however, did provide a consistent story, and it was clear from her friends' testimony that Amanda was popular, involved in lots of school activities, and well-regarded by the faculty and staff. And although many students had seen Amanda that day, no one could give them any information about her after 9 PM that evening, when Heather said she had left their dorm room. No one had seen her that night or witnessed anything out of the ordinary.

Additionally, all of her friends spoke of a content young woman, succeeding in her classes, enjoying her activities, and making plans for the days and weeks ahead. Their accounts did not paint the picture of an unhappy student who wanted to run away or would do something stupid or dangerous. From her friends' effusive descriptions, she was intelligent, popular, and level-headed. It seemed that Amanda was not planning to disappear.

Amanda's teachers would be questioned tomorrow.

As the interviews ended for the day a little past 7 PM, a young male student arrived at the study room to escort Walker back to his residence for the night. A small percentage of the school's faculty lived on campus, situated in a cluster of buildings, similar to a row of townhomes, not far from the girls' dormitory. It was a short walk, but darkness had already descended on the campus as dusk had passed, and the final rays of twilight could not penetrate through the canopy of trees.

Walker carried a small duffel bag he had retrieved earlier from his car with the strap looped over his shoulder as he followed the student up the set of stairs to the front door of the second residence from the end. The student unlocked the door and turned on the lights in the main living space before he handed the keys to Walker and then quickly made his exit.

He dropped the duffle bag on a chair next to the front door and snooped around the apartment, impressed with the exquisite accommodations for the somewhat cramped space. The residence resembled that of a studio apartment, but the interior decorating represented an affluent style with intricate wall paintings and expensive furnishings. He smiled at a beautiful painting of a forest landscape in a thick wooden frame on the far wall. And became lost in the trees.

A voice whispered from behind him. "I figured I would come and find you before you sought me out."

Walker turned to see a woman in her early-thirties leaning in the doorway. She had a slender build and wavy, dark brown hair which fell just below her shoulders. Her complexion was smooth and her hazel eyes were penetrating, behind a pair of gray glasses, giving off an intelligent, yet sexy look. She wore a simple light orange blouse over a denim skirt with flesh-colored stockings and flats. She leaned against the jamb of the open door as if waiting for Walker to invite her inside.

"I beg your pardon?" was all Walker could muster.

She finally reached out her hand, embarrassed. "I'm sorry. I'm Meredith Thomas. I'm a member of the faculty. I teach AP English Literature and Composition."

Walker moved to her and shook her hand. It was soft, smooth. "Nice to meet you."

Meredith regained her composure from the awkward introduction. "I didn't mean to startle you. I actually saw the student bring you up to the residence, and your door was open, so I thought I'd pop in. I actually live right next door," she explained, tilting her head to the left, "in the adjoining faculty residence. It's an end unit."

Walker smiled at the humor. "Does that mean it's a little bigger than this place?"

Meredith smiled back. "Slightly."

"I'll make sure to request an end unit the next time I come for a visit. Do a lot of faculty members live on campus?"

"No. Just a couple of us. Mostly younger ones just starting out. My situation is a little more...complicated."
Walker nodded. "I know all about complicated."
"But I really don't mind it at all; it's such a beautiful campus."
"It is," Walker agreed. "I could certainly live here. No question."
Walker paused. "Were you assigned to show me around?"

"Oh, no," Meredith stuttered, "nothing like that. I just figured you would eventually want to talk with me, so I thought I'd find you first."

Walker gave her a quizzical look. "Talk with you?"

"I taught Amanda Bryson. I had her in class the day she disappeared. I guess it was her last class that day." Meredith paused as her voice dropped. "So I may have been one of the last people to see her."

It suddenly dawned on Walker about the faculty interviews the next day. He jerked back, apologetic. "I'm sorry. I haven't quite gotten that far yet. We just finished the interviews with the students today. Faculty members are slated for tomorrow."

Meredith could obviously see the tired strain on Walker's face, so she gave him a reassuring smile. "You want to start your faculty interviews early? I can buy you a drink."

Walker suddenly realized he had been sober all day. Not one drink. He couldn't actually remember the last time that had happened. *Can I handle it?* he wondered.

Based on his pensive look and delay in responding, Meredith immediately recognized she had put him in an awkward position (again) and tried to smooth out the building tension. "As long as that's appropriate. I'm not a suspect or anything, am I?" Meredith asked with a grin.

"Not yet." Walker shot back, smiling.

Meredith chuckled, then her facial expression turned to one of concern. "Actually, how about dinner? It looks like you could use some."

Walker nodded, realizing he also hadn't eaten in several hours. "That sounds great."

"I know a wonderful place," she said.

CHAPTER 15

The quaint Italian bistro in downtown Leesburg was not crowded at this late hour on a weeknight, so it was quiet as the lights were dimmed and only the slightest sounds of intimate conversations, silverware on plates, and the clinking of glasses could be heard. Two half-empty glasses of wine stood on the table as the waitress took their finished plates and asked if they needed anything else. Walker felt much better after having eaten some food and sipped gently on his second glass of wine, which was perfect in taking the edge off. He thanked Meredith for suggesting it.

The conversation throughout the meal had been pleasant and engaging, mostly small talk about their jobs and families. Walker learned that Meredith, a transplant from upstate New York, had been teaching at the academy for eleven years, her first teaching position after graduating from UVA. Exchanging nuptials with her husband shortly after college, the two had lived in an old farmhouse on two acres of land in Warrenton, Virginia until the marriage eventually ended. Selling the property through the divorce proceedings and moving onto the campus of Washington Academy was Meredith's way of starting over. There were no children.

Walker told her about his former life as an FBI agent, his current life as a private investigator, and his struggle with alcohol after the divorce. He didn't go into details about the sudden collapse of his career or the family turmoil which followed because it was still so difficult to articulate. He simply told her he had made a grave mistake and left it at that. She didn't press.

They had not yet discussed the disappearance, but now was the time, so Walker maneuvered the conversation back to the campus. "Was your move back to campus a good one?" he asked.

Meredith smiled, taking a sip from her wine. "Oh, absolutely. It's really allowed me to clear my head, you know? Focus again on the little things—the subtle beauties that surround us. I sometimes just sit on my porch and stare out at the campus, the gorgeous tree growth, the manicured flower beds, the kids walking to class. I was so absorbed for so long by my crumbling marriage, that I lost sight of the beauty in life. I think I'm finally getting that back again. Plus, living on campus is very convenient and cheap," she said with a smile.

Walker nodded. "Sounds like you've found yourself again?"

Meredith grinned. "Yes, I have. But it wasn't easy. And it took time. I'm not all the way there yet, but better than I was. Certainly improving every day."

"I'm sure it would have been tougher to do that with children," Walker said.

"Exactly. So I guess that was for the best." She paused for a moment, pensive. "That was actually part of the problem. He never wanted kids. I did. I thought I could eventually convince him, but it didn't work out that way. I wonder if we ever would have lasted."

Walker sighed. "We solve all of these mysteries, but relationships still seem to elude us."

Meredith looked him in the eyes. "How old is your daughter?"

"She just turned thirteen."

"And you don't see her at all?"

"No. But it's better this way. I don't want her to see me like this. I'm not good for anyone right now."

Meredith tilted her head. "No one?"

Walker scoffed and looked out at the dining room.

"I see you nursing that wine like it's the last one in the world. How's your drinking? I'm sorry I didn't realize earlier when I offered to buy you a drink."

Walker was solemn. "It's okay. I'm dealing with it. Some days are better than others. I don't need to be completely sober to do the work I'm doing, but I'm trying to keep my wits about me for this case. I need to be sharp, but I think I may have lost that years ago."

"Perhaps you need some time away. Live in a faculty residence on a beautiful private school campus. The residences are mostly for the younger teachers because of their size, but it's a great respite from it all. What better place to live, right?"

Walker agreed. "I was actually just thinking the same exact thing. Does Washington Academy need any criminal justice teachers?" *Or perhaps just criminal.*

"I don't know," Meredith giggled. "You'd have to check with our illustrious leader."

"Ah, yes," Walker leaned back. "The famous Dr. Ellis."

"Quite arrogant, don't you think?"

"I do. And definitely hiding something," Walker added.

Meredith smirked, "Indeed. I think it's the whole private school thing. As I'm sure you've realized, we are a world unto ourselves, beholden to no one, not even the Board of Trustees. They simply do whatever Ellis wants. As long as the endowment holds out and the tuition checks keep clearing the bank, no one is going to speak up."

Walker edged forward, "So you've been there for ten years, what's really going on there, behind all the pomp and circumstance?"

Meredith smirked. "We would need a lot more wine."

"Try me."

Meredith stared at Walker for a long moment, seemingly trying to judge if she could trust him. Then she instinctively looked around the deserted dining room, as though she believed they were listening in on her conversation. She leaned in closer and started to whisper. "Well, first of all, they're very secretive. Both of them. Ellis and his security chief, Castillo. He's with him all the time. It's like the security is paramount to all else, including the academics. I know we have lots of famous children here and maybe some notorious ones as well, but everything we do seems to be centered around protection. I'm just not exactly sure who they're protecting — us or them."

"What do you mean?"

"Well, with Amanda's disappearance, the faculty is definitely on edge, but people are literally afraid to talk about it. I can barely get a word out of my colleagues. Dr. Ellis and Mr. Castillo have spoken to all of us separately on at least two occasions. It's almost like an interrogation. They weren't asking questions pertaining to what we knew about Amanda's habits or routines to help figure out what happened to her, but rather, what we saw or think we saw before she disappeared. It didn't seem right. It was almost like they were asking these questions to ensure Amanda hadn't told us anything that might, you know, implicate the two of them."

"Did they seem suspicious to you?"

"Suspicious? They always seem suspicious to me."

Walker laughed.

Meredith leaned even closer. "Did they really not see anything on all those cameras they have? With all that equipment, shouldn't they know what happened to her?"

"Yeah, all the cameras," Walker said sarcastically. "And only one person has the key. And my access is limited. I only get to see what he wants me to see."

Meredith shook her head and sighed. "It's so sad."

"I know," Walker said. "So tell me about Amanda."

Meredith relaxed and leaned back. "Oh, she was wonderful. A great student. A great person. She was well-liked. I did very well in class. I was always there, stayed after to ask clarifying questions or discuss a grade. She was one of my best. Truly."

"Did she ever give you any kind of sign that she was unhappy or worried or anything out of the ordinary?"

"Not at all. She was very consistent. Always seemed

happy." Meredith paused. "Except with her boyfriend."

"Josh Easterly?"

"Yes, it seemed like the two of them didn't get along very well, based on conversations I would overhear with her girlfriends about him. I didn't know him personally, never had him in class, but he didn't sound like a very good match for her. The small classes here allow us to build meaningful relationships with the students, so you can really get to know them and recognize when something is wrong. Her boyfriend was the only thing that seemed to bother her. All else was good."

"And your class was the last she attended that day?"

"Yes, it was an afternoon class. Again, nothing out of the ordinary. She didn't stay after that day, but I do remember her saying goodbye on her way out. She said something like 'I'll see you tomorrow' so, in my opinion, everything in her mind was fine when she left my class."

Walker nodded. "Okay."

"Do you have any leads?"

"No. Lots of suspicion, but no leads."

"Suspicion with whom?"

Walker leaned back again. "Everyone."

***

As they exited the restaurant, Meredith gripped Walker's arm and held it in hers. She was slightly tipsy from the alcohol and bumped into him as they stumbled to the curb where the Ubers waited. They had called two cars — the same as when they had left the campus — to not draw any undue attention to themselves. Castillo had probably already viewed the footage of them leaving slightly apart from each other and possibly even tailed Walker to the restaurant. When Walker first suggested the separate cars at the residence, Meredith had quickly agreed, and now he knew why. Something was definitely mysterious about this private school, and she was right to be cautious.

Moving slightly in front of her, Walker stepped up to the first car and opened the door for Meredith. She paused, waved to the driver — who returned the gesture — and pulled Walker back from the curb.

"I'll just be one minute," she promised the driver.

She pulled Walker close to her and held out her hand. "I don't know if I can trust you, but I hope I can. You and I both know something suspicious is happening at this school, and I think Amanda may have gotten caught up in it. I want you to find her. I want you to find out what happened to her. And if this school is responsible, I want you to get them."

Meredith opened her hand, revealing a small, white key-card. She lowered her head and stared at the card. "I'm not proud of it, and please don't judge me, but I actually dated Joaquin Castillo for a few months after my divorce. Definitely a rebound relationship."

Walker frowned at first and then simply shrugged his shoulders, trying to avoid passing judgment. *We all make mistakes.*

Meredith gazed at Walker. "But he was too paranoid for me. Too secretive. Too obsessed with campus security and his damn cameras. I have this feeling like I'm always being watched, you know? I haven't found any cameras, I've certainly looked, but I still have that feeling. His OCD and paranoia were simply too much for me." Meredith looked again at the card. "He left this one day at my apartment, and when he came back looking for it, I told him I hadn't seen it. Was that wrong of me?" Meredith asked.

Walker shrugged, again trying to avoid passing judgment. *He was the last one who had the right to do that.*

"I don't know why I kept it," she continued. "Perhaps I thought that one day I would need it...to unlock some secrets that might lay hidden..." her voice trailed off. Meredith quickly placed the security card in Walker's hand and closed it. "It's yours now. For whatever you need. Just find Amanda."

With that, Meredith turned and climbed into the Uber.

The car pulled away. The second Uber pulled up as Walker was transfixed by the keycard in his hand. It was Castillo's key. A key with the power to unlock secrets.

CHAPTER 16

It didn't take long for Walker to make his decision during the drive back to campus. It was a little past 10 PM as Walker thanked his driver, checked in with the security guard at the front gate, and walked onto the quiet campus, except for the faint sound of crickets in the background. Walker noticed the decorative pole lamps, placed every few yards along the tree-lined walkways, casting a soft light on the nineteenth-century revival architecture. Dotting the campus were also emergency phones that gave off a bluish glow in the dark, any potential calls being funneled into one location: the nerve center of the entire campus. His destination.

The administration building was an imposing structure on campus, both for its aesthetic architectural appeal and central geographic location on the school grounds. It also housed the offices of the Dean of Students as well as the Board of Trustees, but it was not the seat of power for that reason. Its real power was buried deep underground in a basement-level complex. Walker remembered his long walk down the antique hallway leading to the next-generation security center. A hall of secrets. If he was going to make any headway in this investigation, he had to uncover what this school's security center was hiding.

The trained professional wondered if the key card would actually work, or if had it been updated or deleted from the system. *Would campus police surround him once he tried to use it? How OCD really was Castillo?*

Walker entered the building using his own keycard, saving Castillo's for as long as he could, surmising that each keycard entry was logged, and the alerts would immediately appear once he used Castillo's card. His time would also be severely limited once he waved the card at an entry point, but it all depended on who was monitoring the alerts and how quickly they noticed it. It was a chance he had to take.

Making his way quickly across the lobby, Walker stepped into the elevator. Only the 'up' button could be pushed. The 'down' button required a keycard. Walker let out a deep breath as he pressed Castillo's card against the button. The button immediately lit up, followed by the reassuring bing, and the doors closed. Walker felt a flutter in his stomach as the elevator descended.

He swallowed hard as the elevator came to a stop and the doors opened into the dimly lit hallway. It was empty. Walker had already strategized in his mind about what he would say to anyone in the hallway, as it would have been difficult to explain why an unauthorized person was down here. Interestingly enough, there were no cameras in this hallway. It was obviously too sensitive a location for cameras, and he was sure Castillo had already made the necessary precautions to prevent entry into this part of the campus. Walker moved swiftly.

The glowing translucent glass at the end of the hall was like a beacon calling out to him, but he was sure he would not be able to enter the main complex as it was likely manned 24-7. However, there were several rooms on either side of the hallway leading to the bright pane of glass, which he assumed his key would also open. Again, all of his entries would probably be recorded, so he figured he only had enough time to choose one room.

Walker stalked down the hallway, staying to one side and focusing on the lights ahead, just waiting for someone to exit the surveillance center and put a halt to his little foray. He paused by each door, trying to decide which one to attempt until finally, he arrived at the last one on the right before the glass. He swung his arm down, swiping the keycard over the keypad, and the door opened slightly. Walker pushed it with his shoulder, quickly made entry, and closed the door gently behind him.

Once inside the small room, he hoped he had selected the right door. Any one of the hallway rooms presented the possibility for a treasure trove of information, but Walker hoped that Castillo put the most important things closest to him. The room was dark and smelled of mahogany and furniture polish. It certainly wasn't like the next-generation complex next door, but rather an aging room from the 1800s. The one modern adornment was a large set of fluorescent lights hanging above the desk, but Walker avoided that wall switch and moved to a small lamp on the desk.

He flipped the switch, emitting a dim glow onto the room, and surveyed its contents. It was sparse. Aside from the large desk in the center of the room with a computer, few decorations adorned the walls and only two filing cabinets and bookshelf buffeted the walls. The cabinet drawers were all locked, as were the desk drawers. Walker moved the mouse for the desktop computer but was greeted with a small popup window — the Washington Academy logo as the background — asking for a username and password. He tapped his thumb rapidly on the desk in frustration, while looking up from the computer and studying the room again.

Finally, he noticed a small door, like a closet, in the far corner. As he approached the door, he recognized a small keypad, which closely resembled the one in the hallway. *Was it possible?* He pulled Castillo's keycard from his pocket and waved it in front of the keypad. Nothing happened. *Dammit.* He waved it again. The door clicked open.

CHAPTER 17

Walker entered into a small space, not much larger than a walk-in closet. In front of him was an assortment of screens and keyboards, similar to what he had seen in the surveillance room, but on a much smaller scale. He stepped closer to the monitors, carefully studying the images move across the brightly colored screens and then peered at the controls below the pictures. Thoughts raced through Walker's head. *Is this where Castillo edited his digital footage? Where he could determine what the outside world saw? Where only Castillo knew what had really happened?*

But he was confused. These images didn't look right. Walker cocked his head slightly to try and make out what he was seeing. Something about these video feeds was different. It was not like the footage he had seen in the surveillance room. These images were not from the cameras that lined the campus. These were from different locations, more intimate locations. One monitor caught his attention. He recognized the location. He peered closer at the brick facade, the rusted railing, the brush which had been stomped down. Walker jerked back as he suddenly realized he was looking at hidden camera footage.

He thought back to his conversation with Castillo in the small meadow behind the female residence hall. The same space at which this camera was pointed, the same feed now showing on this monitor. *That's why Castillo wasn't worried about the blind spots. There were no blind spots.* The visible cameras were only one side of the equation. The hidden cameras were the real power behind the surveillance system. Walker stepped back from the monitors and glanced anxiously across the litany of images. They literally covered the entire campus.

Walker exhaled his surprise, regained his composure, and sat down in a soft chair in front of the array of equipment. He anxiously glanced over at the slightly ajar door, the soft light from the desk lamp filling the adjacent room. There wasn't much time.

Having worked with surveillance equipment during his time in the FBI, Walker played with the controls until he was able to adjust the video feed of the hidden camera behind the girls' dormitory. He scanned through the flickering video images until he arrived back to the day that Amanda disappeared, denoted by the time and date in the bottom right corner of the feed.

At approximately 21:02 (9:02 PM) on September 23rd, a young girl with long black hair appeared in the camera's view. As she peered around, Walker clearly saw it is Amanda Bryson. She reached out her hand, and another hand suddenly came into view, which helped lift her up from the sunken enclosure around the window. The second figure was dressed in a long brown robe with a hood that obscured the stranger's face from the camera. Amanda willingly went with the robed figure, and they moved off into the clearing, the same spot where Walker had stood earlier that day.

Walker rewound the footage and watched it again. He still could not make out the face of the person who helped her out of the enclosure. Walker watched the footage for the third time. Something finally caught his attention, so he paused the tape, zoomed in on the hand pulling her up, and peered at the still image on the screen. There was a ring on the person's right hand, a distinctive ring with the image of an owl scrawled on the top. He had seen this ring before...on Josh Easterly.

At the same time, the door to the outer room made a distinctive click. Someone had used the keypad. The door opened and a person entered the outer room. Walker jumped from his chair and moved swiftly to the closet door, pushing it closed until only a sliver of open space was visible. He peeked into the adjacent room.

Walker didn't recognize the male visitor, but he wore a security uniform similar to the surveillance technicians. The stranger was all business as he glided across the room and started to place a manila folder on the desk. He looked weirdly at the light and called out to his colleague still out in the hall. "Was Castillo in here? The light is on."

"I think so. I saw him earlier." Another male voice responded from the hallway.

The technician simply shrugged and continued placing the file on the desk and walked out. The door closed behind him.

Walker breathed a sigh of relief as his heart settled back into a normal rhythm. He knew his luck was about to run out, so he quickly restored the video feed to its current image capture, exited the small closet, and rapidly headed to the office door.

He swung it open and there in the doorway, staring at him, was Joaquin Castillo.

CHAPTER 18

"I'm telling you...the door was open," Walker pleaded, now sitting in the chair across the wide desk from Castillo, the overhead fluorescents brightly lighting the room. "I swear to you. I was actually looking for you."

"You expect me to believe that? You're telling me one of my technicians left it open?" Castillo demanded.

"Must have."

Castillo leaned over the desk. "That would never happen. Don't lie to me, Mr. Walker. You're here by invitation, and that invitation can easily be revoked. I've been more than forthcoming with you. There's no need to sneak around a secure area to try and find what you're looking for."

Walker returned the stern expression. "Have you been forthcoming with me? Have you given me everything you have?"

Castillo crossed his fingers and leaned on his elbows. "And what makes you think I haven't?"

"Come on, Joaquin, look around. All the cameras. All the surveillance. All the secure areas. Is this to keep the people on this campus safe, or to keep everyone else out?"

Castillo laughed. "My job is the security of this campus, and I will not allow anyone to get in the way of that. Remember, nothing happens here without me knowing it."

"That's exactly what concerns me."

"What's that?"

"If you know everything that happens on this campus,

how did a girl disappear from it two days ago without a trace?"

Castillo glared. "I told you. If you know how to avoid the cameras, you can avoid the cameras."

"All of them?"

"Yes, all of them. It depends on your motivation."

Many thoughts were running through Walker's mind. Firstly, that Castillo obviously knew the hidden camera footage from behind the girls' dorm revealed Amanda's escape, and secondly, if he watched the video, he also knew about Josh. *So why would he be protecting him?* Walker didn't mention the secret footage from the closet or question why Castillo was hiding it from him but thought he would at least plant the seed in Castillo's mind that he suspected him of hiding something. Fortunately, it appeared that Castillo did not yet know his keycard had been used, but Walker wasn't sure how long until they discovered the intrusion. For right now, Walker was in the clear, so his immediate concern was simply to extricate himself from this uncomfortable situation.

"Very well," Walker said flatly. "Can I please go now?"

"Listen, Dr. Ellis agreed for you to be here. I did not. He's asked me to help you investigate. I'm trying to assist you, but I can't do that if you're going behind my back. You had better be careful. Remember, one person has already disappeared," Castillo said with a seriousness that unnerved Walker.

He ignored the threat. "Can I go?"

Castillo waited for a moment then said. "Yes. One of my techs will escort you out of the building. And try not to get in any more trouble, Mr. Walker. We have a busy day tomorrow."

***

Walker was exhausted by the time he made it back to his residence. He hadn't worked this hard in a long time, and he needed some rest. He desperately needed to sleep, but sleeping wasn't that restful. His present-day nightmare would only be replaced by the nightmares from his past. He typically used alcohol to dull his senses and drift to sleep, but this time was different. As he had told Meredith, he wanted to stay alert and aware. He had to be at his best to find Amanda. His other cases simply didn't matter that much to him. This one did.

Walker lay back on the bed, staring at the ceiling. *What was Castillo hiding?* he asked himself. And most importantly, *Was Meredith now in danger? Would Castillo eventually learn it had been her that had given him the keycard and had he just inadvertently dragged her into the crosshairs with him?* Walker wasn't so sure he could answer any of these questions, and he stopped trying as the day's weariness slowly got the better of him. Walker fell asleep, so the nightmares could begin.

CHAPTER 19

Special Agent Walker tugged on his Kevlar vest with both hands, pulling the bulletproof padding down from his neck. Designed to absorb the impact of bullet rounds, the woven vest of laminated fibers was surprisingly light, but it weighed him down now. Still the newest certified member of the Washington Field Office SWAT team, he was well aware of the importance of the gear, had practiced with it many times in training, but he had never quite gotten used to it.

Walker peered around the inside of the armored car, his fellow SWAT teammates readying themselves for whatever they would face, adjusting helmets, checking automatic rifles, and ensuring their equipment was in perfect working order. All police officers were keenly aware that the slightest malfunction in a tool or weapon could cost them their lives, especially in a hostile situation where a SWAT team was required, so ensuring all their various military-style accouterments were ready was of paramount concern.

A human miscalculation, on the other hand, could neither be planned for nor prevented at this juncture in the operation. At this point, each member of the SWAT team would simply rely on their intensive training to ensure a successful outcome. But unfortunately, it didn't always work out that way.

The emergency request for backup came into the FBI field office about 20 minutes earlier — around 8 PM — based on a 911 dispatch call approximately 30 minutes before that. The Virginia State Police were already on the scene, responding to a hostage situation that had developed in an office building on Route 50 in West Falls Church, Virginia. Elements of the state police SWAT team were not in the vicinity because of a training exercise, so the FBI received the call.

From what Walker had gathered from his commander, who was seated in the passenger seat of the vehicle and could be seen through the small bar-covered window separating the cabin from the rest of the armored car, a fight had ensued between a female lawyer and a former client. And now he was holding her — and her daughter — at gunpoint.

State troopers had surrounded the building, which was situated along with a cluster of other businesses in an office park, and negotiations had begun. They needed SWAT to secure the perimeter, conduct reconnaissance, and prepare for a breach if negotiations with the hostage-taker broke down. The situation was standard fare for the elite officers, and they had trained for this very scenario countless times. The armored car lurched to a stop. Seconds later, the rear doors opened and twelve men, clad in their SWAT gear, descended from the vehicle in a single file line into the darkness.

Walker surveyed the scene. Several police vehicles — lights flashing — had formed a semicircle around the front of the office building. Portable lights, placed at various intervals around that same perimeter were also pointed at the building, illuminating it in a white glare, red and blue lights dancing within the glow. A large window, emblazoned with 'Andrea Shelby, Attorney At Law' in gold writing, was the most notable feature of the storefront, next to a standard-sized door with a full-length pane of glass. Through the haze of lights, shadows of movement could be seen inside. A police helicopter thumped rhythmically overhead, its circular searchlight bouncing around the parking lot as it hovered back and forth.

As the SWAT members jogged past a makeshift negotiation station behind a police cruiser, consisting of a small table covered by a radio receiver and schematics of the building, an officer spoke into a cell phone on speaker with the subject. It sounded like a lot of talk from the negotiator with only silence in return. The SWAT commander moved to the next police vehicle and his team gathered around him as he threw a blueprint of the building on the hood of the car, illuminated by the lights from their helmets.

"Alright, gentlemen, as far as we can tell, we have one subject inside with what we believe to be a semiautomatic pistol and two hostages. The first is the owner of the business, a thirty-five-year-old Caucasian woman, and the second is her twelve-year-old daughter. There are smaller offices here and here," he said, pointing to the blueprint, "but we believe all of them to be located in the main office...in the front right here. Hostage negotiations are ongoing, so right now we're the backup."

"Any idea how the girl got in there?" asked one of the SWAT officers.

"Sounds like she was dropped off by her father a short time ago. He's in the back of a squad car over there. Mom and daughter were going to a movie tonight. Dad thinks the assailant is a former client, came back with the gun after he dropped off his daughter," the commander replied.

The SWAT officer nodded as the commander proceeded to assign two-men teams to various checkpoints either around or on top of the building by pointing to the locations on the map. Finally, he said, "Walker and Bingham, I want you two right here on the roof. There's an access panel for an air duct there. Remove the cover so we can gain access if needed, but for right now, just sit tight and observe." Walker and his partner, Marcus Bingham, nodded.

The commander surveyed the group. "Any questions?"

There were none.

"Move."

CHAPTER 20

Walker awoke but still felt drained. He sat up, struggling to catch his breath and groggily returned to his present reality. Unfortunately, his dreams had become a reality as well, but he couldn't change that. His dreams were the mistakes he couldn't correct, the errors he couldn't erase. Making the transition from a reality he couldn't change to the one that he could — but rarely ever did — was a daily ritual, so he was accustomed to it by now.

He stared into the bathroom mirror after splashing water on his face and ran through the previous day in his mind. After last night's threat from Castillo, he was more convinced than ever that Lewis had been right, and the suspicious dean and his security chief were hiding something sinister behind the gilded walls of this exclusive private school. He wasn't sure what it was or how deep it went, but he was certain there were secrets.

The video evidence only proved to complicate that theory. He wasn't sure how Josh Easterly, or any of the dozens of other boys who may have had those same rings, fit into the story. *Was it related to the Sons of Liberty? Or just a ghost story?* It was fairly obvious why Castillo hadn't shared the video evidence with Walker. First, it was a hidden camera which presented a litany of legal issues, and second, it was an image of a stranger cloaked in a robe and wearing a mysterious ring. That image in and of itself would scare the hell out of any parent who wished to send their child here, and it certainly wouldn't be appearing in marketing materials any time soon. But the question still remained: *Was it a dangerous cult or an innocent child's game? And was Castillo aware of it?*

Walker wondered how many other girls may have also disappeared from this campus; how many missing persons may have gone unreported. If Walker hadn't been involved in this case, he wondered where the case would be right now. *Would Amanda simply be just another unsolved mystery, or was Castillo trying to protect someone?* Whatever the motive, Castillo had been hiding a crucial piece of the puzzle, and that was deeply concerning.

However, he had to tread carefully. Any misstep now could result in his expulsion from the campus, and for all intents and purposes, the end of his investigation. As far as he knew at the current moment, Castillo was unaware he had seen the hidden footage, so he had to invoke its existence without tipping his hand. He needed to speak with Ellis again, try to rattle him, and see if any inconsistencies emerged in his story.

Walker decided to place a call to Dr. Ellis' office requesting a meeting, and surprisingly, through his receptionist, he agreed. He imagined Ellis was projecting this facade of cooperation to appease Arcuri, but instead, they simply had to wait it out. Walker only had two days left, so if they appeared to collaborate on the outside while hamstringing the investigation behind the scenes, he would be left with nothing. But at least Arcuri would be satisfied because his private investigator had been given a chance. Or if Walker happened to get too close, he didn't doubt that Castillo would decide to take care of him. He knew the threat last night from Castillo was real. He was former military, meaning he knew how to kill people, and perhaps even make it look like an accident. The closer Walker got to the truth, the more dangerous this investigation became.

After showering and dressing quickly — in a fresh button-down and jeans — Walker made his way to the third floor of the administration building for his second attempt with Ellis. The receptionist entered the office with him. This meeting was certainly not as cordial as the first, no pretentious introductions this time, and Castillo and Ellis were talking as he entered the room. Both men — Ellis behind the desk, Castillo in the same chair as last time — leaned in close toward each other. The secretary closed the door behind her.

Walker approached the desk as Ellis and Castillo halted their conversation and leaned back into their chairs. Before Walker had reached his seat, Ellis spoke. "Joaquin tells me you were in a secure area last night."

Walker sat in the chair, pausing for a moment to decide how best to solidify his lie. "Yes, I lost my way I guess."

Ellis moved forward, his elbows firmly on the desk, his hands folded just below his chin. "Mr. Walker, please remember that we have invited you here. And we have very strict rules regarding entry into certain locations on this campus. As a former member of law enforcement, you should know that."

"Yes, sir."

"But Joaquin tells me you have shown little respect for these rules and no deference to our operating procedures."

Walker looked at Castillo, who was staring at him. He turned back to Ellis.

"Yet we have shared all of our information from this investigation with you. You've interviewed several of our students, and today I'm told you will be talking to the faculty members. We have even given you a keycard for entry into virtually every location on campus, except for our sensitive areas. I'm not sure what you're expecting from us, Mr. Walker."

Bending forward to match Ellis's aggressive stance, Walker said, "I need to know what's going on here that you're not telling me about?"

Ellis started to chuckle and dismissed the suggestion, but Walker continued. "I need to know why you have so many cameras on this campus, but a girl goes missing from these grounds without a trace. I need to know how many other girls have disappeared from this campus that has never been reported. I need to know why Joaquin has been leading me around by the hand and not allowing me to do my own investigation."

Ellis glared at Walker. "Mr. Walker, I know you are frustrated by this case. We're all frustrated by this case. But we did not bring you onboard so you could fling accusations at Joaquin and me and accuse us of not being forthcoming with you. We brought you here because we thought you could help..."

"Did you have anything to do with Amanda's disappearance?" Walker interrupted.

Ellis looked surprised. "I'm sorry. Is this an interrogation?"

"Are you able to answer the question?"

Castillo spoke up, "He doesn't need to answer the question. He's the dean of this school for Christ's sake."

Ellis held up his hand. "It's okay, Joaquin, I'll answer the question." He stared into Walker's eyes. "I had absolutely nothing to do with Amanda Bryson's disappearance. All I want to do is find her and reunite her with her family. And for her to finish her high school career at Washington Academy." He breathed. "Mr. Walker, we cater to a very privileged segment of our society. And for a multitude of reasons — be it the wealth or the power or the sensitive nature of what they do, our parents expect a level of privacy and secrecy from this institution. Please do not assume just because we are not transparent, we are hiding something. We are opaque because it's what our clientele demands."

"Yet Mr. Arcuri asked you to bring me here."

"Yes, but I could have refused. Lorenzo knows full well what we are about here. In fact, he is one of our clients who expects it, and so he fully understood that what he was asking me to do was going against that philosophy. But his father is an old friend, and he's given a lot to this school, so I agreed. But only within the confines of our standard operating procedures," Ellis said, wagging his finger. "Nothing more."

"I can't solve this case if you're hiding anything from me."

"I assure you, Mr. Walker, we are not. But you must understand our need to do this quietly. We must be discreet to honor the wishes of our many other clients and their children, including Lorenzo Arcuri. It would not be wise to draw any undue attention to this matter."

Walker kept his discovery of the video evidence to himself. For now.

Ellis lowered his voice and spoke softly. "I understand that in the absence of any real evidence, it is very easy to suspect us. It makes sense. That we've simply covered everything up to hide the truth of what really happened," he said, glancing at Castillo. "But I assure you, Mr. Walker, nothing could be further from the truth. We want to find Amanda Bryson just as you do. Work with Joaquin, interview the faculty, and whatever you need from me, please don't hesitate to ask. We're all on the same side here."

I very much doubt that, Walker thought to himself as he nodded and thanked Ellis for his support. As far as he could tell, Ellis was telling him the truth. Or similar to Josh's answers, he believed he was telling him the truth. Walker's questions had been direct, but Ellis was able to field them with expert precision. Perhaps that meant he wasn't involved, or perhaps after all these years of hiding so many secrets, he had gotten really good at lying.

CHAPTER 21

Special Agent Walker and his partner easily scaled the wall of the office building through a maintenance ladder on the far side of the complex. They reached the roof, methodically swung their assault rifles to clear the area for any activity, and settled by a large air vent, a rectangular-shaped aluminum structure which jutted out from the flat roof. According to the schematic, this air vent led directly into an adjacent office of the main room where the assailant was holding the woman at gunpoint.

A small electric screwdriver was used to remove the flimsy metal grate which covered the opening of the vent. It was only a short distance to the main floor, and the two SWAT officers could hear the yelling. The negotiations did not appear to be going well.

"Unit two, is the air vent clear?" crackled the question over his earpiece.

"Roger that, command. We have removed the access grate and are holding at the opening. We can hear the subject inside." Walker said into the microphone, attached to his helmet.

"Unit two, move into position. The subject is becoming increasingly erratic and negotiations are breaking down."

The two men exchanged 'anxious but inevitable' glances and Walker replied on the radio, "Roger that. Moving into the air vent now."

The SWAT officers climbed into the aluminum tunnel and crawled a short distance on the flat silver plates until they reached another metal grate, which covered a rectangular opening directly above an office space. This room was adjacent to the main lobby, and the door between the offices was slightly ajar, so the arguing could easily be heard in the next room.

"Command, this is unit two, we are in the air vent above the adjacent room. Permission to enter the room?"

There was a long moment of silence. The commander was most likely checking in with the hostage negotiator. On the continuum of deadly force, the commanding officer had to decide if there was enough cause for an escalation — if a tipping point had been reached to take it to the next level. Making entry into the room was the next level of engagement, not a full breach, but certainly heightening the stakes.

As evidenced by the increased tension and angst in the hostage-taker's voice, the situation was rapidly deteriorating. Literally, any trigger at this point could scuttle the negotiations and send the entire episode south in a matter of seconds, giving law enforcement only a few precious moments to react. Having a SWAT team in position in an adjacent room might be the only chance they had if the subject decided to start killing.

The order finally came. "Permission granted. Enter the adjacent room and hold position."

Walker removed the second grate and passed it back to his partner, who set it gently on the air duct and then swung himself down into the room, holding onto the grate opening for support. He dropped the couple of feet to the floor, went down on one knee, and aimed his rifle at the slightly open door. The ranting in the next room continued unabated, which provided perhaps the best cover for his movements. Moving low in a crouch-like stance, Walker stepped gingerly toward the open door as his partner did a similar maneuver and lined up against the wall behind him.

As Walker reached the slightly open door, he raised his assault rifle through the slit in the entryway and peered into the lobby. Sitting in an office chair in the center of the room was a young girl with long black hair, ensconced in a thick, woven blanket and shivering from fear. Her hands covered her mouth as she wept quietly, her body shuddering as she tried to contain the muffled cries and not draw any attention to herself.

The subject was a white male, approximately six-feet-tall with a buzz cut. He wore camouflage pants and a sleeveless, ribbed undershirt — pejoratively known as a wife-beater — which showed off his bulging muscles. A tattoo on his left arm signified he was probably former military, and that wasn't good. Ex-military meant he was most likely proficient with his firearm, so any advantage SWAT might have with a low-skilled criminal had just narrowed significantly. He had the mother in a stranglehold with his left hand, while his right hand waved a handgun. The negotiator's voice, calm and measured, emanated from a speakerphone on a nearby receptionist counter. In contrast, the perpetrator was irate and loud, shouting back at the phone as though it was a real person sitting there.

The assailant was controlled with his weapon but also moved it erratically, so at some point, Walker could probably get an open line of sight. The subject held his handgun at the hostage's head, but when yelling at the phone, he would point the weapon in that direction, away from the woman. It was in these moments that Walker would have the opportunity for a kill shot.

He whispered into his headset, "Command, unit two has a visual of the subject."

"Copy that. Sit tight."

Walker heard the command, but kept his rifle raised, waiting for either the order to shoot or an irrational move by the subject. Either way, he would take down this assailant before anyone got hurt. As the man continued to shout and swing his handgun, Walker's gun sights were trained on the perpetrator's head. He simply waited for the order.

CHAPTER 22

After his tense meeting with Ellis and Castillo and a brief visit to the Student Records Office on the first floor of the admin building, Walker decided to meet again with his former partner, Mark Lewis. His interviews with the faculty members weren't scheduled until later in the morning, so he had the time. He still didn't trust Castillo, however, so the meeting had to be clandestine. Lewis suggested a remote, wooded park a few miles from campus, so Walker traveled a circuitous route to get there, ensuring he wasn't followed by any security personnel from WA. It appeared he had gotten away without a tail, but he still passed the meager, gravel parking lot — on the edge of the park — to scope out the lay of the land before finally settling on that location.

Lewis arrived a few moments later in a dark blue unmarked sedan. He was alone this time. They walked from their vehicles along a dirt path — conveniently called the 'Hawk Trail' — leading into the woods. The trail was shaded, and the air smelled of pine. Lewis mostly listened as Walker relayed what had happened so far in the investigation on day one. He asked some clarifying questions, but by and large, Lewis was simply intrigued by the insider information about the reclusive school. Intelligence like this on Washington Academy had been extremely hard to come by, so Lewis was appreciative of his former partner's exploits.

They traced the carved path through the woods for about a mile until it circled back toward the entrance. As they neared the end of the path and the woods opening up to reveal their cars in the parking lot ahead, Walker shared his most recent discovery. "There's one more thing. I found my way into Castillo's office."

"How did you manage that?" Lewis asked, surprised.

"Long story."

"What did you find?"

Walker paused for a moment, ensuring he was making the correct choice by telling Lewis. "Hidden camera footage. A lot of it. It looks like he has most of the campus covered. I don't think he knows I saw it. Yet."

"You've got to be kidding me. That's an illegal use of surveillance. I'm sure those proud parents, who pay a fortune to have their kids to go to that school would be none too happy to learn about that."

"Wait, there's more." Walker stopped walking. "I also saw Amanda on that footage."

Lewis halted as well and turned. "What?"

"Being led away by a person in a cloak."

Lewis shook his head in disbelief. "You can't be serious."

"I can't quite believe it myself, but I'm dead serious," Walker said, then paused. "Based on what I could tell about the overall build of the person and a ring that's worn by a lot of boys on campus, I presume it's a male."

"You can't tell from the footage?"

"No, but I think it might be the boyfriend."

"Jesus," Lewis gasped. "What the hell is going on there? Does Castillo know?"

"I can't see how he couldn't. I'm wondering if there's something with the boyfriend."

"Sounds like the boyfriend might need some further investigation," Lewis said. "Any reason why Castillo would be protecting him?"

"I don't know. I looked at the kid's school records before coming to see you, but nothing seemed out of the ordinary, no discipline or anything like that. However, I did discover that his mother is a senator from Connecticut. She sits on the Armed Services Committee. Not sure if that's related to the academy, but perhaps it goes back to Castillo's time with CID. Can you possibly look into that for me?"

"Of course."

"Thanks, Mark."

It was now Lewis's turn to be deadly serious. "Ryan, before you go digging too deeply into Castillo, there's something you should know. I've looked at this guy's history going all the way back to his time with the investigative division. When he left CID, he simply disappeared. I mean we literally have nothing on him. Nothing. He was a ghost for two years before he joined Washington Academy. That can't be a coincidence. He obviously went way underground during the time he was off the grid, and God only knows what he found there. Don't turn your back on him, my friend."

"Understood."

"We haven't looked extensively at his CID files yet, so I'll get to that ASAP. See if there's some connection to this Armed Services senator."

"I appreciate it."

Walker started to move again, but Lewis stood still. He turned to his friend, wondering why he wasn't following.

"There's one more thing I need to tell you," Lewis said nervously, glancing at his car. "I really shouldn't be telling you this, and I could lose my job for it, but you're helping out an old friend, so I think you deserve to know."

Walker edged back toward Lewis. "Know what?"

A long pause. "We're coming in," Lewis said finally.

"What the fuck does that mean?" Walker asked sternly.

Another long pause. "It means we're coming in, buddy. I got the green light. The confirmation of Amanda Bryson's unreported disappearance — in connection with everything else we have — gave us the probable cause we needed. We're coming in. Full force."

"How the hell did you convince FBI brass and a judge

based on my track record?"

"I just told them it was a tip from a confidential inform-ant."

"God damn you." Walker sighed, moving away again.

"With everything else we have, it was simply the straw that broke the camel's back. It didn't need to be solid, just re-liable. Our sources within Arcuri's inner circle confirmed the intel, so that's all we needed."

"You used me."

"I'm sorry, my friend. It was my only option. You've seen it for yourself. You know that school's got corruption written all over it. We've never been able to get this close before. We needed someone on the inside."

"There's nothing in that file is there?"

"No," Lewis said, embarrassed. "We couldn't risk it. It's just some unclassified materials from a closed investigation a few years ago. Wouldn't make any sense to you once you got into it, but I figured you would be too busy with your investiga-tion to even bother."

Walker shook his head in disgust.

"I'm sorry. I truly am. But this is much bigger than one missing girl. There is an unprecedented host of issues here. We need to take this school down."

Dejected, Walker asked, "When's the raid?"

"Tomorrow."

"What? His eyes sprung to life. "What are you doing? You can't conduct an FBI raid on Washington Academy tomorrow. I'm still working on my investigation."

Lewis shook his head. "No, we need to move now. If Cas-tillo gets wind of this through his channels or contacts, we're done. They'll destroy everything—wipe it clean."

"I need more time, Lewis," Walker pleaded. "Once you guys knock down the doors, it's over for me. And Amanda. They'll seize up and I'll never get any answers."

"If we don't move now, we might lose our only chance to put down one of the largest public corruption cases in this country's history. We don't have a choice."

"Lewis, please, I need this one. You have to listen to me. I need more time."

Lewis thought for a long moment, rubbed the back of his neck, and shook his head. Walker saw that his ex-partner was clearly struggling with the decision, and fortunately, he finally conceded.

"Okay, I appreciate what you did for me here," Lewis said, "even if it was unwittingly. I'll give you your two days, but after that, buddy, you have to get out of there. We're coming in with everything we have. They're giving me a ton of resources on this."

"How many?"

"Enough to take down that entire school. You don't want to be around when it happens."

CHAPTER 23

Walker was still seething at the thought of being betrayed by his former best friend as he sat in one of the upholstered chairs that surrounded a thick oak table. The conference room on the first floor of the administration building felt like an empty, cavernous space with just three people hunched at one end of the long table. Because each faculty member was being interviewed individually, only Walker, Castillo, and the interviewee were in the room. In addition to the annoyingly quiet space, the faculty members — nearly without exception — refused to speak above a whisper, so they all sounded like a scratched record because their stories were so frustratingly similar. The monotony was lulling him into submission, so Walker's mind drifted.

Now that Lewis and the FBI were closing in on Washington Academy, Walker realized he was under significant pressure to move quickly. Even if he had found some evidence and convinced Ellis to allow him a little more time, it wouldn't matter now. The FBI could not be stopped. Walker was actually doubtful Lewis could hold off the operation for two more days. He would need one hell of an excuse, and Walker was unsure of what that would be. But he was depending on his friend to come through and give him the time he promised, the time he desperately needed.

Meanwhile, Castillo was slowing down Walker's investigation to a snail's pace, slinking along with just enough lubricant to keep moving, but certainly not getting anywhere. He had been instructed to be discreet with his investigation, so he could only interview additional students, staff, or potential witnesses at the request — and approval — of Castillo. And this was the crux of his inquiry. The empty gesture of giving him a keycard versus actually talking to people was not one Walker would have chosen. *Access to what?* In the absence of any real physical evidence, witnesses were the key to this investigation, and they were essentially being withheld from him. Except in the presence and at the prerogative of Castillo.

The faculty members did not seem to know anything beyond the rumors of Amanda's disappearance anyway, but Castillo already knew that. From the sound of things, the teachers had been summoned individually to speak with the dean and security chief on multiple occasions already. Based on the teachers' reactions, these "interviews" seemed more focused on keeping them quiet than learning any valuable information from them. Most likely, that was their intent. Again, without exception, the faculty members were extremely reserved in their responses, and Walker was learning nothing.

Even the arrangement in the conference room was an exercise in intimidation. Castillo had each faculty member sit at the head of the table, directly across from a huge portrait of Dr. Ellis, hanging above a stone fireplace. Walker sat off to the side, facing the particular faculty member, while Castillo sat right next to him, focusing his gaze on the person the entire time as they recited their answers with the slow precision of an audio recording.

With the interviews almost complete, however, one faculty member, Meredith Thomas, had called Castillo and said she had taken ill, so she would need to reschedule for the next day. Walker smiled when Castillo told him. Since they were now out of witnesses for the day, Walker decided to return to his residence and review Castillo's file on Amanda again to see if he could cull anything about the case that had been alluding him thus far.

As Walker approached his temporary housing unit, sitting on the front steps — her head buried in her knees — was Heather Yates. She was crying.

"Heather?" he said, moving closer.

No response.

Walker sat down next to her on the step and pulled a bag of chips from his bag, which he had purchased from the vending machine as he exited the admin building. He leaned over to her and held out the bag. "Chip?"

She signaled no, her head still on her knees.

Walker shrugged, opened the bag, and popped one in his mouth, trying to act as nonchalantly as possible to not pressure her, but simply to let her speak when she was ready.

After about three more chips, Heather slowly lifted her head but did not make eye contact. "I lied to you yesterday," she finally said.

"I figured you did."

"I just thought this would all go away, you know? Or Amanda would just turn up. I'm really scared that she's still gone."

"Why?"

"Because I think something has happened to her."

"What makes you say that?"

Heather breathed in deeply and looked at Walker, her face wet from the tears. "I'm scared, Mr. Walker. I didn't want any part of this. They told me they would take care of it. But now, I don't know what they did."

"Who's they?"

Heather ignored the question. "I remember that night. I remember her leaving. I remember the fight with her boyfriend."

"Heather, who's they?" Walker repeated.

Heather steadied herself, a look of resolve stiffening her face as though she had just made a fateful decision. She obviously wasn't sure about it, but the choice was made. "Amanda didn't take her backpack with her that night."

Walker tilted his head, "What?"

"She didn't take her stuff with her. It was gone when I came back that night. I'm positive she didn't take her stuff, which I thought was odd at first, but then when I came back, it was gone. If she had come back to our room, she would have left a note or something. A text maybe. But it was just gone."

"Did you tell Mr. Castillo about this?"

"Yes, that night. When I called Campus Police. He arrived with them. After the officers had searched the room and left, I told him about her stuff, told him that I was sure it was here when I left." Heather paused for several seconds, exhaling loudly. "He said I was probably confused and told me I should just say that she took it with her. That it would all be better that way."

"You're absolutely sure she didn't take it with her?"

"Yes, and if she came back, she would have told me. That was our thing, remember? We always kept each other informed."

"But she may have simply forgotten."

"True. But then there was the next day."

Walker leaned in closer. "What happened the next day?"

Heather paused again and swallowed hard before starting again. "The next day, I was called to Dr. Ellis's office. He and Mr. Castillo were both there. They asked me more questions about the disappearance, told me a private investigator was coming, and that I should simply tell you that she had taken her belongings with her. They said if I told you too much, it might involve me somehow, and they didn't want to see that happen. That this could just as easily be blamed on me because I was the last one to see her. They even said they could help me with my grades if I cooperated and stayed quiet about her personal belongings. I was scared. I didn't know what to do, so I lied to you."

Walker leaned back on the step. "Is everything else you told me true?"

"Yes, of course. I know you don't believe me now, but it's all true, I swear. She did get a text and left at about 9 PM, but she didn't tell me where she was going. I thought it was to meet

Josh, but I really don't know for sure. That's the truth," Heather said, starting to cry again.

Walker wrapped his arm around Heather to comfort her, and she lay her head on his shoulder, still sobbing. He looked around and immediately spotted two cameras pointed in their direction. *These damn cameras are everywhere.* Walker wondered if the cameras were capable of audio as well. Probably not. But knowing Castillo, the security chief most likely had directional microphones at his disposal, which could be used for that purpose if needed. He imagined Walker wasn't enough of a threat to warrant to use of those devices just yet. Still, Walker scanned the immediate area around him for anything suspicious-looking. Nothing seemed out of the ordinary. *The story of this entire case.*

However, what was clear to Walker was that anyone watching this video feed could easily discern that Heather Yates had just told Ryan Walker a very important secret. What wasn't certain was how far Joaquin Castillo would go to keep that secret quiet.

CHAPTER 24

Heather Yates had convinced Walker that Castillo was definitely involved with Amanda's disappearance in some capacity. He couldn't yet pinpoint exactly how or why, but there was too much circumstantial evidence building up against him. It was moving into the realm of beyond a reasonable doubt, and that was a difficult threshold to attain for any criminal investigation and subsequent prosecution. Couple that with the warning from Lewis and the fact that Castillo was off the grid for two years, and all the arrows pointed to Joaquin.

So why would your chief of security be involved in Amanda's disappearance? Walker wrestled with the question. Castillo's involvement could probably only indicate a select number of possibilities, most of which would lead one to believe that Amanda had stumbled onto something she shouldn't have. Whether it was a skeleton in Castillo's closet, some kind of corruption related to Ellis, or a discovery that could smear the school's reputation—it didn't matter. All indications were that Amanda vanished because she was supposed to and someone went to extraordinary lengths to cover his tracks. The only person with the necessary tools and talent to accomplish that task, as far as Walker had seen, was Castillo.

Confronting Castillo at this point without any hard evidence would be fruitless, so Walker had to search for that initial discovery: the reason why Amanda Bryson was targeted, the reason why she had to go missing. Walker remembered that Amanda worked at the Tuition/Student Aid Office, which provided a unique opportunity for her to see financial records. If Lewis was right and Washington Academy was indeed laundering money for Arcuri, it would most certainly move through the tuition office. If Amanda had uncovered some kind of sensitive material, which made perfect sense assuming the suspicious business dealings of this institution, it was entirely plausible that Ellis had asked Castillo to take care of her. *Whatever that meant.* And so if Walker could retrace Amanda's steps, follow the trail of what she had been working on, he might be able to figure out the impetus which led to her disappearance.

Walker introduced himself to an older woman, referring to herself as Ms. Watkins, at the front desk of the Tuition/Student Aid Office, located in a whitewashed building near the western end of campus. The polite woman was more than happy to oblige, speaking highly of the sweet young girl that had gone missing and even leading Walker on an unprompted tour of the entire building.

As they made their way into the last room of files, stacked neatly on color-coded shelves, much like a doctor's office before the digital age, Walker asked, "Is this where Amanda worked?"

"Oh, yes," the woman replied excitedly, but then her voice trailed off as she immediately realized the reality of the situation. "This was the last project she was working on."

Walker scanned the folders. "What was she doing?"

Ms. Watkins paused for a moment, appearing to be caught up in her own thoughts, then spoke with authority, as if remembering a directive. "Yes, of course. She was reviewing our tuition records from the last ten years. We are actually in the process of updating our financial records database, so Amanda was going through all of these old files and uploading them into a new online system."

"Can I look through the files she was working on?" Walker nodded to the stacks on the shelves.

"Unfortunately, no."

"Excuse me?"

The woman smiled politely. "I'd be more than happy to

share them with you, but they're no longer here. They've been sealed and moved to a new location. The moving gentlemen were here just two days ago."

"Do you know why they were being moved?"

"Not exactly, but I imagine it was decided that this process was more economical to outsource to a smaller company. They can typically do it much more quickly and for a lower cost. We actually do it quite often."

"Do you use the same company?" Walker inquired, intrigued by the prospect.

"Ah, yes, a little firm in Alexandria. Tuition Associates."

Walker took a mental note of the name and would give it to Lewis. Perhaps a shell company for the next step in the laundering process. "Okay, Ms. Watkins, thank you so much for your time."

"Of course, Mr. Walker. But you can still search those records if you'd like."

"Pardon?"

"They haven't been sent to Tuition Associates yet. They've only been moved temporarily to a storage facility on campus," the woman said, blissful in her ignorance.

"Do you know where?" Walker said excitedly.

"Absolutely. I can show you. They will be a little hard to sort through, but perhaps you could still find what you're looking for. But of course, you will need Mr. Castillo to assist you. There's no key card at the storage unit. It's an old fashioned lock and key."

Of course, it is. "That would be great," Walker replied.

"I can call Mr. Castillo for you right now."

"That won't be necessary. I'll be meeting him in a few minutes anyway," Walker lied.

"Very well. Then I'll just show you where to go," she said, pointing back to the front lobby, where Walker had seen a campus map under a plate of glass on the counter.

"Just one final question," Walker said, as the two started to exit the room. "Who told you to move these records?"

Ms. Watkins turned to him and chuckled as if the answer was blatantly obvious. "The same person who always handles these records. Dr. Ellis, of course."

CHAPTER 25

The storage facility was a short walk from the Tuition/ Student Aid Office, located on the edge of campus just below the crest of a hill. It was a small, wooden shed — its light red paint flaking off its aged barn boards — and the only dilapidated structure Walker had yet seen on campus. Glancing back, he could no longer see the campus but was instead surrounded by the thick woods which encircled the school. Everything was quiet.

He knew he needed Castillo to enter the facility, but emboldened by his most recent discovery, Walker decided to have a look for himself. Perhaps there was a way inside without the security chief at his side. If he did ask Castillo, he was sure it would take a full day to arrange, and by that time, there would certainly be no documents of any interest remaining in the storage shed when they finally entered.

The building's wooden structure had been worn down and not recently repaired, but the door looked relatively new, and just as Ms. Watkins had noted, it was secured by a silver-colored lock. No keycard here. But as Walker moved closer to the entrance, preparing to look for other possible entry points, he noticed that the traditional lock, hanging on a metal clasp attached to the door, was not closed.

Walker instinctively paused and looked around. *Had someone forgotten to lock it? Or was someone inside?* He removed the lock from the clasp, laid it gently on the ground, and pushed on the door. The hinges creaked as it swung open.

Walker entered and intently scanned the small space, adjusting his eyes for the low light. There were no visible light fixtures or switches in the cramped space, so the only source of illumination was from the natural light through the open door.

There was a narrow passageway through the middle of the shed, buffeted on both sides by several columns of boxes stacked to the ceiling. Each box was the same size and labeled with a white tag on the front. Upon closer inspection of a box near the entrance, Walker could see that the label denoted the department from which the case had originated. This was obviously the storage location for all of the old paper files from the school, including the tuition records destined for Tuition Associates and their digital database.

Walker made his way through the gauntlet of boxes, peering at the various containers as he made his way through the stacks. He didn't exactly know what he was looking for, didn't think he would actually make it inside this space, but now that he was here, he was curious as to what it contained. Because of the darkened space, Walker needed to squint to read the labels on the boxes.

As Walker neared the rear of the building, he heard a slight rumble to his right, immediately followed by a cascade of boxes from one of the columns. The boxes were filled with documents and made of thick cardboard, so they crashed upon his back and shoulders, pushing him to the hard ground. More boxes pummeled him as he lay there. Struggling to free himself from the avalanche of boxes and lift himself from the floor, Walker heard a rapid echoing of footsteps as they moved away from him. Pushing a box to clear his view, he saw a figure, dressed in jeans and a hoodie race to the front door, exit, and slam it behind him.

Next, he heard the familiar snap of a lock. The lock he had left outside had just been used to barricade the door. Then Walker heard something else, something far more sinister, followed by a distinctive smell. Craning his head toward the spot where the column of boxes had crumbled, Walker saw that it was now replaced by a flickering orange flame and a rising line of smoke. The acrid smell of burning paper and cardboard immediately filled his nostrils, followed by his mind's anxious realization that a fire had been set to the boxes.

Walker shoved the last of the boxes from atop his body and stood amongst the garbage heap of cardboard, feeling the aches from the bruises on his neck and shoulders. He stumbled through the fallen boxes toward the door, knowing full-well it was locked, but pushing on it anyway with his already aching shoulders. It didn't budge. Walker turned from the door to see the fire spreading rapidly and the room quickly filling with thick black smoke. Burning paper and cardboard — much different than a piece of firewood — produced a dark, dense smoke that would engulf the entire inside of the shed within minutes. And Walker with it.

Scanning the room for another exit, behind the fallen timber of boxes, he could see a window with one pane of old glass. But the fire was building rapidly and had already reached the bottom layer of that window. Turning his attention to the opposite side of the shed, he assumed there would be another similar window directly across from the other. He hoped he was right.

Immediately moving to that section of boxes, Walker pushed the lower ones until the column collapsed, some boxes bouncing across the center, becoming fuel for the ever-expanding fire. Sure enough, a window was there. He moved several more rows of boxes, flinging them into the fire, and formed a makeshift staircase to the window. The smoke was thickening as it filled the interior of the shed and started to block out the window. Walker pulled his shirt up over his mouth but the ash and soot were already blinding him and he instinctively coughed as the smoke entered his lungs. He knew he didn't have much time.

He climbed to the window and banged on it with his hand, but the glass was thick and sturdy. He pounded again, but the window refused to break. Finally, as he struggled to hold his breath in the suffocating smoke, Walker forced his elbow through the glass. The center of the window cracked and then shattered. Walker used his elbow, blood seeping through his shirt, to remove the remaining shards of glass and pushed his head out of the window.

Walker gulped in the fresh air with long deep breaths like a stranded castaway finding freshwater as the smoke billowed from the broken window and encircled him. The window was just large enough, so he lifted himself up and pushed out of the window as the flames ignited the first boxes on this side of the shed.

Tumbling as he fell, Walker landed hard on his back about six feet below. The force of the impact took his breath away but expelled the dirty air from his lungs. He instinctively coughed, both from the smoke inhalation and the pain he now felt in his chest. Although soot was smudged on his face and eyelids, Walker could see the flames above start to escape from the window and curl into a hand-like motion, its fingers gripping the surrounding walls. Dark smoke now engulfed the shed, until it was barely visible, wafting up through the branches and leaves of the overhead trees.

Staring at the burning shed, Walker knew that whatever evidence might have been locked away in that storage facility was gone. He was simply lucky he wasn't also a casualty of the fire. Although he had indeed contemplated dying many times, this wasn't exactly the way he wanted to go out. At least not now, knowing he was perhaps Amanda's only chance. He hadn't felt a sense of value in a long time, but at this moment, he was glad to be alive. It felt good. His body did not, however, so Walker collapsed back onto the ground and savored the fresh air as he could hear the faint sound of sirens in the distance.

CHAPTER 26

Walker rested on the rear bumper of the ambulance, breathing oxygen through a mask, his face covered in black smudges of ash and soot. The ambulance had pulled onto the grass just at the crest of the hill, parked alongside the two fire engines that had arrived at the scene. A crowd of students had also gathered on the hillside, pulling out their phones to snap pictures or record video of the exciting event, and campus police officers had been stationed on the ridge to keep the onlookers at bay.

The fire had been extinguished, but there was essentially nothing left of the storage shed except for a skeleton of timbers and piles of wet burnt paper. The shed still smoldered as firefighters sifted through the ruins to ensure nothing was going to start up again since the entire shed was literally a tinderbox.

Walker stared hopelessly at the storage shed, his breath clouding the oxygen mask with each exhale. Any evidence that might have been there was now ash. He was lucky to be alive. That deadly smoke could have incapacitated him within minutes, and he would have been dead long before help arrived. Whoever set that fire had either wanted to destroy the evidence inside or kill him. Perhaps both.

He had told the campus police what he could remember about the suspected arsonist, but even he realized he was a terrible witness. The vague description of the nondescript person he saw running away from under a pile of boxes did not instill confidence in the note-taking officer. And of course, there were no cameras back here. Then again, maybe there were, but only Castillo would know what those cameras may have seen, and Walker would never be permitted to view that footage. It was hard to believe, but things may have just gone from bad to worse.

A friendly face appeared around the corner of the ambulance, and Walker smiled as Meredith sat down next to him. She looked at the smoking ruin before them. "I understand you wanted to make an impression while you're here, but did you really have to burn the place down?"

Walker laughed into his oxygen mask, immediately triggering a guttural cough, which lasted for a few seconds.

Meredith put her arm around him. "I'm sorry. The last thing I want to do is kill you after you were able to survive this. Please don't tell me you were inside."

Walker simply nodded.

"Oh, my God, Ryan," Meredith said, exasperated. "Why don't I help get you back to your place, so you can get cleaned up and tell me what you were doing down here?"

He smiled through the oxygen mask.

As Walker strained to lift himself up and pull the mask from his face, Joaquin Castillo strode over to the ambulance. Both Walker and Meredith paused as he approached and returned to their seats on the bumper of the rescue vehicle. Castillo did not look pleased.

"Mr. Walker," Castillo said, harshly rubbing the bridge of his nose with his thumb and forefinger and breathing deeply. "You've caused quite a little mess down here."

"I didn't actually cause the mess. I didn't set the fire."

"But my officers tell me you were inside, were you not?"

"I was, but..."

"Then how do I know you didn't set the fire?" Castillo interjected.

Walker glared at Castillo. "You think I set a fire inside that shed while *I* was inside that shed?"

"I don't know what you're capable of anymore, Mr.

Walker. First, I find you in a secure area of our surveillance center, and now I find you covered with soot after you were somehow involved in the destruction of one of our buildings."

Walker shook his head while Meredith just stared at the ground.

"How did you even get inside the shed? The closed lock is still secured to the door."

"It was unlocked when I arrived."

Castillo broke into laughter, and Walker suddenly realized how preposterous it sounded.

"It was unlocked? How convenient. Then how do you think it became locked again?"

"Whoever attacked me locked it when they ran out."

Castillo smirked sarcastically. "Really? Please tell me about this attacker."

Walker lowered his head. "I can't. I didn't get a good look at him. I was under boxes, remember? He was wearing jeans and a hoodie."

"He? You sure it was a male?"

"No."

"How about a physical description?" Castillo rattled off the attributes. "Approximate height, weight, age, hair color, race? Anything?"

Walker just shook his head, unable to answer any of the questions.

Castillo glared at Walker and shook his head. "Get out of here. Go get cleaned up. I'm going to be here for a while cleaning up this mess, so our little investigation is put on hold for right now. I'll contact you when I'm done. And from now on, you don't go anywhere on this campus without me. Is that understood? Why don't you do us all a favor and stay in your residence for a while? It seems like that's the only way you're going to stay out of trouble."

CHAPTER 27

After a well-deserved shower and change of clothes, Walker stepped out into the miniature living room of his residence, still drying his hair with a towel. Sitting on the only sofa in the room and flipping through a magazine, Meredith looked up and grinned. "Just like new."

"I wish," Walker responded. His body still ached, both from the boxes and the fall, and his lungs still felt heavy from the smoke inhalation. He sat down in the only chair in the room, which was facing the sofa.

"So," Meredith asked, "do you think Castillo was angry with you? I couldn't quite tell."

Walker laughed but quickly stopped because it hurt his chest to do so.

"I'm sorry again," Meredith said, seeing Walker wince at the pain.

"It's okay. I've been through worse. Castillo was the least of my problems today. If I hadn't made it to that window, I wouldn't be here right now."

Meredith whispered, "What exactly were you doing down there?"

Walker leaned his head back, covered it with the towel, and grunted. "I was looking at old records. Records that were going to be shipped to a company to become digital."

"And why were you looking for these records?"

Walker pulled the towel down off his head. "I was trying to locate any records Amanda may have had access to before she disappeared."

"You think there may have been something important in there?"

Walker took a deep breath and let it out slowly. "All I know is that everything I've seen and heard and witnessed so far tells me this abduction was an inside job. Everything points in-house. You don't have this much security and this much secrecy without finding ways to get rid of problems. It's very possible Amanda stumbled onto something and Ellis ordered Castillo to silence her."

"You really think they're capable of that?"

"You don't go to all of these lengths to have this much surveillance unless you have something to hide. Like you said before, those cameras are not meant to keep people out; they're meant to keep all of you in."

Meredith recoiled at the thought. Although Walker knew she had already considered the possibility, when a private investigator told you — especially with all his experience — it became very real. And very frightening.

Meredith paused for several moments, as though she was trying to process what Walker had just told her. "Why?"

Walker breathed out forcefully. "No idea. They're obviously hiding something. I just don't know what it is yet. That's why I went to the shed."

"What were you hoping to find there?"

"A link. Something to help me."

"I guess you don't have that problem anymore," Meredith said, trying to lighten the mood.

"Yeah, you could say that," Walker grinned.

"You didn't see the person who knocked you over? Started the fire?" she asked.

"Barely. Not enough for an eyewitness."

"So whoever started that fire, were they trying to burn those files or kill you?"

Walker put the towel over his head again. "Great question."

Meredith looked down at the floor, shaking her head in disbelief.

The cool towel felt refreshing on his warm skin, so Walker rubbed his face with it one last time and placed it on his lap while staring up at the ceiling. "Can I ask you something?"

"Absolutely."

"Do you think Castillo is capable of murder?"

"Whew." Meredith winced. "That wasn't the kind of question I was expecting."

"I know," Walker confessed. "But you know him. You've been with him. Is he capable of something like this?"

Meredith sighed as she settled back into the sofa. "I don't know. Like I told you before, he was simply too much for me. Maybe it was all his training, perhaps it was his life experience, but he was always overly concerned with secrecy — what he could say, what he couldn't say. It was unnerving."

"Is it all about the security of the school for him, or is it something deeper?"

"I think it starts there, but then it goes deeper. Almost like he has something to prove. Something to atone for. You know what I mean?"

Walker huffed, "Unfortunately, I know exactly what you mean."

"I'm sure he's good at what he does, but it's almost as if it haunts him. So...would he do something like this...to protect the school...to protect the security of the school? I don't know."

"How about protecting someone?"

"Protecting someone?"

"Like Amanda's boyfriend, Josh Easterly, for instance. Would he protect him? Hypothetically?" Walker asked.

"Well, I know Easterly is from a very well-to-do family. He's a Congresswoman's son, I believe "

"Really?" Walker faked surprise. "We're certainly in the halls of power here, aren't we?"

"Indeed. And their troubled kids."

"Troubled?"

Meredith laughed. "Yes, you certainly can't come from all that wealth and privilege and not be a little troubled, right? I think it's probably their own form of rebellion, revolting against the establishment so to speak. Their parents are all well-connected and very powerful, so the only way these kids can express themselves is a kind of secret organization, somewhere they can be who they are. Sort of break the rules without breaking the rules, you know? Almost like a *Dead Poet's Society* kind of thing. Only these guys aren't reading poetry."

"Like a satanic cult?"

"I wouldn't go that far, but definitely a secret society. Rituals. Initiations. Codes."

Walker leaned closer. "This secret society — the *Sons of Liberty* — is it real?"

"I don't know, but the rumors never seem to die. What do you think that means?"

"Is Josh a part of this secret society?"

"I have no idea, but I can only imagine that if it actually existed, Ellis would certainly want to keep it quiet, don't you think? It's almost like the boogeyman. Especially at a place like this. I'm sure they would go to great lengths to keep it quiet."

"I'm sure," Walker responded. Then asked, "Enough to abduct a student?"

The question was rhetorical, but the silence — as the two people mentally considered the possibility — was deafening.

CHAPTER 28

Special Agent Walker peered through his assault rifle scope into the adjacent office at the man with the gun. "Command, I have a clear line of sight on the subject. I am prepared to eliminate the threat," he whispered into his headpiece.

"Negative, unit two, stand down. The negotiator wants a little more time."

Walker shrugged off the order. The negotiator might be hearing the subject's voice, but Walker was seeing the assailant first-hand and clearly had the best vantage point. His mannerisms and uncontrollable urges told the seasoned FBI agent there was no longer any amount of reasoning that would be effective with this perpetrator. He was simply too far gone, too irrational, and it would only take seconds to kill both the mother and daughter if he decided that as his best course of action. Right now, Walker was the only one in a position to eliminate the threat.

"Command, say again, I am prepared to take out the threat. I have a clean shot."

Longer silence. "Negative, Walker, give us a few more minutes."

The FBI sniper bristled at the command. They used his real name over the radio, which meant quite simply to *shut the fuck up*. Walker exhaled his frustration while removing his finger from the trigger guard. His instincts were getting the better of him, and he needed to calm down. As a federal agent in the most elite law enforcement agency in the world, he wasn't accustomed to taking orders — at least not in this regard — as he was typically in charge of his own investigations and called his own shots. This situation and what had to be done appeared to be crystal clear, yet he was being asked to stand down.

In the meantime, the increasingly violent subject was becoming more irate, meaning time was rapidly running out. Walker carefully unsnapped the buckle from under his chin and removed his helmet with one hand, while still staring down his rifle's scope at the gunman, the crosshairs pinned on his adversary. He breathed in deeply and pressed the switch to turn off his weapon's safety while placing his finger back inside the trigger guard and pressing it lightly against the trigger.

Without warning, the subject suddenly lowered his handgun and fired at the telephone on the desk. The telephone exploded as the mother and child instinctively shielded themselves from the flying shards of debris, while the gunman reacted to the disintegration of the phone with a triumphant gesture and blood-curdling howl as he raised the gun in the air. The negotiation was over.

With the assailant's handgun momentarily pointed away from the hostage, Walker placed the man's forehead directly in the center of the scope's crosshairs and his entire focus narrowed onto his lone target.

His headpiece crackled. "Unit two, weapons-free. Take out the subject."

Walker did not respond. No response was necessary. He simply let out a slow breath to steady his weapon and pulled the trigger.

CHAPTER 29

Walker startled awake, then calmed. He was sitting on the sofa in his faculty residence living room, his head arched back against the thick upholstery. As he brought his head forward, he noticed Meredith was sitting next to him, sleeping, her head propped on his left shoulder. Her soft body was brushed up against his, and he realized he hadn't been this close to a woman in a long time. He hadn't respected himself enough to be with anyone, and nothing about that had changed, but Walker had to admit the warmth of her body felt good.

He hadn't meant to fall asleep with her and immediately regretted it. He had been so exhausted after the fire that he literally couldn't keep his eyes open, so he took a few moments just to rest his eyes, and Meredith said she would stay with him. Obviously, they both fell asleep. Her kind gesture was heartfelt and Walker truly appreciated it, but this case was not anywhere close to being solved by sleeping on the sofa.

Walker wasn't sure if he was attracted to Meredith, or if this relationship had any kind of future, but there was a definite emotional connection between the two of them. Although inadvertent at first, it probably stemmed from their shared loneliness, and they simply found what they needed in each other for the moment. *Was it sustainable? Probably not.* Walker wasn't sure what that meant for the two of them, but he couldn't think about that now. It was simply too much to try and make sense of, and he was in no condition for it, so his mind drifted back to the case.

The dead ends. The storage shed. The fire. He tried to

weave together the loose ends mentally, focus on a puzzle with its missing pieces, concentrate on that one piece of evidence that was eluding him. He struggled to see the completed picture in his mind.

Meredith moved her head slightly and opened her eyes. She looked up at Walker, trying to determine where she was and what she was doing. Immediately making the realization that she was laying on his shoulder, and may have drooled on his shirt, she pulled back and sat up straight. "I'm sorry," she instantly apologized. "I guess watching you sleep made me tired." "It's alright," Walker said, finally able to move his arm and tactfully stretch out the cramp that had developed there.

She smiled, "I guess you're going to be okay."

Walker nodded. "Yeah, still sore as hell, but it looks like I'll survive."

"I would love to know what's going through your mind right now," she whispered.

Walker smiled. For one brief moment, the pressure had left, the pity was gone, and the self-loathing was taking a short break. "That there are no clues to this case on this sofa."

Meredith laughed. "I would have to agree, detective, but you did need some rest."

"Right."

Meredith turned and lay her head back on the cushion. "I wish I could just stay here. Block out the world a little while longer, you know?"

Walker stared up at the ceiling fan in the center of the living room, watching the fan blades make their rhythmic rotations. "I do."

Silence lingered for a few moments until Meredith spoke. "So what's next for the case? Now that the storage shed is no longer available?" she asked.

Walker grinned. "Back to square one, I guess. I might go back to the tuition office."

Meredith chuckled. "Why would you go to the tuition office?"

"Well, that's how I got to the storage shed in the first place. I was looking for tuition office records."

"Records?"

"Yeah, Amanda worked there."

Meredith laughed again. "Oh, I don't think she could have stumbled upon a massive conspiracy in that short of time."

Walker sat up from the cushion and turned toward Meredith. "What do you mean?"

She mirrored his posture, looking confused. "Well, she was only there for maybe a month or so. I remember her talking about it in class."

"What? That's why I went there. It was in Castillo's file. I thought she may have found some incriminating evidence in the financial records. Are you saying she didn't work there?"

"Oh, yes, she worked there, but she was only recently transferred. She used to work for Dr. Ellis as his receptionist."

Walker was incredulous. "What?"

Meredith smirked., "I guess he didn't disclose that to you?"

"No! I knew he was hiding something. Dammit!" Walker huffed.

Meredith put her hand on his arm. "The rumor is that something happened between them, which is why he transferred her."

"What?" Walker felt as though he was about to lose his mind.

Meredith just shook her head, matching the disbelief in Walker's face.

"Does Castillo know about this?"

"I don't know. But it was all done very quietly. I just remember Amanda talking about her new job in class, having previously worked for Ellis. I heard the rumors like everyone else, but I never asked Amanda directly."

"What was the rumor?"

"Just that something inappropriate had happened between the two of them, and so he had to transfer her to keep everything quiet."

"What happened?"

"No one knows."

"No one?"

Meredith paused. "Well, I guess there are two people you could ask. But unfortunately, one is missing, and the other...is the person who invited you here."

CHAPTER 30

The Washington Academy residence for it *Dean of Students* was an opulent Virginia mansion near the northwest corner of the campus built in 1832. Although slightly altered and refurbished throughout the years, it still maintained its nineteenth-century character, staying true to its southern Virginia charm. Originally built for Washington Academy's first headmaster, and aside from a brief hiatus during the Civil War, the residence had been home to every subsequent dean for the prestigious academy ever since.

Augustus Becker had served as the school's first headmaster when the academy was founded twenty-seven years earlier, but with increasing student enrollment and sprawling campus growth during the 1820s, he stepped down from that position to assume the role of President of the Board of Trustees with its many responsibilities. Before his death in 1858, Becker ensured the residence remained a permanent fixture on the Washington Academy's campus and a non-negotiable feature of any potential candidate's employment contract. The clause was never opposed by any incoming leader, and there had been twenty-three of them, including Becker, since the school's inception.

The mansion's current residents were Dr. Robert Ellis and his wife of thirty-two years, Gloria. They had requested some minor upgrades when they moved into the home eighteen years earlier — mostly interior furnishings — but aside from that, the mansion still looked much like it did in the 1800s. A long paved driveway led from the main road to the detached two-car garage, which was added in the 1950s. The dean's residence was slightly removed from campus, separated by a line of trees and shrubs, so Walker assumed it was outside the far reach of Castillo's monitoring system, but wasn't entirely sure. He had stopped at Ellis' office first and been told that the dean had left for the afternoon, so Walker figured that meant he had returned home.

Walker was approaching the residence uninvited, hoping that Ellis wasn't aware of his visit. He wanted it that way, so he could surprise Ellis and possibly catch him off guard. Knowing he was currently a stranger on the property, Walker moved stealthily along the garage and peeked inside the windows along its doors. Only one car was present, a shiny black Mercedes, so he figured either Ellis or his wife was at home.

Making his way up the small set of steps leading to the wraparound porch, he knocked lightly on the door. His main purpose was to speak with Ellis about why Amanda had been transferred. The good doctor hadn't volunteered this important tidbit of information, and since it was an extremely valuable piece to the puzzle, Walker wanted to know why. A sudden transfer to a new position followed by a mysterious disappearance was simply too much of a coincidence. *And what exactly had happened between them?* That all-important question needed an answer. *Now.*

The front door swung open. An older woman, distinguished with slightly graying hair, stood in the entryway. She smiled at Walker and was exceedingly polite.

"Can I help you?" She asked in a slow southern accent.

Walker, surprised at first by the regal woman before him, smiled back and reached out his hand. "Yes, ma'am. My name is Ryan Walker, I'm..."

"The private investigator," she interrupted, her sweet accent making it sound much more important than it actually was.

"Yes, that's right."

"I'm Gloria Ellis. Pleased to meet you." She took his hand in hers and returned a delicate handshake. "I do hope you find that poor girl. It's just so tragic what's happened," she said, shaking her head in disbelief.

Walker returned the gesture. "Yes, it is. And that's actually what brings me here today. I was hoping to speak to your husband. His office told me he had taken the afternoon off."

"Yes, that's right. He needed to travel to Washington today for a meeting. I'm sorry, but he probably won't be back until this evening. Please come in though. Perhaps I can help."

"Thank you," Walker said, as he entered the foyer and took in the splendor of the gorgeous mansion. The expensive art which decorated the walls and intricate sculptures that hugged the corners created almost a museum-like feel but was softened enough by the shades of color and furnishings that it felt like a home.

"Your home is beautiful," he finally said, still gawking at the priceless artifacts.

"Oh, thank you," said Gloria as she led him through the foyer into a large sitting room, decorated with more stately furnishings and anchored by a large stone fireplace at the head of the room. She pointed to an overstuffed chair with a quilted pattern on its lush cushion. "Please sit down. Can I offer you some coffee or tea?"

Walker sat in the large chair. "No, thank you, I'm fine."

Gloria sat across from him in an equally large chair. Walker had not yet met Ellis' wife, had only seen pictures of her behind his desk, and she appeared just as in her photos: the quintessential Stepford wife. Walker imagined she spent her days taking care of the home and keeping up appearances for her high-profile husband, her southern charm on full display as she attended gatherings and hosted cocktail parties for their wealthy friends.

Gloria sighed. "It's so very dreadful what happened to that girl. It's just awful. Have you discovered anything, Mr. Walker?"

"Not yet, but we're making progress," Walker stated, matter-of-factly.

"I do hope you find her. These young people have so much to live for. Please know that I am praying for her."

Walker ignored the religious reference but acknowledged the sentiment. "Of course, thank you," he said. Then asked, "Did you know Amanda?"

Gloria sighed. "No, I did not, but my husband has been talking about her much as of late. He's been very upset about this entire situation. To have one of your students...he thinks of them as his children, you realize? To have one of your children disappear, it's just unthinkable. We don't have any children ourselves, so I think he sort of adopts them all."

Walker nodded to be polite but was unsure of exactly what Gloria was trying to say. He had just heard from Meredith that Ellis had some kind of encounter with Amanda, and now his wife was saying that Ellis felt like these were his kids. *Adopts them? In what way?* The only parallel Walker could fathom was that Ellis believed he held some kind of authority over them and used his powerful presence as a way to exert pressure against his own students. If that was indeed the situation — as twisted as it might be — Ellis had just become much more dangerous than Walker had ever anticipated. He treaded lightly. "Has he given you any indication of what he thinks may have happened?"

"Oh no, just lamenting that a poor girl has disappeared from our campus, vanished under our watchful eye. Robert would do absolutely anything to protect these students."

"Yes, you have quite a security system here."

Gloria dismissed the notion with an elegant guffaw, shaking her head. "My goodness. Security. Too much security if you ask me." She rolled her eyes. "Please don't tell Robert this, but I really don't care for that Mr. Castillo. Much too serious. And all those cameras...what an eyesore on our beautiful campus. So unsightly. But alas, he insists on it. My husband has asked him to tone it down, but he simply refuses. I wonder sometimes how much power you hold when you can see everything."

"I didn't see any cameras around here?" Walker mused.

"Oh no, I won't allow it. I will not feel like a prisoner in my own home. This was actually one of the first houses built on campus, about the same time as the faculty housing. I absolutely love the Virginia charm. But I also love the mystery."

"Mystery?" Walker asked, surprised by the choice of words.

"Oh, yes, Mr. Walker. This campus is so rich in history, and as anyone knows, that history always hides a fair amount of mystery."

"I'm actually quite a history buff," Walker said, glancing at the paintings which lined the walls. "What happened here?"

"Well, this campus is haunted."

"Haunted?"

"Yes. By Mosby's ghosts."

"I'm familiar with Mosby. Partisan ranger. Loudoun County was his base of operations."

"Yes, Mr. Walker. This is Mosby's Confederacy. When the 'war against northern aggression' wrought its havoc upon us, he protected us from those terrible Union invaders. I'm originally from this area of Virginia myself. My grandfather owned a cattle farm just a few miles from here." She paused, shifting to a somber tone. "Our family lost it all," she said quietly.

Walker abruptly realized that Gloria was a native Virginian, a southern belle, and she was just at about the right age to have been born and raised on the *Lost Cause* theory of the Civil War. It was an argument that the American Civil War was one of the noble Southern gentlemen defending their homes against the tyranny in the North, led by the greatest tyrant of them all: Lincoln. As a student of historiography, the interpretation of the past based on the thinking of the present, Walker knew the *Lost Cause* theory was indeed a concerted effort by southern historians to limit the impact of slavery as the primary cause of the war. Instead of casting the South as honorably protecting their way of life versus defending a peculiar institution that had already been outlawed by the rest of the world.

Walker imagined that Gloria was a confederate sympathizer, still angry that the South had lost the war and still bitter that her father had lost everything in the process. Walker knew Ellis was originally from Maryland — a neutral state — which made sense, as it would have been doubtful that her father would have allowed her to marry a Yankee. Walker felt like he had just stepped back in time.

"I'm so sorry to hear that," Walker said with as much empathy as he could muster. "But did you say...ghosts?" he asked.

Gloria paused for a moment, appearing to reflect on her family's history and the tragic loss they suffered at the evil hands of the North, but then seemed to be reaffirmed by the stories of her Confederate saviors. A smile wrinkled her face and she leaned forward.

"Well, Mr. Walker, the story goes that Mosby's Rangers actually used this campus to move their men and supplies. Supposedly, they built an elaborate series of tunnels beneath the school grounds to hide and transport their contraband. That's how they were able to surprise those Union troops all the time...because they were *underground*. It's rumored that when the war ended, many of his rangers wanted to stay here and continue to fight a guerrilla war against the North. Although Mosby eventually surrendered, some of his raiders did stay here and died in those tunnels below us. Today, their spirits still wander the campus, protecting us from harm. Remember, this will always be Mosby's Confederacy."

CHAPTER 31

Walker was startled by his conversation with Gloria Ellis. If things weren't already weird enough, they had just taken a definite turn for the surreal. *Ghosts? Tunnels? Spirits of the Confederacy?* Walker wondered if a seance would be better than an investigation at this point. This mystery was only getting more complicated, and Walker did not believe in ghosts.

However, he did believe in a corrupt person in a position of power at an elite private school who could use that position to assert his will on his students with near impunity. Especially if he was assisted by an ethically-challenged security chief with complete control over the eyes and ears of the campus. Walker needed more background on Ellis. Immediately. Perhaps Meredith could shed some more light on the *good* dean who had not been telling him the truth since he first stepped into his office two days ago.

He returned to his residence, for some reason expecting to find Meredith still there, but she was not. He quickly went to her residence next door and knocked several times on the door, even peeking in the windows, but it was dark. She was gone.

Walker didn't want to jump to any conclusions, but after the time he thought they had shared together, he doubted she would simply leave the campus without telling him. It was a Saturday, so there were no classes today. He checked his phone. No texts. No calls. Perhaps he was simply overreacting. Or perhaps he felt more of a connection than she did. Walker obviously wasn't a great judge of character, but the way they had talked gave him the distinct indication that she was going to help him with this investigation. And now he needed her more than ever. Her experience with Ellis for all of these years could provide some valuable context on the enigmatic dean.

Walker suddenly had a sinister thought. He remembered Gloria's comments about Castillo. *Out of the reach of the cameras.* She definitely did not like him, but *out of reach*, that was a unique way of phrasing it. Walker looked at the sofa where he and Meredith had been resting earlier, then scanned the room slowly with his eyes. He moved around the living room, peering closely at the paintings, running his fingers along the edges of the frames. He circulated around the room several times but found nothing. He stopped again in the center of the room, stared at the sofa again, then gazed upward toward the ceiling fan.

Pulling a chair over, he stepped onto the makeshift pedestal and reached the centerpiece of the fan box. He turned the box counterclockwise, unscrewing it with several rotations until the covering finally fell off into his hands. Walker stared into the inner compartment of the fan mechanism, which housed a small camera, a red light flashing and its wires disappearing into the ceiling. He instantly recognized the camera model from his days at the FBI, but this particular unit was much more advanced. It was clear this camera was providing a live recorded feed of the entire room — audio and video.

As Walker attempted to make sense of the foreign device in the fan blade, the realization hit him with the power of a freight train. *Castillo had been watching him this entire time.* His every move. This was simply another circuit in his elaborate hidden camera system. The security chief could be watching him right now, smiling that it took so long for him to discover the hidden surveillance camera. Walker wasn't sure if more devices were hidden in other rooms, but there was no need to look for them now. It didn't matter. The game was over, and Walker had already lost. Castillo had been playing him from the beginning.

Walker's next realization, however, almost knocked him from the chair. *Meredith.* Castillo had heard their conversations. Watched them together. She was now compromised. *But where was she?* Only one person would know.

CHAPTER 32

Walker pounded his fist on the translucent glass for several minutes until it finally slid open. He had traversed the campus in under five minutes, making his way from his residence to the subterranean surveillance center to find Castillo. He even used Castillo's keycard again in the elevator but didn't care who noticed this time. As Walker entered the space, he felt the chill. The room felt colder and appeared darker than he remembered. And empty. Except for one occupant, sitting in an executive chair at the back of the darkened room with his feet crossed up on the counter.

Walker stood at the front of the room, silhouetted by the video screens playing silently behind him, the campus on full display.

Castillo broke the silence. "You know, I could sit here all night watching these feeds." he mused. "It's so quiet and God-like. You can literally watch the world from here."

Walker marched his way up to the counter, not interested in the philosophical and emotional amusements of a deranged person. He stood directly in front of Castillo, blocking his view of the screens, and slammed the video camera onto the counter. Castillo nonchalantly cocked his head and looked at the broken video camera on the counter surface, its severed wires like spider legs sticking upward.

"Can you explain this?" Walker said in a measured low voice.

Castillo smiled, huffed, and looked away.

"What the fuck is this?" Walker demanded.

Castillo looked up. "That, Mr. Walker, is a very expensive camera."

"And what was it doing in my living room?"

Castillo was abrupt. "Are you really that dumb?" A slight pause. "Or are you just drunk?"

Walker began to protest, but Castillo loudly pulled his feet away from the counter and stood up to face his opponent. "Did you really think you could just walk onto this campus and be able to solve a missing persons case almost seventy-two hours after the fact? That you could do more than all of the equipment and personnel I have at my disposal? Solve this mystery with a case file and a keycard? Did you really expect us to just open all of our doors for you, expose all of our inner workings, so you could sling accusations at us? Of course, I watched you. Because I don't trust you."

Walker straightened and calmed his voice. "What are you hiding, Castillo?"

The security chief laughed. "Please. Spare me your conspiracy bullshit. I gave you access to everything."

Everything? Not quite. Walker simply couldn't tell Castillo what he knew — what he had seen in the office down the hall — or it could jeopardize the pending FBI raid. He couldn't do that to Lewis because the corruption was literally seeping through the walls at this school. Even if he couldn't find Amanda, at least he would have some solace in the fact that the FBI could take down this school, and that would be a win. A win for Amanda. But there was still a device sitting right there in front of him and perhaps a vague reference to others. "What about your hidden cameras?"

Castillo flinched, but did not probe deeper, did not ask why Walker had made it plural, but probably making a mental note to figure it out later. "Listen, those are invaluable to the overall security of this campus."

"You've been watching me, manipulating my every move since I got here."

"I am the head of security, Walker. It's my job to know what is happening on this campus. Did I spy on you? Yes. But it's because that's what I do. I protect this school. Were you actually foolish enough to think for one second that you ever had full reign here? You were always under my control."

"You think putting a camera in my residence is controlling me? That's just voyeurism."

"What do you want from me? I didn't tell you to get close with Meredith."

"You sick bastard," Walker said. "Is that was this is about? An old fling? A former girlfriend who knows your secrets?"

"You be careful with that girlfriend. She's got some issues. But perhaps you already know that...now that the two of you are so close. I wondered how you had gotten my keycard and access to my office. But now it all makes sense. You have no idea what you're getting yourself into."

"Don't worry about me. I can take care of myself. As long as you aren't looking over my shoulder, trying to stop me from investigating this case."

"I told you from the very beginning, my priority is this school, and no one, including some washed-up private investigator, is going to get in the way of that. Like I said before, you had better be careful because no one is going to miss you."

"Are you threatening me?"

"You can call it whatever you want, but you jeopardize the safety of these students in any way, and you won't be around much longer." Castillo paused and looked at his watch. "As far as I can see, you have one day left, so yelling at me is not helping you to solve this case, now is it?"

"Where is Meredith?"

"How the hell should I know?"

"You're the one with the camera feeds. So where is she? Did you have to take care of her, too? Does she know too much about Amanda's disappearance?"

Castillo chuckled loudly. "Have you listened to yourself? You can't solve this mystery, so it must be us. Jesus Christ. Do you have any other theories?"

Walker paused, unsure if he wanted to play his next hand, but he was reaching the end of the line, so it was at least worth a shot. "What do you know about the tunnels?"

"What tunnels?"

"Don't bullshit me. I've heard the stories."

Castillo sighed, looked down for a moment and then stared at Walker. "This school has been here since 1805. You don't think we have our share of legends and myths for something that's been around for that long? The ghosts of Washington Academy," Castillo said, rolling his eyes. "Yeah, we've got our underground tunnels, our secret societies, and now, a missing student. They must all be related."

"What are you trying to cover up here?"

"You have no idea what you're talking about."

"I'm going to find out the truth. I will find it. And if you're a part of this," He pointed his index finger at Castillo, "I'm going to bring you down."

Castillo shook his head. "You can threaten me all you want, but I want to solve this as much as you do. I'm not hindering your investigation, I'm just making sure you stay in line. I've tried to solve this one, too. And even with all this surveillance," Castillo said, waving his arms at the screens. "I still can't figure it out."

"What did you mean when you said they're all related — the tunnels and society and Amanda?"

"I didn't say that. You know what I meant."

"No. What did you mean?"

Castillo lowered his head and waved his hand dismissively. "Forget it."

Walker edged back toward Castillo. "No. What are you talking about? Why do you think they're related?"

Castillo sat back down in the chair and sighed heavily as he leaned back. There was a long moment of silence as Castillo stared at Walker. Finally, he said, "Supposedly, our little secret society uses the tunnels to sneak into the surrounding wooded areas undetected."

Walker was dumbfounded. "What? Is that true? Where are these tunnels?"

"Don't get your hopes up." Castillo huffed. "I've never seen them. I don't actually know if they exist, but the legend is that Mosby built an elaborate series of tunnels under the campus, connecting some of the buildings with the surrounding woods, which would enable him to move his forces quickly or hide supplies. Several of the original buildings were here at the time, so it makes sense. You saw that big painting of Mosby outside Ellis's office, right? Well, there you go. He's a real hero around here."

Walker was intrigued. "Where do you think these tunnels might be?"

"Not sure. We did some searching a couple of years back but came up empty. Honestly, I don't have time to be digging for tunnels. I have enough to worry about above ground."

"What about this secret society...the *Sons of Liberty*? Have you ever followed its members, tried to find the entrances to the tunnels?"

"As I told you before, we don't even know who's a member or if it actually still exists, so there's no one to follow. And we've never picked up anything on the cameras. It's almost," Castillo paused and chuckled, "It's almost like they're ghosts."

Walker wasn't amused. "Did it ever occur to you that the reason you couldn't confirm the existence of this secret society is that they *were* underground, far beyond the reach of your elaborate camera system?"

"No, it hasn't." Castillo stood up. "Because it's not real. They're just stories, Walker. Nothing more. And if you waste your valuable time attempting to uncover some mysterious tunnel or track down some secret club, that's time that Amanda doesn't have. And according to my calculations, you only have one day left. You really want to go back to Arcuri and tell him his daughter was swallowed up by a folktale from the Civil War?"

Walker glanced down, dejected. For all the security chief's faults, he knew Castillo was right. Chasing down some 100-year-old myth that may or may not prove to be true would take too much time, and the clock was running out. Walker also realized he was literally grasping at straws because he needed this victory so badly. He needed to find Amanda for a plethora of his own reasons, least of all to provide closure for her father. Therefore, following his only lead — a dubious story about a labyrinth of secret, nineteenth-century tunnels built beneath a prestigious private school — was his only chance, but it was simply too outlandish to be taken seriously. It finally occurred to Walker that he had lost his grip on reality, and along with it, his last best hope to find Amanda.

CHAPTER 33

Walker exited the administration building into the cool night air. He was deflated. All dead ends. No leads. And Castillo had hamstrung his investigation from the beginning. This school was not going to give up its secrets — not without one hell of a fight — and Walker just wasn't prepared for the battle. With the backing of the FBI he might have had a chance, but on his own with no support and everyone working against him, discovering the truth was a nearly insurmountable task. He was alone.

The former agent was reminded of his crucial moments in that adjacent office, his rifle carefully slid in the small space where the door was ajar. The fateful shot. The feeling of emptiness afterward. Like the ghosts of Mosby, the past was coming back to haunt him. He obviously couldn't save Amanda, was grasping at Civil War folklore to do so and may have put Meredith's life in danger. Perhaps his own. *How far would Castillo go to stop him? And what was happening here that was so important to hide?* Walker didn't know if he cared anymore.

He trudged to his vehicle, still parked in the lot across from the admin building, and opened the driver-side door. Slumping into the seat, he pulled a half-empty bottle from the floor. Walker had managed to stay away from the alcohol for two days, but now he desperately needed it to ease the pain. As he unscrewed the bottle's cap, he could feel the darkness returning, the headache getting stronger, the sickness overwhelming him. He needed this drink to settle him down, remove the anxiousness and bring upon the numbness, which would soothe the pain and help him forget. Take him to another place. A quiet place. At least temporarily.

Walker concluded that he really didn't care what happened to him at this moment, almost wished for Castillo to carry through on his threat, or for Arcuri to kill him after he couldn't find his daughter. For all its good intentions, this investigation was over and the case was closed. There was simply nothing else he could do. His feeble attempt to crawl his way back to the surface by finding a criminal's daughter was foolhardy at best, and his misguided quest for some type of redemption had failed miserably. It was over. Walker reached over and opened the glove box, the handgun falling into his hand. He held it for several moments and stared at it while making a momentous choice.

He turned his attention from the gun and lifted the bottle to take a long drink, needing some liquid courage to go through with the unthinkable. The bottle vibrated in his unsteady hands as he raised it to his lips. As the liquid touched his tongue, a light from far off on campus, shined through the bottom of the brown-tinted bottle and reflected brightly in his eyes. He stopped before the liquid entered his mouth and slowly lowered the bottle, as the source of the light came into focus. Walker admired the three-story brick building with the smooth white pillars adorning its entrance. His eyes tightened on the ancient-looking columns, and he instantly realized the importance of the building and how it might assist him.

***

The Map Room, located on the basement level of Douglas Library — named after the famous inventor who graduated from WA and gave a large donation for the new structure to be built shortly before he died in 1973 — was no larger than a closet and dimly lit. It obviously wasn't the most popular location in the library, but the cramped space and low lighting did not deter Walker from his very important task.

After he had inquired about old maps of the campus at the circulation desk, a student led him downstairs and almost looked embarrassed as he announced this small space as 'the map room.' Contributing to the claustrophobia were the shelves that surrounded the interior of the room, each containing maps from the time period neatly typed on the tiny name tags below each shelf. Walker studied the shelves for several minutes, finally pulling some maps from the earlier dates as well as the more recent collections.

He spread the maps out on the only other space — a rectangular wooden table which was worn and splintered, probably its final destination before it was thrown out — located in the center of the room. Walker sat in the only chair — another potential yard sale buy — and oriented himself with the most recent drawings of the campus layout to confirm what he could already picture in his mind based on his brief time at the school. He then compared the current campus layout to the construction and architectural designs through the years, which were also stacked neatly on the shelves. These blueprints were then compared to the earliest map renditions of the campus until he found what he was looking for. And there it was.

The oldest buildings on campus were the current administration building and the dean's residence. Both of the buildings had been updated, as evidenced through the construction records, but largely maintained their original cosmetic appearance with only underlying structural repairs.

However, one of the campus's other original buildings had been completely redesigned and only a small portion of the initial structure remained. It had been extensively refurbished in the 1990s and its outward modern appearance was now significantly different than its previous architectural design. However, according to the construction blueprints, an older section of the building still remained, hidden deep within the confines of the present renovation. Walker knew that if an entrance to a tunnel system existed, it would be there.

CHAPTER 34

Walker exited the library with a bounce in his step, buoyed by his discovery and emboldened to uncover one of the secrets of this campus. He cleared the pillars and bounded down the front steps of the library toward the Center Grove, a tree-lined and sidewalk-crossed quad in the center of campus which formed the nucleus of Washington Academy. The library sat on the edge of the Center Grove, an intersection of human architecture and natural beauty, which had gone back to the earliest designs of the campus.

Darkness had fallen, so the trees had become shadows and the cool breeze rustling through the school grounds sent a shiver down his spine. He had only reached the second landing and was about to span the last set of steps when a figure emerged from the darkness below him. Walker halted, dead in his tracks. It was Castillo.

The security chief looked up at him with a renewed sense of purpose. "The boys' dorm," he said excitedly.

Walker was stunned and stood breathless, but said nothing.

"The boys' dorm," Castillo repeated. "That's where we need to look for the tunnel."

"How did you?" Walker started to ask, but before he could finish, Castillo began walking up the stairs, until he was only a few steps from Walker.

"After you left, I started thinking that maybe you were right. Why didn't I have video footage of Amanda? Why couldn't

I figure this out? As much as I'm sure you hate me right now, I'm an investigator just like you. And just like you, I've been immensely frustrated by this case. But what if we couldn't figure this out because they were underground? I think you might be right."

Walker was stunned by the admission from his nemesis, someone he didn't necessarily hate, but had certainly written off as no help to this investigation whatsoever. And based on what he had just discovered in the library, he agreed with Castillo's assessment about the male residence hall. He simply nodded.

Castillo continued. "We have a complete collection of the campus's schematics in our database when we installed the security system, so I just checked. And aside from the admin building and the dean's home, a section of the boys' dorm was the first on campus. And if I was looking for a perfect staging area from which to launch a secret society, that would be it."

Still in shock from his own discovery and Castillo's sudden revelation, Walker didn't know what to say. "I didn't think you were on my side."

Castillo quickly shut down the good feelings. "I'm not. But if there's something there, I need to know about it. Remember, this campus is my top priority."

Walker didn't really care why, but for the moment at least, he had a partner. "Let's go."

***

The two men hurried across the campus and entered the male dormitory only minutes later. The investigators immediately traveled to the oldest section of the building, based on the schematics Castillo had downloaded onto a small tablet he had brought with him. Castillo held the device like a Geiger counter in front of him as they descended a set of stairs into a basement hallway where multiple rooms existed for the various clubs and organizations on campus.

They moved down the hallway methodically, studying the doors, each decorated with an array of symbols and words representing the club that it housed. As they neared the end of the hall, Walker's attention was drawn to a blue door with an assortment of decorations denoting an environmental club on campus. However, directly in the center of the door was a drawing of a tree that struck a remarkable resemblance to a famous one.

Walker halted and pointed to the door. "That looks like an elm tree to me."

Having already passed the door, Castillo paused and turned. "So?"

Walker grinned as he knelt down and ran his finger over the outline of the tree. "This is a very famous elm tree, Mr. Castillo. An elm that was located near Boston Common, where one of the very first protests against the British government took place. It's called the Liberty Tree."

"The what?" Castillo asked.

Walker laughed as he made the connection in his mind, still tracing the tree with his hand. "You ever hear the Jefferson quote? *The Tree of Liberty must be refreshed from time to time with the blood of Patriots and Tyrants.* It was during the American Revolution when this tree became a symbol of the growing rebellion against the British."

Castillo looked down at Walker. "Rebellion? By the thirteen colonies?"

"Yes. Led by none other than the *Sons of Liberty*."

CHAPTER 35

Similar to the many other doors on campus, this one was secured by a keycard system. The security chief swiped his card in front of the black pad to the right of the door, and it unlocked with a distinctive click.

"Who has access to this door?" Walker asked.

"Only the students presently enrolled in this organization. We enter the access code onto their individual key cards, but I won't be able to check that list of names until I return to the security center," said Castillo as he entered the room.

Walker stepped cautiously behind him, knowing the names on that list would be important to see eventually, but for now, the cryptic symbols on the door were enough of a reason to search the room and possibly move this investigation forward.

The room was about double in size to the dormitory room Walker had seen earlier, and it was furnished much more as meeting space than living quarters. Two ugly cloth sofas, obviously hand-me-downs from another generation, lined the walls and an assortment of metal, padded, and wooden chairs were arranged awkwardly about the space. The floor was covered with a dark blue shag carpet with stains of varying degrees and sizes spread throughout the thick fibers. On the walls hung an assortment of annual club photos — the school year prominently featured on the decorative frames — which included all the members of the organization for that particular year with their accompanying student portrait. Walker glanced at the framed pictures, but could not locate a current one as they all appeared to be at least ten years old.

Castillo made his way to the right side of the room, where a four-feet-high, wooden counter extended out from the wall. He searched the cluttered shelves built into the back of the counter, rifling through craft supplies, file folders, and some old snack bags, but found nothing of any interest. He turned and noticed a second door, a hollow door with a cheap brass handle that appeared to lead into a closet. Castillo reached for the handle and opened it. A cold rush of air met him at the entryway. Surprised by the rapid change in temperature, he stayed silent but motioned for Walker to follow him by snapping his fingers. Walker hurried across the room and followed Castillo as he stepped inside the closet.

Darkness. Castillo felt around for a light switch, but there wasn't one. He put his hands out in front of him, feeling his way through the black void. More shelves made of untreated and splintering wood lined the walls of the narrow space, again stacked with what felt like old art supplies and boxes of tossed-out materials. Walker stood motionless while Castillo moved to the back of the small closet and pushed against the surface. The wall moved with his hand. He instinctively pulled back, bewildered by the pliability and feel of the wall. It was cloth. Castillo surveyed the back wall again with both hands, gripped it tightly, and yanked on it with a violent tug. Ripped from its nails, a long black drapery dropped to the ground and soft yellow light instantly flooded the room. Walker squinted as he tried to make sense of the passageway before them.

The two men exchanged glances as Castillo pulled a handgun from the shoulder holster under his windbreaker and stepped into the tunnel.

CHAPTER 36

Now that the closet was somewhat lit by the glow from the tunnel entrance, Walker studied the inside of the space and realized that had entered some sort of inner chamber. The texture of the walls appeared to be rough and cracking as was the uneven floor, reminding Walker of masonry work from the 1800s. Thick wooden beams ran across the length of the ceiling and decaying plaster was smeared between the beams. The shelves were obviously a recent addition, used for simple storage, but it was clear the space itself was the remaining section of the original structure that had once stood here.

Walker exhaled as he realized the story of the tunnels was real. He wondered how many other underground passageways traversed the layout of the campus deep beneath its surface. He was curious who had discovered these tunnels and when, but that was a mystery for another time. Right now, it was about Amanda Bryson, and this tunnel could very well lead him to her. He slowly entered.

***

The two men walked gingerly along the dirt floor of the tunnel, attempting to stay quiet, unsure of what was ahead of them or what they might encounter. The lighting in the man-made channel was intermittent and dim, so they were also being cautious of how they stepped. Walker assumed Castillo was carrying a loaded weapon, so any kind of slip or fall could have tragic results.

And of course, Walker still didn't trust Castillo, so he was more than happy to let him go first. The dark tunnel provided an entirely plausible opportunity for an "accident" to happen, and Walker didn't want to end up with a gun pointed at him from behind. Although shooting Walker may not have been Castillo's intention when they first entered the tunnel, it might simply present itself as too precious an opportunity for him to pass up. As far as Walker was concerned, no one else even knew this tunnel existed, so being shot in the back and left for dead would have been all too easy.

But Castillo had seemed genuinely interested when they discovered the passageway and was almost excited to enter it. Perhaps this would now be a joint investigation. It was possible that Castillo really didn't know who had done this and was merely defensive from the beginning about his inability to protect the students and identify the culprit on his cameras. *Had Castillo been purposely obstructing his investigation just so he could save face? Simply make himself look better when the former FBI agent couldn't figure it out either?*

Perhaps this was Castillo's chance to make amends, or an opportunity to solve this case and get back into the good graces of Ellis, so he could declare with confidence that his campus was safe once again. Or maybe it was simply his law enforcement background — that no matter what you did or how corrupt you had become — you still believed that it mattered. Whatever the reason, he was sure it was better to have Castillo on his side than not.

As Walker's thoughts drifted, he also studied the inside of the tunnel. A string of cords had been rigged along the upper edge of the dirt ceiling, and about every twenty feet or so, a small lightbulb had been latched. Because of the distance between bulbs and the low wattage of each one, the tunnel was dark, but still relatively easy to negotiate with their footing. Unfortunately, the ceiling of the tunnel was barely five feet high, so the men had to crouch as they hiked through the narrow passage.

The two men followed the cramped tunnel through several oxbow bends and turns until finally, the dark passageway unveiled a stronger natural light from up ahead, appearing to be moonlight shining in from the other end of the tunnel. Walker encountered another wall of cold air, indicating the exit was near. He calculated they had marched just over two hundred yards from campus, so they were now well into the wooded acres that surrounded the school.

After one last bend, the tunnel's floor inclined upward to an opening which was barely larger than a small door, surrounded by large rocks and vegetation on both sides. This entrance was well hidden from the outside world, and if Walker had been a partisan ranger, he could see how the tunnel had been extremely effective for hiding men and material. Both men slowed their movements and tracked at a slower pace as they neared the exit of the dirt and rock enclosure.

Castillo instinctively moved to the right side of the holed opening while Walker edged to the left, both men naturally channeling their law enforcement training. Castillo reached into the back of his jeans with his left hand, removing another firearm, and handing it to Walker without looking as he closed in on the opening. In his peripheral vision, Walker glimpsed the offer of the gun, and although initially surprised by the gesture, intuitively grabbed the weapon as the two former police officers reached the end of the makeshift tunnel.

Both men emerged from the tunnel at the same time, but neither could immediately make sense of the frightening scene before them.

CHAPTER 37

Directly in front of the two men in a small clearing amongst the dense forest, ten cloaked figures were arranged in a circle, each facing inward. The faces of the figures were merely shadows as dark hoods were pulled over their heads and long robes, which extended to their feet, concealed their bodies. Each of the robed strangers held a lantern, casting a soft light into the center of the circle. On a large flat rock in the middle of the circle, illuminated by the dim glow of the lanterns, was a woman's naked body. She was lying flat on her back, like a sacrifice to be offered to the gods, her arms and legs outstretched over the edges of the rock.

The woman appeared to be semiconscious and was moving slightly, but seemingly unaware of her precarious position. Her pseudo-paralysis signified that she had probably been drugged and was most likely an unwilling participant in this deadly spectacle. The cloaks looked exactly like the one Walker had seen on the hidden camera footage, so the connection was beginning to form in his mind. But before he could finish his thought, one of the cloaked figures stepped forward and entered the inside of the circle.

He slowly approached the helpless victim and methodically ran his hand, just barely visible from beneath the baggy sleeve of his robe, over her entire body as though he was a predator admiring his prey. His fingers moved carefully from the contours of her face over the mound of her breasts, sliding across her stomach and touching her genital area. The molester stood motionless for several moments until finally lowering his hand to his side and returning with an object, removed from his cloak.

As Walker strained to make out the object in the dim light, the other cloaked figures began to chant as they raised their lanterns above their heads. With the light from the lanterns shifting, Walker could now see the victim more clearly and realized it is not a woman at all, but a young girl. Seeming to be somewhat awakened from her drugged-induced state by the chants growing ever louder, the female victim turned her head slightly toward Walker, and he immediately recognized the ear piercings and slightly colored hair of Heather Yates.

As the figure in the center of the circle raised the object higher, the chants seemed to be reaching a crescendo, and Walker could now decipher the object in the assailant's hand. It was a hunting knife. A white bone handle — wrapped in his fingers — was attached to a long silver blade with one edge smooth and the other serrated. Heather started to awaken and wearily realized there was a large knife hanging over her. She attempted to scream, but before the cry could even leave her throat, the deafening chants that engulfed her suddenly stopped, and the figure plunged the knife downward.

CHAPTER 38

Akin to the sound of thunder after a lightning strike, a collective grunt from the unknown figures rose up into the night air as the knife found its destination. Walker was paralyzed, motionless, still shaken by the horror he had just witnessed. A stark realization swept over him. *He had failed again.*

He was suddenly jolted from his paralysis by two gunshots, which rang in his ears and echoed as the sound ricocheted off the surrounding rocks and trees. The macabre ceremony ended abruptly as the robed figures scattered in all directions, ripping off their cloaks, dropping their lanterns, and tripping over each other as they tried to escape. As the hoods came off, Walker could see they were boys from the school. *Cowards.* The toughness they displayed moments ago over a terrified and helpless girl was now gone, replaced with their own horror at being discovered. They were nothing more than scared kids.

Walker glanced at Castillo, anger contorting his face, smoke rising from his gun where he had just released two rounds into the air. The sharp smell of gunpowder awakened Walker from his trance, and he jumped from the tunnel entrance, chasing whatever cloaked criminal was still visible in his sight as Castillo rushed to Heather. Walker's target happened to be the one with the knife, directly in front of him.

Everything transpired in seconds, but it seemed like an eternity to Walker. The killer was noticeably stunned by the gunshots, dumbfounded by the sudden end to his murderous rampage, so he did not move as quickly as everyone around him.

He was still standing upright, attempting to decide the best course of action, when Walker rushed toward him in a fit of rage and grit. He immediately dropped the knife into the dirt and turned to run as Walker collided with him, grabbing a firm hold of his cloak and forcing him to the ground.

The unknown figure struggled to free himself, throwing the lantern at Walker, and then out of sheer desperation, wildly punching at his captor, many of the blows missing. He mobilized his legs as well, kicking furiously until his cleated shoe cleaved into Walker's face and tore a wide gash into his cheek. Walker was immobilized for a moment, giving his opponent just enough time to tear off his robe and get to his knees. Walker swiped at the laceration on his face with the back of his left hand, streaking the blood across his torn flesh. He raised his right hand. It held the gun, which was aimed directly at his adversary, who without his cloak was now completely visible in the low moonlight. Josh Easterly.

Josh stared at the barrel of the gun and followed the outstretched arm of its owner back to the bloody and determined face of Ryan Walker. The two exchanged a long stare, a test of wills, a reflection of how far each of them had fallen and what they were still capable of. Walker wanted to pull the trigger, furious over the merciless killing he had just watched this young man commit, but he couldn't quite do it. Although he had certainly reached the depths of this world by killing many others, there was something about the innocence of a child.

Walker had convinced himself all these years that the people he followed were grown adults who had made terrible choices, had gone to the dark side and deserved whatever punishment might befall them. But the young man in front of him was different. Although this person had certainly chosen his fate and made tragic mistakes in the process, he was still a child and did not deserve to die. In his soul, Walker was still an agent, still a law enforcement officer, and still bound by the rule of law. And for that reason, he could not pull the trigger.

Seeing the hesitation in Walker's movements and capitalizing on the moment of humanity that had just returned to the ex-agent, Josh rose to his feet, turned, and ran away. Walker lowered his gun as Castillo, who had been tending to Heather, rushed by him and pursued Josh into the dense woods. They both disappeared into the darkness as the sounds of crackling leaves and snapping branches eventually faded to silence.

Time returned to its normal rhythm as Walker grunted loudly, turning over and sitting up, exhausted from the scuffle with Josh. He crossed his arms on his knees as he looked at the discarded robes and broken lanterns which now littered the clearing. It was eerily quiet.

Trying to avoid the inevitable as long as possible, Walker finally brought himself to look at the girl lying motionless on the flat rock a few feet away. He rose to one knee and took a deep cleansing breath, trying to prepare himself for what he was about to do. He didn't bother to brush himself off as he struggled to his feet and eventually willed himself to begin the slow march toward the victim. It reminded him of another time.

CHAPTER 39

As Special Agent Walker pulled the trigger, the assault weapon released its deadly ammunition, nearly without sound. The silencer had muffled most of the explosion from the barrel, so instead of a loud gunshot blast, it was more like a hushed airgun. But the .45 caliber round in the barrel was anything but harmless, and moved across the space of the lobby at lightning speed, impacting the assailant's head with remarkable precision. The result was immediate. The left side of the hostage-taker's head exploded in a mass of blood and brain tissue, spraying bits of both onto his hostage. The subject was propelled to the floor, but he pulled the woman with him as his arm was still wrapped around her neck.

Both fell hard to the floor as Walker sprung from the side room, flinging the door open, his rifle outstretched to finish the job if needed. It was a headshot, so most likely the man was already dead, but more importantly was the condition of the woman, who was very close to the blast. As Walker took giant steps across the lobby, he saw the woman — dazed and confused — lift herself up with her arms from the body splayed on the floor and look back at him racing across the lobby. Although her face was covered in his blood and her tears, she appeared to be unhurt.

Walker had just reached the daughter, still cowering in the chair, when he felt a sudden punch in his back. It took his breath away. He was forced to the floor and the intense pressure in his back was now releasing to all parts of his body as he smashed into the hard cement floor. Disoriented by the pain, but working to recover from the fall, he rolled slightly to locate the source of the impact.

A second subject, who had been sitting in a chair in the corner of the lobby, obscured from Walker's limited view through the slit in the doorway, was now standing behind him. For this new unknown subject, the SWAT team had just breached the lobby and killed his partner, so his only resort was to go out in a blaze of glory.

Still smoking from the first shot that had hit Walker squarely in the back, the gunman's pistol was now pointed directly at his head. His vest had taken the first bullet, and although the force of the impact had knocked him down, he was unharmed. He would not be so lucky with the second. Walker rapidly tried to lift his rifle toward the new threat, but from his vulnerable position on the floor, he knew would his reaction would not be fast enough.

As the gunman centered his aim and prepared to pull the trigger, his chest suddenly exploded. Two bullets exited the man's torso, tearing gaping holes through his flesh, which burst open with blood splatter and fragments of fabric. As the assailant's body was pushed forward from the blast, Walker could see his partner, rifle raised, behind the gunman. His life had been saved, but Walker's sudden relief was quickly replaced with unspeakable horror as the gunman's arms swung to the side and the handgun in his right hand, through an involuntary reflex of the fingers, fired.

The single shot from the pistol was all that was needed to kill the young girl sitting next to him. Her mother, still propped up on her arms, let out a blood-curdling scream, watching her dead daughter fall from the chair.

Everything moved in slow motion as Walker was momentarily stunned by the sight of the young girl lying motionless on the bloody floor and shook his head in disbelief as he turned back to the mother, who was still wailing at the top of her lungs. As his partner entered the lobby and immediately moved toward the girl to check her vitals, Walker could not quite comprehend what had just happened nor what he had just done.

CHAPTER 40

Emotions were flooding through Walker like a raging river as he approached Heather. As he neared the hard stone where Heather lay, he realized that the knife had not actually struck her. Instead, there was a jagged gash in the rock, about six inches from her neck. *Had Josh missed? On purpose?* Walker couldn't quite reconcile his confusion as Heather abruptly moved her head as if waking from a dream. The shock of seeing the knife in her delirious state may have caused her to pass out, so she was just now finding her way back from the blackness.

Heather appeared to be in a fog as she slowly opened her eyes and looked up at Walker. He immediately grabbed a nearby robe from the ground and covered her with it while putting his hand on her forehead and held it there. Heather managed to curl her lips into a smile through the grogginess as though she intuitively realized she was now in safe hands.

Lowering his weapon and reaching for his cell phone, Walker placed the call to 911, determined that he would stay with her until the ambulance arrived. Indistinct shouts and radio static could be heard through the thickness of the woods in the direction of the school, campus police officers most likely barreling their way toward the sound of the gunshots. As they approached his position, he watched their flashlight beams dancing among the trees.

Walker climbed up onto the rock and Heather curled into his lap, shivering under the thick cloak, as the reality of her situation became clear. The chemicals in her system were now wearing off, so the catatonic paralysis induced by the drugs was quickly replaced by the very lucid and very real emotions of fear and relief. Walker held her tighter as the bouncing lights drew closer and the faint sound of sirens were carried to them by the crisp breeze.

He took a deep breath and exhaled slowly. Although it wasn't all of his doing and perhaps more luck than anything else, this girl was alive because of him. And he was now holding her close, comforting her from the ordeal she had just endured, as he wasn't able to do so many years ago. He hadn't felt this way in a long time, felt like he had made a difference, saved a life. He still wasn't sure if he was any closer to finding Amanda and uncovering what had happened, but at least for the moment, he had rescued another child and it felt good. He had hoped his mission to Washington Academy would provide a chance for redemption, and in some small way, he may have found some.

CHAPTER 41

Walker sat alone on the rock as police officers from the Loudoun County Sheriff's Department and EMTs from Leesburg Emergency Dispatch encircled him like sharks around an evening meal, but unlike the sharks, they weren't interested in Walker, only the sundry clues that surrounded him. He was in a deep place, far beneath the surface of what had just happened, filled with every emotion he had ever experienced. He still struggled to make sense of the last few minutes — the lingering memories, emotional turmoil, and refreshing conclusion to this most recent episode of his life.

He looked down at his hands, filthy from a dried mixture of dirt, blood, and tears. He had just held a young girl in these hands, alive and breathing, taken away in an ambulance with only superficial wounds. The bizarre ritual in the woods wasn't meant for him but had exorcised some of his demons nonetheless. As he rested on the natural alter — a symbol of his deliverance — he realized there was still good in him, he had not completely lost that internal drive to help others. After his last assignment as an agent, he didn't think he was meant to do this anymore. He had hurt too many people and made too many tragic decisions, but now he was moving toward the right side again. And it was where he knew he belonged.

Walker had spent so much time wallowing in his own self-pity and doubt, that he didn't believe he could still save people, still make a difference. He had been living a life of death and decay for so long, he was consumed by it. But now, he could feel the fresh air, a way out of the hole he had dug for himself. All he needed to do was start climbing.

Another person suddenly brushed up against Walker, startling him from his catatonic trance. He turned to see Castillo talking to him, but the words sounded distance at first, almost garbled until finally Castillo shook him and the command became clear. "Hey, Walker, watch out."

He stood and moved from the rock just as Castillo, dragging the young man by his shirt collar, threw Josh Easterly into his vacated spot. Josh's hood and robe had been removed, his white shirt was now wrinkled and dirty, untucked from his equally mud-streaked khaki pants. Josh resisted Castillo's offer of a seat, so the security chief manhandled the student by roughly sitting him down and holding him on the rock in front of them until Josh finally gave up and stopped struggling.

Castillo stood upright, crossed his arms, and stared down at the pathetic excuse for a criminal. He was still breathing heavily from his pursuit through the woods, so he took a few moments before speaking. Finally, he said, "So, what do we have here, Josh? The *Sons of Liberty* in all its glory? The first thing you're gonna do is give me the names of all the other assholes that were out here with you."

"Fuck you!" Josh glared.

After a quick glance to his left where two officers were absorbed in a conversation, Castillo swung back quickly with his right hand slamming hard into Josh's cheek. Josh's head flung to the left, and he fell off the rock into the dirt. Walker was startled by the abuse, so he stared at Castillo, who simply smiled.

Reaching down with a grunt, he picked up Josh by both hands and sat him back on the rock.

Now bleeding from his right cheek, Josh appeared dazed, his head down — probably throbbing — as he tried to recover from the open-handed punch.

"That was for my friend here," Castillo said, looking down at Josh with superiority. "'Now you having matching scars."

Josh glanced away as though trying to ignore Castillo's

comments.

Castillo reached down and grabbed the boy's chin, moving it up and back to face him. "And what do we have here? A bruise from the ground..." Josh fought against his grip and pulled away. "...when you were being chased by officers after you tried to stab a girl," Castillo said with the persuasion of a prosecutor. Josh sat still, looking away, but Walker was sure the implication was not lost on the supposedly smart, private school student.

Leaning in closer, almost whispering, with a delight in his voice, Castillo continued. "That's right, Josh, you see what's happening here? None of your friends are around. It's just you. We've got a missing girl on our hands, and your fingerprints are all over a knife that nearly just killed a girl. You see where this is going? You better start talking because the way I see it, the only thing that's fucked here...is you."

Silence. Josh continued to stare at the ground as the two investigators leaned over him, like police officers with a suspect. Castillo abruptly stepped closer, as if deducing that Josh needed some further convincing, and the boy instinctively recoiled.

"Alright, I'll talk," he said.

Walker stepped into the conversation. "Alright, what?"

Josh huffed loudly and looked up at Walker. "Alright, I'll give you the names. There were only ten of us. We didn't mean anything. We were just messing around."

"Messing around?" Castillo interjected.

Josh reluctantly turned to Castillo. "Yeah, we weren't going to hurt her. We just wanted to scare her. I heard she's been telling you that I killed Amanda, that she thinks we did it as part of our club."

"Did you?" Walker asked.

"No!" Josh shouted to both men. Then, in a lower voice, "Of course not."

Walker and Castillo, both realizing they had finally broken through the boy's defensive wall, exchanged glances and paused, giving Josh time to collect his thoughts and explain.

"I loved Amanda. Yeah, we fought, but I still loved her. I would never hurt her. I swear to you. I don't know anything about her disappearance."

Walker believed Josh for the first time.

Waving his hand at the clothes and lanterns still discarded in the clearing, Castillo asked, "Then what is all of this shit? What is this club all about?"

"I don't know," Josh said, shaking his head. "Rebellion. Going against the establishment. Giving us a chance to be free. We've had this club for a few years. We sneak out, come to the woods, chant, listen to music, drink, do drugs. You know? Live a little. This place is stressful."

Castillo sighed. "Jesus Christ! Give me a break."

"Well, it is, you know?" Josh pleaded.

"How did you know about these tunnels?"

Josh shrugged his shoulders. "Well, we had always known about the legend. Didn't know if it was true or not, but it was an interesting story. We'd also heard about the secret society that started a few years ago. I guess it disbanded when the administration came down hard on it, but we wanted to bring it back. Restore it to its former glory, you know? So, we did some research, and low and behold, we found this tunnel. Took us almost a year, but we did it."

"And the tunnel is how you kept the *Sons of Liberty* a secret? You never had to leave the boys' dorm, so you never came up on the cameras?"

"Exactly."

"Why the robes and the chanting?" Walker asked.

As if those particular additions were his creation, Josh smiled. "Role-playing, man. Makes it more fun. More mysterious. You can't have a secret society without cloaks and lanterns, right?"

"So you're the head of this little rabble, huh?" Castillo said.

Josh cocked his head slightly as if still wondering how

exactly he had gotten caught. "I was."

"You're damn right there, kid. You were." Castillo confirmed. "First intelligent thing you've said all night."

Castillo turned to Walker, and the two stepped away from Josh, currently lost in his confusion. "What do you think?"

"I don't know," Walker said, "let's get the names of those other kids and talk to them." He glanced back at Josh. "I don't think he's got it in him. One of the other kids perhaps, but he's no sociopath. Sounds like they were just letting off some steam."

"And my gunshots were after the knife had already come down, so if he had wanted to kill Heather, he could have done it," Castillo added.

Walker thought for a moment. "Yeah, but anyone can be a killer. Unfortunately, you don't need to have experience. He could have missed. And we still haven't found Amanda."

"I agree. Let's turn up the heat. Arrest him. Turn him over to the police. See if they can rattle him a bit and get whatever they can from him."

The two turned back to Josh, and Castillo spoke, "Josh, I don't know if we believe your story or not, so we're going to turn you over to the police for questioning until we can get to the bottom of all this."

"Okay, whatever." Josh conceded. "I'm telling the truth."

Castillo picked up Josh — more gently this time — and walked him toward the Sheriff's deputies standing nearby. "Okay, but you need to cooperate with them, you understand?"

"Yes, sir."

The security chief turned Josh over to the nearest police officer and whispered into his ear to apprise him of the situation. The deputies nodded and led Josh away as he returned to Walker, who was running his fingers through his hair. "Okay, what's next?"

Just as Castillo started to speak, another uniformed officer — an old friend in the Sheriff's office — bounded out of the woods with a flashlight and approached the two men. "Joaquin, we found something. You need to see it."

The two men followed the police deputy back into the darkness of the trees along a meandering route for several yards until they reached a slight ravine. At the natural depression in the landscape, they came upon two other officers with their flashlights trained upon a spot on the muddy ground.

As Walker and Castillo moved closer, the lights illuminated an object that was half-buried in the soft earth. Only portions of the fabric were visible and smudged with dirt, but even in the low light, it was clear that the object was a backpack, and its colors were distinctly red and gray.

CHAPTER 42

The natural clearing nestled in the wooded area bordering the southwest corner of Washington Academy was officially a crime scene. But a rather innocuous one. Though a bizarre ceremony had occurred here, based on what had transpired, it would be a misdemeanor charge at best — indecent assault or reckless endangerment — but nothing more. Attempted murder would have been a stretch unless Joshua Easterly or one of the other boys gave a full confession about their intent to murder Heather Yates, but in the absence of that, no prosecutor would even attempt to bring the case in front of a jury.

However, the discovery of the backpack — combined with the disappearance of Amanda Bryson and the strange ritual — turned this relatively benign crime scene, which could have easily been handled by the local authorities, into a much larger affair, involving multiple state and federal law enforcement agencies. The backpack provided a clear piece of evidence that foul play had been involved and immediately catapulted this missing persons case into a full-fledged homicide investigation.

The great lengths that Ellis and Castillo had taken to keep Amanda's disappearance quiet had suddenly evaporated as calls went out to all pertinent agencies, including the Virginia State Police and the FBI. The crime scene investigators arrived shortly before the news vans. Police scanners had been abuzz with the night's events — a bizarre display in the woods surrounding Washington Academy, an injured female student, and a missing girl from several days ago. Leaks to the press were now unavoidable, and the intriguing headlines were already appearing online on the local news sites, quickly being picked up by the national broadcast networks. By daybreak, the pace of the news coverage had become unstoppable and people from the Midwest to the West Coast were talking about the unusual story coming out of that prestigious private school in Virginia.

In the shallow ravine just beyond the clearing, a pack of crime scene investigators — equipment in hand — descended on the obscure location of the backpack. A makeshift path of trampled plants and crushed twigs had formed from the glade to the ravine as more police found their way to the discovery. There was no need for a display of crime scene tape in this remote location, but a cordon had been established just on the edge of the clearing and sheriff's deputies were stationed on the perimeter to approve all who were permitted entry. Walker and Castillo were already there.

While multiple officers with flashlights focused their aim, two crime scene investigators carefully removed the backpack from its resting place in the pulpy ground and laid it on a large piece of plastic. The red and gray stripes were barely visible, the red block darkened with mud, almost looking brown. Using delicate silver clamps to grip and maneuver the backpack, one officer held it stationary, while another unzipped it. When completed, the officer gripped the top edge of the fabric with his clamp and pulled back the outer sleeve. All eyes turned to the inside of the backpack. It was empty.

***

Castillo pushed 'end' on his cellphone after the line went dead, Robert Ellis abruptly ending the call. He turned toward Walker. "Ellis is mad as hell. He can't believe this has turned into a fucking circus."

Having made their way back out to the perimeter while the investigators continued their work at the ravine, Walker was blinded by the bright and flashing lights from the throng of police cruisers, ambulances, and news vans. *Ellis was right. It was a circus.*

"We need to conduct a massive search of this entire area. All the personnel we can assemble as well as search dogs," Walker stated.

Castillo nodded. "Agreed. I'll talk with the state police sergeant from the local barracks. I think she's the one in charge of the scene now, so it will be up to her at this point."

Walker shook his head in affirmation, exhaling a long breath, his first respite from the long night. His body ached and his eyes were heavy.

Castillo looked at him. "Why don't you go back and get some rest. There's nothing more you can do here. If we find anything, I'll wake you. If not, I'll see you back here in the morning."

"I think you're right. Thanks."

Placing his hand on Walker's shoulder before the two parted ways, Castillo said, "Although I hope to God we don't find Amanda out here, I think we might be one step closer to solving this case. Thanks for getting us this far."

It was the first sincere thank you Walker had received in a long time. He nodded and walked away from the flashing lights. He hated the lights.

CHAPTER 43

Special Agent Ryan Walker could only hear his own breathing. Everything else around him was muffled and played out in slow motion as he struggled to come to his senses. He was in shock by the events of the last few moments and could not quite piece together the reality of what had just taken place. It wasn't how it was supposed to have happened, it's wasn't how they had trained. All Walker could do was sit up, place the rifle across his knees, and watch the aftermath of the botched raid unfold before him.

The remainder of the SWAT team with rifles raised swept single-file through the front door and fanned out across the lobby. They quickly secured the area and immediately began attending to the multiple people on the floor, including himself. His body felt heavy as he watched the agents kneeling above the little girl shaking their heads in disbelief at the tragic loss. Walker knew that the two assailants were also dead, according to the movements of the agents hovering over those bodies.

Hoisted up by two agents, the mother was still releasing her blood-curdling screams and resisting the officers, attempting to crawl across the floor to her dead child. Walker went limp at the sight of the broken woman, so when another agent grabbed him under his arms to pick him up, Walker's body wouldn't budge. The agent moved backward and simply dragged Walker along the floor away from the scene. As they reached the front door; the flashing colored and white lights from the parking lot flooded the darkened room and cast a shadowy effect on the officers still inside until everything blurred into darkness.

He could still only hear his own breathing.

CHAPTER 44

Walker made his way back to the search area at dawn. Castillo hadn't contacted him during the night, which meant they hadn't yet found Amanda. This was positive in that the discovery of a body would have signified a tragic end to this girl's life and meant a murderer was out there somewhere, but negative in the respect that without definitive proof of death, Amanda's fate was still unknown.

As Walker approached the southern edge of the campus, where the school's property bordered the thickly forested area, Virginia State Police troopers had established an entry point into the woods. White sawhorses — stenciled in blue with the words 'State Police' — marked the entrance to a makeshift path that curved its way through thick vegetation and brush to the open clearing and shallow ravine a few hundred yards away.

A fine mist of milky fog was rising up from the school's manicured fields just before the boundary to the woods, giving the entire area a surreal spookiness. Blurred images of red and blue flashing lights could be seen through the translucent fog, while police uniforms and FBI windbreakers faded away as the state and federal officers descended into the valley. The news vans were stopped at this perimeter, but a perfect row of reporters, holding microphones close to their faces and talking into the rolling cameras, stood against the picturesque yet eerie backdrop.

Walker nodded to the uniformed officers at the artificial gateway to the crime scene and recognizing him from the night before, allowed him to proceed. He immediately saw Castillo, leaning on a police cruiser, partially obscured by the surrounding fog, smoking a cigarette. It was the first time he had seen Castillo smoke but figured it was probably because he had been up all night. Walker held two cups of coffee, purchased from the student union building moments earlier, in his hands and offered one to Castillo as he leaned on the cruiser.

Castillo was surprised at first by Walker's sudden appearance through the fog but then beamed with gratitude as he gladly accepted the coffee. "Ah, thank you, this is much appreciated." He quickly threw the half-smoked cigarette on the ground and stomped it out with his foot. "Haven't had one of those in years. Borrowed it from a sheriff's deputy. Tastes horrible."

"You've been out here all night?" Walker inquired.

"Yes, sir," Castillo answered firmly. "This is my campus, my responsibility."

"What's the situation?"

Castillo paused, taking a long sip from his coffee and savoring it for a moment. "That's good." He lowered the cup and pondered his thoughts. "Well, the situation is...we haven't found anything yet. We've got fifty officers out here, including the FBI, as well as search dogs, and we've found nothing to indicate that Amanda Bryson is in these woods. No clothes, no blood trails, no hairs or fibers. The only thing we *do* have is her empty backpack."

"So her backpack was just dumped here? Along someone's escape route?"

Castillo winced. "Perhaps. But no footprints either. We did have a light rain two days ago, so it's entirely possible that evidence was washed away, but overall, no sign of a struggle, shallow grave, or escape route."

"What about her cell phone or laptop?"

"No sign of either."

Walker groaned. "I thought we were going to find her. I really did. I didn't want us to find her, but I thought we were close."

"Me, too," said Castillo. "We've searched a radius of a quarter-mile around that backpack. If there was something to find out there, we would have found it."

"What about the tunnel?"

"Right. I went back through it myself. Twice. We've sealed off the entrance from the boys' dorm. Officers are still searching that inner chamber we found, but the tunnel's clean."

"There must be other tunnels, right?"

"I would imagine, but we'd have to go back to the drawing board. Literally. We'd have to look at original drawings and schematics of the campus again, compare it with today, and see if we could possibly locate any other tunnels. Other entrances. It could take us a while. And I don't think Amanda has that much time. If any at all."

"And Josh didn't seem to indicate there were other tunnels or at least ones that he knew of," Walker added.

"Right. He seemed so happy to have just found that one, I doubt they ever looked for any more." Castillo paused, appearing to still be frustrated by the entire affair. "Unfortunately, it was all they needed."

Walker nodded in agreement. "Where is Ellis?"

Castillo glanced back toward campus. "Meeting with senior officials from the sheriff's department, state police, and FBI back at the admin building. They're working on a joint statement. I think they're planning on a press conference soon. This story is simply out of control right now. It's all over the place. Rumors are flying everywhere."

"Why aren't you with them?" Walker asked, smiling.

Castillo huffed. "I don't give a shit about the politics of this thing. Ellis can have all of that as far as I'm concerned. I just want my campus back."

"Behind the cameras, huh? Not in front of them."

"Exactly." Castillo grinned.

Walker was serious now. "I need to talk with Ellis again."

"Come on, Walker, we've been through this," Castillo said,

the anger rising in his voice. "He's got nothing to hide. He's just looking out for his school. Why do you keep badgering him?"

"Because something happened between Amanda and him before she disappeared," Walker stated forcefully.

Castillo looked surprised. "Who told you that? Meredith? I'm telling you, you're putting a little too much trust in her. You find her yet?"

Walker ignored the question, realizing he still hadn't heard from her but was adamant about his request. "Joaquin, I need to speak with him. I think he holds the key to this whole thing. He's definitely hiding something...from you and me. And you're the only one that can get me in there. Please."

Taking another long sip from his coffee, Castillo grieved. "Alright, I'll get you a few minutes with Ellis, but after all the shit that's just gone down, your little visit here might be cut short. This will probably be your last conversation with anyone on this campus. Understand? You sure you want to do that?"

Walker knew Castillo was probably right. Ellis was now clearly on the hot seat. The twisted events at his school over the last forty-eight hours were a front-page news story across the country and most of the blame for that notoriety could be placed squarely at Walker's feet. It would not be a pleasant conversation.

The same could also be said for Castillo, as the security chief had tried but failed to control Walker, but now that everything was crashing down, it really didn't matter anymore. Ellis would take most of the heat, with all of this craziness occurring on his watch, but the first bit of collateral damage would most likely be Castillo. Realizing his days were probably numbered, Castillo knew it was already too late for him, so he finally decided to be more of a help than a hindrance. And for that, Walker was grateful.

"Yes," the private investigator affirmed. "He's our last chance to find Amanda."

"Okay," said Castillo, seemingly resigned to the bad idea. "But I'd pack your bags first."

CHAPTER 45

The United States Department of Justice Office of the Inspector General is the agency tasked with investigating misconduct in the FBI. The hearing with the Inspector General Review Board took place in a small conference room in their suite in downtown D.C., which did not seem fitting to the huge implications which would result from their decision. Walker sat with his attorney at one end of the conference table while the three panel members huddled at the other end. The two men and one woman — finely tailored in their dark suits — sifted through files and documents, the results of a month-long investigation into the FBI raid that cost the lives of three people, including a child.

An internal FBI investigation was always conducted whenever a civilian had lost his or her life, but in this case, one death — that of twelve-year-old Erica Shelby — was being blamed on the FBI. A wrongful death suit was also being levied by the family against the Bureau because of the outcome of the raid. Specifically, the suit alleged, and the investigation confirmed, that the FBI agent who stormed the room after firing the fatal round that killed the hostile subject had acted recklessly by not properly clearing the room upon entry. Not realizing that another suspect was hidden in the corner, this federal agent was struck by gunfire and unable to return fire. The threat was neutralized by the second SWAT team member to enter the room, but only after the suspect had positioned himself in close proximity to a bystander, resulting in the death of a child.

Although the breach had been successful and the threats had been eliminated, it was not before a civilian life had been taken. Investigators contended that if Walker had properly cleared the room, he could have easily taken out the second suspect before that assailant was able to cause harm. Proper tactical procedures for forced entry dictated that the first SWAT officer to enter a space should clear that space to eliminate any and all threats that existed, while his partner would approach the downed suspect. Ensuring all threats were properly accounted for would not unnecessarily risk the lives of fellow SWAT members or innocent bystanders in the vicinity. Although Walker had taken out the primary threat, he had not neutralized all threats, which caused the collateral damage. It was a terrible mistake with devastating consequences.

The conclusions of the investigation were clear and the lawsuit was splashed all over the news, so the FBI's hands were tied. They could have released Walker from culpability, but it would have appeared as favoritism, and so settling the lawsuit was simply one step in the healing process. The other was to fire him. The members of the review board spoke for several minutes about how they had reached their decision, and of course, gave Walker and his attorney the right to appeal that decision. That did not happen. Walker had taken an oath when he joined the FBI to protect and serve, and he did neither in that case. His career with the FBI was over.

This hearing was followed shortly after by additional hearings at the Arlington County Domestic Relations section of the downtown courthouse, as his wife filed for divorce and they fought over custody of their daughter. Walker had been emotionally crushed by the raid, was suspended while the investigation ensued, and fell into an irreparable depression. His relationship with his wife crumbled rapidly as he became despondent, and because she had begged him not to join the SWAT team in the first place, she blamed him for destroying himself and their family. Walker was soon ordered by the court to vacate their home as the spousal relationship became untenable.

His daughter tried desperately to maintain their relationship, but Walker was simply too swallowed up in self-pity and regret to be able to show love to anyone, and so that bond, too, became toxic and infrequent. As Walker's self-flagellation continued to spiral downward, his wife convinced the judge to strip Walker of his custodial rights, including visitations, which only quickened his descent. As the outcome of the investigation became clear and the loss of his family was inevitable, Walker started drinking heavily and taking drugs—prescription at first then illegal as needed—to take away the pain.

Soon, he required more to sustain the level of pain relief, so he desperately needed money to maintain his destructive habits. It only took a few visits to a dance club in a seedy area north of the U.S. Capitol to convince the clientele he was no longer with the FBI but had learned some valuable skills that could easily be put to good use as a private investigator for hire. A few jobs later, and his reputation only grew.

Eventually ceasing with the drugs because he needed more lucidity for his investigations, Walker still relied on the alcohol to provide a layer of comfort. It was an escape from the reality that a person who had always dreamed of being in law enforcement was breaking the law on a regular basis.

It had been a long and treacherous plunge to the bottom, but in the cold and dark abyss of his current situation, Walker always knew there would be a way out. A way back from the depths of his self-imposed prison.

Three years later in late September, Lorenzo Arcuri summoned him to his sprawling estate on the Potomac River.

CHAPTER 46

Walker now sat in front of Dr. Ellis's desk in a different chair this time — Castillo's chair — as if perhaps the change in position would tip the scales of fate in his favor. Or Ellis would think he was talking to Castillo and reveal more than he normally would. He didn't care if it was a shift in the cosmos or mental laziness on the dean's part, because either way, he needed answers.

Ellis stood behind the wooden desk, his back to Walker, glaring out the large glass window at the beautiful campus below. Walker had entered the silent room moments earlier, as the other officials were scurrying out and making final plans for the upcoming press conference. Ellis had yet to speak. Nor had he budged from his fixed position behind the desk, nearly comatose in his movements, slowly surveying the grounds.

"I've always loved this campus," Ellis said finally, still gazing out the window. "From the first moment I saw it, I knew this was the place I wanted to be." He paused for several beats. "It's been almost twenty years now. Twenty years," he whispered. "It's amazing where the time goes."

Walker stayed silent while the dean reminisced about his time at Washington Academy. He figured Ellis was only a couple of years away from retirement, and as all people do when they near the end of their careers, he was mentally reflecting on the legacy he was going to leave behind. It was a legacy that had been steeped in prestige. Until now.

It must have been a crushing weight on Ellis to have

worked for so many years building something only to witness it all come crashing down around you. Castillo was coping with the end by smoking a cigarette in the woods, but he was young and would be employed again soon. Whereas Ellis's life's work was almost over, and he could no longer control how he would walk away. Regardless of what happened now, the lasting impression of Dr. Robert Ellis would be one of disgrace and shame. Walker was sure the Board of Trustees were already secretly meeting to discuss the terms of Ellis's removal and whatever other sanctions they deemed appropriate.

The silence lingered for several moments until Walker spoke. "You have to tell me the truth, Dr. Ellis. It's over. All the lies and cover-ups are exposed. The secret's out, and whatever protection you think you had is gone. It's only a matter of time before the FBI comes knocking on your door." *Sooner than you think.*

Ellis turned his head from the window, his face sculpted into a solemn expression. "I know," he whispered, then turned his gaze back to the window and was silent again.

Walker shifted in his seat, frustrated by the delaying of the inevitable. "What did Amanda discover, Ellis? What secret dealings are you trying to hide?"

Ellis scoffed, still looking out the window. "The dealings aren't important, Mr. Walker. They have absolutely nothing to do with this. There was no grand conspiracy to abduct a young girl because she discovered some secret file, I assure you."

"So why all the lies?"

Ellis exhaled, turned slowly, and sat in the large chair behind the desk. He leaned back and crossed his hands over his chest. "Because...there *was* a moment of weakness. A sexual advance. An awkward moment in which I broke a sacred trust. It was through no fault of her own, she was completely innocent, and it was all my doing. I'm an old man, Mr. Walker, who has been happily married for thirty-two years, but we all still have needs, don't we? They just can't manifest themselves in that way. I deeply regret what I did, apologized more times than you could possibly imagine, but alas, it was a terrible mistake."

"What exactly happened between you and Amanda?"

Relief soothed Ellis's expression. "Oh no, you misunderstand. The sexual advance wasn't with Amanda. It was with Meredith. Meredith Thomas."

Walker was dumbfounded. And speechless.

Seeing the look of shock and awe on Walker's face, Ellis explained. "Meredith came to visit me at my office a few months back, shortly after she moved onto the campus into one of our faculty residences. She was obviously upset about her husband, and so she was very needy at that moment. I had a few too many scotches that day and as the evening rolled around, I was a little less reserved than usual. She sat in the very chair you're sitting in now, and I was in the seat opposite her. One thing led to another and in her weakened state, simply needing someone to comfort her, I started to come onto her. She was receptive at first, but I mistook her helplessness for affection, and as I became more aggressive, she resisted. I regret to say that I did not stop immediately. Nothing happened, I promise you. I did not sexually assault Ms. Thomas. But she did yell out at one point, which brought my student assistant, who was working late in the outer office, bursting into the room. And of course, what she saw was me accosting Meredith. Unfortunately, my student assistant was..."

"Amanda Bryson," Walker interrupted.

Ellis sighed. "Yes."

Walker exhaled loudly, lowered his head, and massaged his forehead with his fingers. "Why did you not tell me this before?"

"Because when you get to be an old man like me, Mr. Walker, you don't have many career options left to you. The one thing you can hope for at this late stage in the game is to be able to determine how your career will end. Walk away on your own terms and leave behind a lasting legacy. I've worked for many years creating that legacy, and to see it all destroyed in one moment of weakness, I just couldn't do that."

Walker's eyes widened. "What are you telling me?"

"I'm telling you that's why I couldn't share this information. Why I was never going to share this information. My entire career, my legacy, was at stake."

"So Meredith and Amanda were now liabilities to you?"

"Of course not. I would never do anything to harm either one of them. I simply apologized profusely to both of them and begged them not to disclose what had happened between us."

"And they agreed?"

"They did. Meredith was incredibly understanding about the whole thing, and she certainly didn't have to be. I even offered for her to speak with our school psychologist, but she refused. Amanda, on the other hand, and for obvious reasons, was quite rattled by the entire episode, but Meredith was actually the one who convinced her to stay quiet. We even decided to put Amanda into Meredith's English class for the fall semester, so she could keep an eye on her. Meredith was extremely strong."

"So why did you transfer Amanda?" Walker asked.

"I needed to. She certainly didn't want to go, but I had to do it. We simply couldn't work that closely together anymore because my guilt was too overwhelming. I couldn't bear to see her every day and be reminded of what she had witnessed, the look of disdain in her eyes, the complete loss of respect. It was too much for me, so I transferred her."

"Did she ever report you?"

"No, but that was much more than I expected, I assure you. I thought my tenure as dean of this school was effectively over, that I should tender my resignation before anyone found out before the Board of Trustees decided to fire me." Ellis paused pensively. "Or before Mr. Arcuri decided to send one of his assassins after me."

"But nothing happened?"

"No. I was too much of a coward to resign, so I anxiously waited for whatever fate was to befall me. I was convinced my career — and maybe my life — was over. So I simply made my peace with it."

"And then Amanda disappeared?"

"Indeed."

"Did you speak with Meredith?"

"Yes. The next day. But she was different. More combative. Accusing me of doing something to Amanda because of what had happened. I tried to convince her that I was not involved in Amanda's disappearance in any way whatsoever, but she wouldn't believe me. She kept talking about the loss of her husband and how I took advantage of her while she was struggling with her grief."

"From the divorce?" Walker clarified.

Ellis twitched at the question.

"Divorce? Meredith's not divorced, Mr. Walker. Her husband is dead."

CHAPTER 47

"Dead?" Walker audibly gasped.

"Yes, heart attack. Quite sudden. Far too young."

Walker lost his balance. Meredith's story about the divorce had been a lie. *Why? What else about her background was also untrue?* "Do you know where she is?" Walker asked.

Ellis looked surprised. "Why? Is she missing?"

"For several hours now, yes. Do you have any idea where she might be?"

"I have no idea, Mr. Walker, but how is it that you know her so well?"

"It's a long story, but more importantly, how is it that the two women who can threaten your career have disappeared?" Walker asked sternly.

"Pardon me?"

"You heard me. Why is it that Amanda and Meredith are both missing, and they're the only two people who can attest to what happened in this office? Have you done something with Meredith to keep her quiet, too?"

Ellis was flabbergasted. "God no! I have no idea where she might be. I had no idea she was missing."

"You've told me a lot of lies, Dr. Ellis, why should I believe you now?" Walker said with a fury in his voice.

"Mr. Walker, please look at this from my perspective. I know I made a horrible mistake, and I regret it terribly. I truly do. And I know now that I must admit to that mistake and take responsibility for my actions, along with all the shame that I will bring to this school and my family. But do you really believe I would abduct two women to cover up for my indiscretions?"

"Dr. Ellis, with all due respect, from my perspective, the two people with the power to ruin your career are now missing."

Ellis chuckled grimly. "My career is already ruined, and nothing can change that at this point. But I do see how this probably looks to you. Do you really think I'd be telling you all of this if I took either of those women? That I would be incriminating myself like this?"

Walker exhaled and stared at Ellis. "*Why* are you telling me all of this?"

"Because I want to help you understand what happened here. Provide you with some much-needed context. I think it's about time, yes?"

"Why did you wait so long? I could have used this information two days ago."

"Forgive me, Mr. Walker. I was simply still trying to protect my reputation, solidify my legacy as dean of this prestigious school. At the time, I thought that was still possible, that Amanda would simply turn up and everything would go back to normal. But as we now know, that happy ending just wasn't meant to be. I think I probably knew it the moment you walked through that door, but I couldn't quite admit it to myself. I actually thought there was still hope for a positive outcome. But now my career has ended. My marriage could very well be over. And the reputation of this school will be tarnished for years to come. But I still want you to find Amanda. I still want you to solve this case. Amanda Bryson does not deserve for anything to happen to her because of my transgressions with her teacher."

"Are you suggesting Meredith is somehow involved in Amanda's disappearance because of what happened the other day — her negative demeanor toward you?"

Ellis shook his head. "I regret to say it, but I do. There was just something about her that wasn't right. Something that frightened me."

Walker tried to absorb everything he had just heard. The incongruities were astounding to him. Meredith had been his closest ally the entire time he had been here. She had genuinely shown warmth and compassion for him, especially after the fire. Her conversations led him to uncover clues that otherwise would have stayed hidden. Yet she had lied about her husband, lied about her background, and who knows what else. And now the dean of the school was talking about her abnormal behavior and accusing her of being involved in Amanda's disappearance. If Walker's grip on reality hadn't been completely loosened, it was hanging on by a very thin thread.

Trying to seek other possibilities and knowing full well that hidden cameras were probably lurking in this office as well, Walker asked, "Do you think anyone else could have seen what happened between you and Meredith?"

"I don't think so. No. Who else could have seen?"

"Could they have told anyone? No one is trying to blackmail you or force your hand with the knowledge of what happened?"

"Of course not."

He obviously wasn't taking the bait, so Walker decided to go direct. "Does Castillo know?"

Ellis thought for a moment. "Unless either Amanda or Meredith spoke to him about it, I would not believe that he knows. I've never told him."

You wouldn't have to, Walker mused to himself. "And he's never mentioned it to you?"

"Absolutely not."

"And you never mentioned Meredith's erratic behavior to him?"

"No. I actually dismissed it at first. Just thought I was overreacting, but as the days wore on, I reflected upon it and realized it was probably more serious than I originally thought, which is why I'm telling you now."

"But if you knew all of this from the beginning, why did

you bring me here? Why go through all the trouble of this charade of an outside investigation?" Walker begged.

Ellis lowered his eyes. "Guilt, Mr. Walker. Plain and simple. I thought that if I allowed you to investigate, even if you didn't find anything, that my conscience would be cleared."

"And now?"

"And now, I understand that we all pay for our mistakes. One way or another, and as much as we attempt to avoid the inevitable, we all pay." His voice trailed off.

Walker got up from his chair and stared at Ellis who was now deep in thought. "I need to find Meredith," he said vehemently. "I'm going to need an escort downstairs, so the techs there can help me pinpoint her location on campus."

"Certainly," Ellis agreed, jolted from his stupor, leaning forward to pick up the telephone on his desk.

As Ellis put the receiver to his ear and pushed the button to dial the security center, Walker said, "I just need to ask you one final question."

Ellis looked up at him and nodded.

"If you wanted me to be here, why did you let Castillo hinder my investigation?"

Ellis pulled the phone away from his mouth. "Hinder your investigation? Why would he do that? Joaquin was the one who convinced me to bring you on board."

"Excuse me?"

"Indeed. When Lorenzo asked me to permit you on the campus to investigate, even though I was guilt-ridden, I was still very hesitant, but Castillo told me he knew of you, respected your skills, and believed you could help us. Tragically, it seems his confidence in you has led to my downfall, but at least we may still find Amanda."

Walker stepped closer. "Wait. Castillo wanted me here?"

"Yes, very much so."

Walker mentally searched his mind, trying to determine a plausible explanation for what he was hearing. "Do you know anything about a relationship between Meredith and Joaquin, either in the past or recently?" he finally asked.

"No, I don't believe so," Ellis answered.

"An affair perhaps?"

"I really don't know. I'm sorry. I'm not aware of any relationship."

"Forget the security center. I need to speak with Joaquin. There's something he's not telling me. He's at the tunnel exit at the southern end of campus, so I'm going there now."

Ellis hung up the phone. "Please be careful, Mr. Walker. There have been so many surprises during the last few hours, I simply don't know what to expect anymore." Walker turned to leave as Ellis finished his thought. "I still can't believe they found that tunnel where they did. The boys' dorm? That's baffling."

Walker abruptly turned. "Why is that, sir?"

Ellis leaned back in his chair again. "Because that original section of the male dormitory wasn't actually one of the first buildings on campus."

"It wasn't?"

"No. The earliest drawings of the campus were lost during the Civil War, so the ones we have in the library were actually created years later, as the campus really started to expand in the late 1800s. So if there were tunnels, I'd expect them to have been constructed under those original buildings."

Walker advanced back toward Ellis. "What were the original buildings?"

"There were two. A dormitory and a lecture hall. The school's first lecture hall was this building we're in now and the original dormitory, which predated the school's late-nineteenth-century expansion, was completely refurbished in the 1920s and again during the 1980s to serve a new purpose for the campus."

"Which was?"

"Our faculty residences."

CHAPTER 48

After exiting from the admin building and stopping briefly at his car to remove the Glock and a small flashlight from the glovebox, Walker sprinted across campus to the neat row of faculty residences he had called home for the last three days. He leaped up the set of steps to the front door of Meredith's unit but didn't bother to knock. Removing his handgun from the back of his pants and pointing it downward, Walker kicked just below the door's handle. The wooden frame cracked and splintered as the old door swung open, revealing a largely empty living space that was dark and quiet. He stepped patiently across the threshold, his handgun drawn, the flashlight held just below it, scanning the room for any movement or activity. There was none.

Walker slowly entered the main living area, which was similar to his own residence next door, but this one didn't appear to have anyone actually living in it. He didn't bother to move toward the light switch, but even in the semi-darkness, with his narrow beam of light tracking across the space, he could see that the room was spotless. Nothing was out of place.

The furniture and wall hangings were neatly arranged as the books and folders on the desks and lamp tables were perfectly stacked and tidy. Walker immediately recognized a distinct pattern of organization and symmetry as he moved into the kitchen. Again, everything was neat and clean — no dishes or silverware were present on the main counter or kitchen table in the corner. The refrigerator was free of magnets or papers, and all the appliances were properly spaced apart and reflected a metallic shine when hit by the illumination from the flashlight, as though they had just been cleaned.

If Meredith actually lived here, he couldn't quite believe she had grown tired of Castillo's OCD. These two rooms were all the evidence Walker needed to deduce that whoever lived here suffered from an acute obsessive-compulsive disorder. So he wondered if that had been a lie as well. *Had she actually ever been with Castillo? Or did she even live here?* Walker had never seen her place before, just taken her word that she lived next door to him, but right now, he didn't trust anything that had come out of her mouth.

Meredith had certainly played him, withheld her many secrets, and lied to him about nearly everything, but the strange appearance of her residence was unnerving on an entirely new level. Walker couldn't figure out exactly who was he dealing with here and that was frightening. He couldn't imagine where this ended, felt as though he was closer than ever to the truth but unsure of what that truth was going to be.

Crossing the linoleum floor, Walker noticed a metal door at the far end of the kitchen. Walker approached the door and raised his gun as he carefully turned the knob. Opening the door with his left hand and pointing his gun and flashlight into the dark space with his right, Walker stared down a steep staircase leading into a basement level. He maneuvered his way down the stairs, peering through the sites of his gun, with the flashlight irradiating the way. Each worn, wooden step creaked as he climbed his way into the underground chamber. The walls were damp, and it smelled of mildew and rot.

Finally stepping onto the cement floor of the basement, Walker could feel that it was uneven and cracked, deteriorated from its centuries of use. Through the darkness with only the dim stream of light from his handheld flashlight, he approached the far wall of the basement. A large armoire hugged the stone wall, but was slightly askew, revealing the partial entrance to another tunnel, similar to what they had discovered in the inner chamber of the boys' dorm.

He paused, mesmerized by the threshold to the tunnel. He could picture Mosby's rangers, lugging supplies and weapons through this underground labyrinth, plotting against the Union soldiers above. So much had happened down here, so much secret history had passed through these subterranean passageways. And even now, these tunnels were still protecting secrets.

In his soul, he could feel this journey was nearly at an end. The answers he sought were about to be revealed. He did not know what he was going to find, but he hoped it would be the truth, regardless of what it would cost him. He slid his body past the thick armoire and moved cautiously into the tunnel. But unlike the other, there were no lights dangling from wires. It was complete darkness. Walker held his flashlight tightly alongside his gun, projecting a thin layer of light forward through the sepulchral darkness.

He had only walked a few yards before he saw an opening up ahead and a soft glow emanating from what appeared to be a larger chamber. He stepped toward the growing light and the tunnel opened into a large room, built into the shape of a dome, with high ceilings and makeshift wooden counters encircling the interior walls. It appeared like some sort of ancient workshop with various archaic instruments as well as metal and wooden tools littering the counters. A web of cords crisscrossed the dirt floor, carrying electricity to a number of small lamps, attached by silver sconces to the walls just above the cluttered shelves, casting a dull light on the bizarre collection of spare parts from the last century.

As he entered the chamber, Walker was momentarily stunned by the surreal sight of the underground workshop. He peered around the entire room, moving his firearm in complete synchronization with his eyes as he scanned the strange lair. He finally settled on a lone figure who was facing away from him and working diligently at a space on the counter near the far left side of the room. His gun's sites lined up on the back of the darkened figure, and he immediately recognized the body structure and the unique stance of the person he had spent so much time with during his time here. On the shelf next to the figure were a cell phone and laptop.

Not uttering a word, the shadowy figure cocked his head slightly, hearing the visitor enter the quiet cavernous space and knowing this stranger to his workshop was staring at him. Walker immediately tightened the grip on his weapon, removed its safety, and pulled back the cocking mechanism with his thumb. The cocking of the handgun echoed loudly in the hollow chamber. A slight smile creased the stranger's face, and the figure — hands raised — slowly turned to confront Walker.

The low light from the nearest lamp cast a pale shadow on the figure's face, and Walker instantly recognized the person before him. Standing there motionless, his hands held up at his sides and a smirk on his face was Joaquin Castillo.

CHAPTER 49

Walker kept his weapon trained on Castillo, positive that if he made even the slightest of movements, the former FBI agent wouldn't hesitate to fire until the clip was empty. He stepped closer, only looking at Castillo through the thin triangle of his gun's sites. Walker wanted nothing more than to pull the trigger, but he knew if he did, the answers he so desperately sought would remain elusive. So for now, Castillo was safe, but in Walker's mind, the situation was remarkably fluid.

The smirk remained on Castillo's face as he glanced at his hands raised to about eye level at his sides. He finally bobbed his head in satisfaction and chuckled. "Well, I'm must say, Mr. Walker, I drastically underestimated you."

Walker did not respond and took another step closer, his weapon still aimed at Castillo's chest.

"I didn't think you would figure it out. I mean, I gave you enough clues, but I didn't think you had it in you anymore. I know you've probably wrestled with a lot of demons this week, so I figured that would ultimately cloud your judgment and prevent you from discovering the truth. But then again, here we are. I must say, I'm impressed."

Walker lifted the Glock a little higher, moving the barrel toward Castillo's head, "Where is Amanda?"

Castillo chuckled again. "That's odd. I thought you would ask about Meredith first."

"Where is she?" Walker demanded.

"Which *one* exactly?" Castillo motioned with the fingers

on his hands, darting his eyes back and forth between both hands.

"Don't fuck with me, Castillo!" Walker shouted, then calmed into a reassuring voice. "The games are over. The lies are done. What have you done with Amanda? And Meredith?"

"Ah yes, Meredith. Dear sweet Meredith. You took quite a fancy to her, didn't you? She really pulls you in with that innocent, yet sexy seduction of hers, doesn't she? Believe me, she's not that innocent."

Walker ignored the taunting. "What have you done with them?"

"It's not what I've done with them. It's what I'm going to do with them," Castillo said with an immense degree of satisfaction.

"They're still alive?" Walker asked, surprised. He honestly expected them to be dead.

"Oh, yes, very much alive, but not for much longer."

"Where are they?" Walker repeated.

Castillo turned slightly and pointed to another tunnel entrance near the rear of the chamber. The faded light made it hard to distinguish the dark entrance against the facade of dirt and rock, but Walker peered at the rear wall and was able to barely see another passage leading out of this room. "After you, Mr. Walker. If you want to find Meredith and Amanda, this is the only way."

Walker motioned his gun toward the tunnel entrance. "No. You lead the way."

Castillo shook his head and laughed. "I don't think you're in any position to be giving orders. Are you really going to shoot me? Do that and you risk never finding them. Knowing you were so close, but yet so far away from solving this intriguing mystery. I don't think so."

Walker swung the gun back on Castillo. "I made it this far. I don't need you to finish this."

"Really? You made it this far. All on your own, huh?" Castillo said, grinning. "You are only here because I wanted you to be here. I led you here, Walker. I brought you down here because I wanted to give you a chance to go down the rabbit hole and find out the truth, pull back the curtain on this entire charade, and give you the opportunity to know what happened before you died."

"You're in no position to be threatening me. I could kill you right now and be perfectly within my rights to do so, even if I cared about the consequences, which I'm not sure I do anymore."

"Would you still kill me if I told you that Josh Easterly is innocent. Oh, I don't mean he's completely innocent. He's still a troubled kid with a leadership role in a weird society, but it's far from secret and light-years from dangerous. But a killer? No. Josh is not a killer nor is he an abductor. He had absolutely nothing to do with Amanda's disappearance.

Walker was curious. "You framed him?"

"Did I mention stupid? It was almost too easy. His insane jealousy and his constant fights with Amanda made him a perfect suspect. And the secret society — God help me — that was a stroke of sheer luck. We've known about it for years, mapped all the tunnels and secured all the escape routes. And then just monitored the activity, ensuring it was never a threat. That's where the hidden cameras come in handy. You know about those, right?"

Walker winced. Castillo obviously knew he had seen the hidden camera footage, probably knew that Meredith had given him the key, a gesture that may have cost her life. "But the footage, it showed Josh with Amanda..."

Castillo sneered. "One more piece of the mindfuck, my friend. I needed you to think Josh was involved, so when we started to chase Mosby's ghosts, you would play along. You really didn't think that footage was real, did you? You think I would allow you access to one of the most sensitive areas on this entire campus? Sounds like you drastically underestimated me, Mr. Walker."

Walker grimaced, realizing he had been played.

"We pretended over the years to go after the *Sons of Liberty* to push it further underground, but that was just a ploy to see what they would do. We've always allowed it to thrive, instill a sense of fear in the students, knowing someday we could use it to our advantage. And here we are," Castillo said smugly.

"What about the ritual? The backpack?"

"Those kids might be dressing in cloaks and chanting in the dark, but they're still kids. They conduct those rituals like clockwork, so I knew exactly when it was going to happen. I was surprised you had made it to the library that night; I guess I really pissed you off. But remember, I found you. I was coming after you anyway to lead you to the boys' dorm; I just had to make a quick detour to the library. Did you really think we were partners?"

Walker looked down the barrel. "Go on."

"All I had to do was convince Josh that Heather was ratting him out, and he decided to scare her. And the backpack, well, I planted that little beauty that morning. At first, I thought it might be a little over the top, but after that perfectly timed ritual and your priceless scuffle with the boys, it was just one more piece of evidence in the circumstantial case against Josh Easterly and his *Sons of Liberty*. Prosecutors probably won't even need a body at this point. They could easily charge him with third-degree murder or manslaughter based on the overwhelming evidence against him. As I said, it was almost too easy."

"My God, you're sick."

"I'm not the sick one, my friend. Did our esteemed Dr. Ellis tell you what he did to Meredith?"

"Why are you protecting him?"

Castillo huffed. "You still don't get it. I'm not protecting him. I can destroy him. I'm just waiting for the right moment. The good Dr. Ellis knows deep down who controls this campus. He knows who has the real power here. Once he decided to join forces with a den of thieves and bring me on board as the intermediary, his days were numbered. A respected professor like

Ellis would never survive in the company of crime lords. It was only a matter of time. Amanda simply sped up the process for him."

"What are you saying?"

"I'm saying if Amanda wouldn't have disappeared and caused this entire affair to spiral out of control, Ellis would have been done anyway. Remember, I have hidden cameras everywhere. I know all of his secrets. Talk about sick. Ellis is a disease all by himself."

"You have footage of him?"

"Indeed. And all I have to do is release it."

"But now you won't have to."

"Exactly. So I'm just going to save it for a rainy day. My 'get out jail free' card, so to speak. Just in case he tries to take me down with him. But that's not going to happen."

"You had it all figured out, huh? From the beginning."

Castillo laughed. "Ah, yes, but you were the X factor. I did know your best days were behind you, so I knew you could be easily manipulated. Did you really think finding Amanda was going to erase your past, put an end to those violent nightmares I saw you struggle through on the camera, put you back in the good graces of the FBI? You're damaged goods, Walker, and nothing was going to change that."

Starting to feel weak, Walker could sense his grip on the handgun loosening. His grasp of reality, or what he thought was his reality, was slowly slipping away. It was all a facade, a massive charade with him at the center. He had been played from the moment he had stepped onto this campus. His life had never been his own, and he had almost lost it in the process. "I suppose you set the fire at the storage shed as well?"

Castillo nodded. "We needed to get rid of some old files anyway, so if it killed you in the process, that was just a bonus. No hard feelings for that one, right? At least you survived."

Walker began to lower his Glock, realizing his desperate quest for redemption was now at an end. He had not discovered the truth; he had only uncovered the lies which had led him to this place. There was no escape from the nightmare. What he thought was a way out was merely a mirage in the deserted wasteland his life had become. A life he was now convinced was over.

As the lowered gun reached his waistline, Castillo sprung into action, tackling Walker with the weight and muscle of a trained fighter. Walker was crushed into the hard dirt, his gun released from his hand. Taken by surprise and still recovering from his inner thoughts, Walker was delayed in defending himself against Castillo's fists, several blows landing hard on Walker's head and face before he succeeded in knocking the larger opponent off of him.

Walker rolled onto his stomach as Castillo fell into one of the wooden legs holding up the old counter which circled the room. Through blurred vision — caused by the punch to his left eye — he searched the dirt floor for his gun. Only off balance for a moment, Castillo quickly rose, scanned the materials on the historic workbench, and grabbed a blacksmith's hammer from the shelf. Larger than a traditional hammer with a head made of thick iron for forging steel, the blacksmith's hammer made for a deadly weapon.

He turned and descended on Walker, who was crawling away from him, by bringing the hammer down with ruthless force upon his body. The thick hammer slammed into Walker's shoulder blade, the pain pounding through his muscle and reverberating through his bone. His left arm immediately went limp and the hammer struck him again in the center of the back. Walker felt the sharp blow recoil through to his chest along with a discordant cracking of bones. He instantly stopped moving, fiercely gasping for air to refill his bruised lungs, instinctively coughing and wheezing loudly as he tried to inhale.

Castillo stood over his opponent, looking down at Walker's battered body, blood seeping through his shirt, black bruises forming underneath the clothing, where the hammer had done its cruel work. He held the weapon high, enjoying one more moment of satisfaction at finally eliminating his nemesis, before going in for the death knell. Castillo set his sights on the back of Walker's head. One more swing of the hammer and it would be over.

The blacksmith's hammer plunged downward with all the force Castillo could muster, but before it reached its target, Walker turned over, gun in hand, barrel pointed at Castillo's chest. The .40 caliber bullet fired from the Glock hit Castillo squarely in the chest, and his body jerked back as the crude hammer fell from his hand and bounced along the ground. Castillo stumbled forward to catch his balance and looked down at the single spot of red in the center of his shirt, which rapidly expanded into a widening circle of blood that seeped through the cloth. He stared at the red hole in his chest, unsure of what to make of it, seemingly trying to process that he had just been shot. His face distorted by anger, Castillo lifted his head and glared at Walker with more rage than the veteran FBI agent had ever seen. And charged.

Walker fired two more shots in quick succession, each hitting Castillo in roughly the same spot as before, this time the force of the impact pushing Castillo backward as his feet left the ground. The first bullet punctured his left lung. The collapsed organ immediately began filling with fluid and would cause Castillo to drown in his own blood within minutes.

The second bullet hit one of Castillo's ribs, shattering it, and sending fragments of bone into two of the four chambers of his heart. The bone fragments severed the soft tissue protecting this vital organ and easily spliced the arteries and vessels in their way. His heart instantly collapsed, and Castillo was dead before his body hit the ground.

CHAPTER 50

Walker held his weapon in the same position for several moments after Castillo crashed to the floor. Castillo hadn't moved since landing on the dirt ground, so Walker assumed he was dead. His three shots had impacted Castillo center mass — what they had been trained — because the vital organs housed there were the most susceptible to injury and eventually death. A headshot would have done the job as well, but Walker was in no condition for that. He had barely been able to reach for his gun and fire, let alone aim for his head while Castillo brought the ancient hammer down on him again.

Convinced Castillo was no longer in this fight and would not be getting up again, Walker fell back to the earth with a grunt. He stretched his arms out next to him and took several long cleansing breaths. He could feel the pain of every inhale and exhale through his chest and back, and he was sure his shoulder blade was broken. Because the pain was so intense, he could barely move his left arm.

After several minutes of lying motionless on the hard ground, Walker eventually, with another labored grunt, brought himself to a sitting position. He craned his neck as much as possible until the pain prevented further movement, and tried to massage his left shoulder blade with his right hand, but it was painful to the touch. He finally exhaled once more and got to his feet, stumbling at first because of the need to compensate for his immobile left arm.

The severely injured detective used the counter to brace

himself, pushing whatever supplies had been sitting with his gun, and they crashed to the floor. Finally stabilized, Walker looked down at Castillo — his eyes wide open — as if still in shock that he had actually lost the fight. The former agent knew he had barely won the melee and was lucky to be alive. If his gun had been just two more inches away, he would be the one lying dead on this dirt floor.

However, this was not the way it was supposed to end. Although Castillo had certainly deserved to die, Walker still had more questions for him. Needed more answers. But it was too late for that now. Walker wondered how Castillo had orchestrated this entire episode. *And why? To what end?* And how had Walker been so blind not to see it?

Did he really think that solving this mystery would have saved his reputation, restored his status with the FBI, or repaired the damage he had caused to his family? Was he really that short-sighted? It suddenly materialized in Walker's mind that he had been so focused on seeking atonement for his past that he lost sight of the truth right in front of him.

All of a sudden, Walker's hand gave way from the counter and he almost fell, jolting him back to reality and making him realize this wasn't the time for self-reflection. There were still two women missing, and although the likely culprit was now dead, it was still possible for Walker to find them. He turned toward the tunnel entrance at the rear of the chamber and exhaled as he pushed away from the counter and shuffled gradually across the room, his gun at his side.

Walker had no idea what to expect on the other end of this tunnel. Nothing had met his expectations thus far, so he was sure there would be more surprises ahead. For a man who had often contemplated death, he hoped at this moment at least, he would live through it.

CHAPTER 51

The final tunnel sloped downward, and Walker lost his footing multiple times as he navigated the rocky ground. Because it was further buried in the earth, this passage also seemed darker than the others, and there were no lights this time, no openings ahead. He continued to use his only source of light — the scuffed flashlight which was now beginning to wane — as a meager signpost to lead the way. His cell had also been cracked during the life-and-death struggle with Castillo, so a phone call was out of the question, but Walker doubted he could actually get a signal this far below ground anyway. At this moment, he was most assuredly on his own.

Walker heard the faint sound of running water about the time he estimated he had traveled about a hundred yards. He slowed his pace as he reached the exit of the tunnel, opening up into an underground cavern. This dungeon-like complex was the largest of the structures he'd seen, but it was mostly rock covering the floor and the walls, so it was also probably the deepest. In the center of the cavern was a circular hole, man-made, surrounded by uneven, yet expertly-cut masonry stones. The sound of the water grew louder and Walker realized it was coming from this pit. A well.

Listening closely to the sound of the running water, Walker could feel the dampness in the air on his skin. He quickly deduced that an aquifer ran through this subterranean structure, providing the remote underground location with a constant supply of freshwater. What began as a natural cavern had probably been further carved out by Mosby's rangers as it would have made for a perfect hideout — or staging area — and could have been occupied for longer periods of time.

Impressed by the feat of human engineering, Walker was startled as his flashlight caught a flesh tone in the far corner of the cavern. He immediately centered his gun and light toward the human color, which was followed by a murmured groan. He strained to see in the corner of the chamber, but no shape was immediately visible. Walker stepped slowly in that direction, still unsure of his footing on the uneven ground.

As he edged closer to the outer wall, a dark figure came into view. Sitting in a chair. Head lowered. Long hair. Hands tied behind her back. Although much more dirty and disheveled, he instantly recognized her from the picture he had been looking at for three days. It was Amanda Bryson.

Walker rushed to her, partially stumbling, partially kneeling in front of her. He dropped his gun and flashlight on the hard ground and reached his working hand up to her neck. Her skin was warm and he could feel a pulse. She was alive. He pushed the hair out of her face and lifted her head, shaking it slightly to wake her. She appeared to be heavily sedated, so her eyes stayed closed, even with the jostling. He instinctively ran his hand over the rest of her body, looking for any blatant injuries, any signs of trauma. There were none. At least on the outside. The emotional trauma on the inside would take years to heal.

Still kneeling, he moved around the back of the chair and fumbled to find her hands. They were tied together with a worn and fraying piece of twine. He gripped the thin rope and reflexively pulled on it as if he thought it would break at the first tug. The twine was weak but had been wrapped around Amanda's hands several times and secured with multiple knots. Walker didn't have anything sharp enough to cut through the threads, but he thought back to Castillo's workshop and surmised he could retrieve something from there to cut through the bonds.

He put his hand on her arm and patted it gently, knowing

she couldn't feel it, but it was more for him than her anyway, relieved that Amanda was still alive. After all that Walker had been through to find her, he certainly didn't want to leave her now, but if he was going to mount any kind of rescue and get her out of here, he needed to get back to the workshop without hesitation. He slid himself back to the front of the chair, adrenaline pumping through his body, assisting him to move his torn muscles and broken bones. He reached for his gun and flashlight. But they were gone.

Walker was confused. He thought he had put them right here. It was too dark to see clearly, so he moved his hand in concentric circles over the damp rock, searching desperately for his lost items. His hand finally touched an object. But it wasn't a gun or a flashlight; it was a boot. And it belonged to someone standing over him.

As Walker looked up, a wooden bat swung from out of the darkness and struck him on the left side of his head, the blow pounding his skull and blurring his vision as he landed hard on the damp stone floor, and everything faded to darkness.

CHAPTER 52

Walker awoke to a massive pounding behind his eyes. He squinted as the pain drifted upward to his forehead and temples and ensconced him in a mental fog. He was seated upright, but lurched over, his head laying on his chest. Blood seeped down from the large bruise just below his hairline into his left eye and dried there, so his one eyelid was crusty and difficult to open. He was unsure how long he had been unconscious.

As he gradually regained consciousness, Walker attempted to move his arms but realized they were pulled tightly behind him, feeling the scratchy twine on his bound hands. Looking downward with his one good eye, he realized he was seated in an old wooden chair — like one you'd find in a classroom — with another length of rope wrapped around him several times, securing him to it. He wiggled his hands, tied behind his back, but it only made the thin cords of twine cut more deeply into his skin. He was now exactly in the same position as he had found Amanda — another captive in this deep hole in the ground.

A figure approached him, carrying a dingy yellow bucket by the handle, water sloshing around inside. As the stranger neared, the bucket was upended and a gush of freezing water slammed into Walker's head and torso. He shuddered as the water whipped against his skin and irritated his open wounds, further ripping him from his grogginess. He shook the water from his face and tried to regain his bearings, focusing on the person standing before him. At that moment Walker's faith in everything that was real drained from him like the excess water dripping from his body onto the stone floor below.

Meredith Thomas tossed the plastic bucket to the side, and it clattered against the nearby wall. She slid another wooden chair along the hard floor and stopped directly in front of Walker. She sat and looked at him, a long hunting knife — similar to the one he had seen in the woods the night before — gripped in her right hand. She cocked her head as if surveying the damage she had done to his skull while also reveling in the satisfaction of the ropes she had tied and smiled. "Surprised?"

Walker stared at Meredith through his opened right eye and partially opened left, but was unable to speak because he couldn't quite believe what his damaged vision was supposedly showing him.

"Did I surprise you, Ryan? Especially after that time we shared together. You should never be too careful about who you meet these days." She grinned, waving the knife at him as if accentuating each word with a swing of the knife.

Walker blinked his eyes, trying to knock the pain from behind his sockets and focus on Meredith.

She spoke softly, almost in a whisper. "I really wish you hadn't killed Joaquin. He was so instrumental in this whole affair. But I guess he was just trying to protect me. I do think he loved me. I heard him telling you the story, all the things he did for me, but he would have done anything for me. That's love, don't you think?" Meredith reached out and gingerly touched the bruise on his forehead. "He was even willing to kill for me. I heard the two of you fighting. It was so violent. I really thought he was going to kill you, but you survived. Well done. Now I can kill you myself," Meredith said, as she moved her hand down to his cheek, swung back, and slapped it loudly.

Walker's head swung to the right, and he let out a long sigh as the sudden movement reverberated through his body and thrashed at his previous wounds. He slowly brought his head back to its original position, blinking several times to try and recover from the stinging whiplash.

"Ah yes, my dear Ryan" Meredith said loudly as she rose from the chair and bent over, pushing the blade to within inches of Walker's face, putting her own face directly behind the handle, "this was all a setup. This entire episode was a massive stage play and you, my private investigator, were one of the actors."

Meredith stood up, glancing at the walls around her, deep in thought. "I've always loved plays, you know? Ever since I was a little girl and my father would take me to performances at the local theatre. In high school, I fell in love with Shakespeare, and could simply not get enough of those beautiful words, those enchanting stories. I think he's what actually started my love of literature and my passion for the English language, a playwright who could put words to paper so powerfully...it literally took my breath away." Looking back at Walker, Meredith said, "And so you should be very proud, Ryan. You've been cast into this play, unwillingly of course, but thrilling nonetheless."

Meredith sat back in the chair and positioned her face close to Walker's, whispering again. "You have played a very important role for us. A role that no one else could have played. We needed someone who was damaged, struggling to cope with a mistake that was unforgivable. A mistake that had cost a life...a child's life...and ruined him in so many ways."

Walker knew this story all too well, but hearing it again in the cold dampness of a dark cavern gave it enormous weight and his shoulders slowly buckled under the pressure. He slumped down as he again relived the nightmare which had haunted him for years.

"We knew you had always wanted a chance to make amends for that poor little girl and her grieving mother. And so we would give you that chance. A chance to save another little girl and finally move on from that tragic mistake." Meredith paused for a moment, then asked, "Did you think finding Amanda would stop the nightmares? I watched you in your apartment, tossing in your sleep, restless, unable to find peace. I was sad for you. I still am. But I needed you. I needed you for a very specific role. And now that you've fulfilled that role, I'm going to help you find that peace you so desperately sought."

Walker lowered his head as an awkward sense of relief swept over him. Although he guessed that Meredith was about to kill him, he didn't fear it. Everything she said had been correct. He had been struggling, was not who he used to be, and could not find peace with his place in the world. He did believe that rescuing Amanda may have given him some relief from the pain, but now he knew it wasn't real, so in the end, he was right back where he started. He deserved the end that was coming. But before he died, he had one final question, the same question he had posed to Ellis. "Why did you bring me here?"

Meredith leaned back in the chair and smirked, moving the blade lightly along her lips, as if trying to decide if Walker deserved the truth before she killed him. After a few pensive moments, she made her choice. "We needed you to ruin that son of a bitch Ellis. A disappearance alone was not going to do it. He could hide it too well, especially working for a devil like Arcuri, so we needed something more. We needed a high-profile investigation, headline-grabbing stories of strange rituals and buried backpacks, and a man that would have to admit to his transgressions and be ruined by his own hubris. The only way that was going to happen was if you were involved, and Joaquin and I could control how it all played out. You would think you were solving the case, but we were merely pulling the strings."

Walker exhaled. "Why Ellis?"

Meredith laughed loudly. "That was just *your* part. The entire play was much bigger than that. This isn't just about Ellis. It's about three evil men who needed to pay for their crimes. Forget redemption. How about punishment?"

Shaking his head in disbelief, Walker hopelessly tried to make sense of what Meredith was saying until it suddenly dawned on him in the darkness of the cavern.

"That's right," Meredith said, noticing that Walker was beginning to put the pieces together. "The dean of our esteemed academy, Dr. Robert Ellis, was laundering money for a wicked crime lord, Mr. Lorenzo Arcuri, who hired a private investigator, Mr. Ryan Walker, to hunt down an accountant who was embezzling money from both of them."

"Edward Collins?" Walker whispered, the missing link finally falling into place.

Meredith smiled proudly at the realization. "Yes. He was my husband."

CHAPTER 53

Stunned by Meredith's revelation, Walker didn't say a word, simply stared at her face, seeing the various emotions flicker through her expressions — anguish, loss, and resolve.

"I had never changed my last name after we were married. I had already started a career with my maiden name, so I decided to keep it. After Edward went to work for Arcuri, we simply decided to keep using my last name as a security measure, allowing me to more easily disappear if something ever happened, which unfortunately, it did," Meredith said, her voice trailing off. She breathed heavily.

"I was the one who actually introduced Dr. Ellis to my husband shortly after he lost his job. I had been working at the school for many years at that point, and I think Ellis was slightly infatuated with me. He knew we were struggling, and so as a way to show how much he cared for me, he approached Edward with a job offer. At first, we were grateful, didn't quite realize at the time that Ellis was in bed with a mafia lord, but eventually, it became clear that my husband was now working for the Arcuri crime family. And by that time, it was too late."

Walker feigned empathy. "I'm sorry."

"Don't be," Meredith snapped, "because that wasn't the worst part. Once Edward was in too deep, Ellis approached me again and confirmed that my husband was indeed laundering money for the Arcuri empire. However, he told me that in order for Edward to stay in Arcuri's good graces, Ellis now needed something in return. That's right. Dr. Ellis, revered Dean of

Washington Academy, forced me to have sex with him. Or perform sexual favors for him whenever he demanded. If I refused, he said he simply would tell Lorenzo that Edward was cheating him, and my husband would be killed."

"My God."

"I never told Edward what was happening. It was just too painful. But eventually, I convinced him to get out from under them, and we hatched an escape plan. Edward was a great accountant, so over several months, he skimmed off money for himself—for us—that we were going to use to relocate and disappear. But we didn't leave fast enough. Arcuri realized he was embezzling the money and sent you after him."

Walker closed his eyes and shook his head, a tight knot forming in his stomach over his involvement with this tragic story.

"They left me alone obviously. Probably because Ellis had asked them to, so he could keep me as his sexual slave a while longer. He called me into his office, expressed his deepest sympathies for what had happened to Edward. But then told me that he and I were going to continue with our *relationship* unless I wanted him to tell Arcuri that I had been working with Edward to steal the money, too. I went berserk on that son of a bitch, blamed him for everything, and told him that I was no longer going to be his toy whenever he wanted. Ellis became extremely irate and attacked me, just as his student assistant, Amanda Bryson, walked in on us.

"Ellis told me a different story."

"Of course he did," Meredith replied, "he's made a career out of telling lies. But now he was caught. Amanda had witnessed him attacking me, so he had no choice. He had to transfer her and leave me alone, at least for the time being. However, I wasn't going to give that bastard another chance to strip away any more of what was left of me, so I came up with my own plan for revenge. For all three of you."

"How?" Walker asked with a morbid curiosity.

Meredith grinned. "Joaquin and I did have an affair years

ago when Edward and I were having some marital issues after he was fired from his firm. It was short-lived, a respite from my life perhaps, but Castillo had always maintained a special affection for me. I knew he was the one person on this campus with the power to help me execute my plan, so I rekindled a relationship with him to learn all I could about how things operated here. And as I'm sure you know, he's spent a lot of time in the underworld, so he knew all about Ellis, Arcuri, and a former FBI agent named Walker. There was certainly no love lost between him and Ellis, so he was more than willing to help me. Love is blind, right?"

Walker rocked his head back and forth as Meredith explained the elaborate scheme.

"A simple text to Amanda, telling her I had to speak with her about Ellis, was all that was needed for her to venture over to my residence, where Joaquin used chloroform to incapacitate her. He also ensured no surveillance techs were working in the security center at that exact time, so he could easily delete the footage of Amanda walking across the campus to my front door. When you control the eyes of the entire campus, you can close them whenever you want."

"What are you going to do with Amanda?" Walker asked.

Meredith glanced over at the unconscious girl tied to the chair, then spoke with an eerie precision. "She's so innocent, isn't she? I feel badly for her since none of this was her fault. She obviously doesn't deserve a brutal death like the one my husband received at the hands of Arcuri's henchman. I have a syringe for her. I'll administer the drug while she's passed out, so she won't feel a thing. Then I'll throw her body into that underground aquifer, and Arcuri will never know what happened to his daughter. Not knowing will be my ultimate revenge. A man as powerful as Arcuri will always be reminded that he was powerless to find his own daughter."

Walker sighed heavily.

"But you," Meredith said, pointing the blade at Walker again, "you will be awake for your death, so you can experience it slowly and painfully. You will feel every inch of this blade, and the pain I inflict upon you will linger until you die."

She suddenly plunged the knife into Walker's abdomen, and he grunted loudly. The pain was intense — a massive burning sensation — radiating into his chest and arms. His neck stiffened as he wrestled at his ropes, the futile attempts merely weakening him further as she pushed the knife deeper into his body.

Walker gasped and grunted, trying to shift his body away from the knife's blade, only resulting in Meredith pushing harder into his stomach, holding the handle of the knife firmly in her hand as he struggled. Although he had reached a peaceful resignation with death minutes earlier, the excruciating pain gave him second thoughts. Walker almost wanted to beg her to stop. But it was too late now.

The large blade was nearly gone, had torn through his skin and muscle and was ripping a gaping hole into his torso. Blood was forming around the entry wound, drenching his shirt in dark red and smearing the color along the silver blade, which continued its penetration inside of him. He suddenly felt cold, his arms and legs starting to shake, barely able to perceive that he was going into shock.

His vision starting to blur, Walker studied Meredith's face, a maniacal smile forming with her lips as she admired the deadly knife and seemed to take great pleasure in causing him pain. She finally glanced up, a stern expression on her face, as if to say that her fun was over and it was time to finish the job. As an experienced police officer, Walker knew what was next.

A single knife wound would not immediately kill him. It would take some time as he slowly bled out onto the stone floor and eventually slumped over from blood loss. He would probably lose consciousness before his heart actually stopped pumping blood, so Meredith appeared to want to end his life more quickly, while he was still cognizant of what was happening to him.

Now that the sharp knife had taken its initial toll, Meredith could end it all and watch closely as the life drained from Walker's eyes. To accomplish this, she would need to quicken the bloodletting, which meant either stabbing him several more times or twisting the knife to further open the wound and speed the rate of blood loss, bringing a rapid end to Walker's life.

Meredith had enjoyed herself enough. Watching him struggle, seeing the anguish crinkle his face, and feeling his body losing its will to live had given her the satisfaction she had been seeking for so long. She looked back at the knife and regripped her hand, preparing for the final blow: the twist of the knife.

There was nothing left to do. Walker accepted his fate and a rush of relief washed over him. He sagged into the chair and no longer struggled against the steel object tearing through his flesh. *It was over*. As a final thought, Walker wondered if anyone would ever follow this tunnel, find this chamber, and solve the mystery of what had happened to Amanda Bryson. He didn't know the answer to that, but *his* quest for those answers had come to a tragic end. Shakespeare would have been proud.

Meredith glared one last time directly at Walker as she gritted her teeth and twisted the knife. Walker could feel the life finally fading from him. Everything went blurry, then black, then was followed by a blinding white light.

CHAPTER 54

The blinding light was instantly followed by a deafening explosion, which rattled the subterranean chamber. The loud noise shattered Walker's eardrums and an incessant ringing immediately filled the void. Through the intermittent ringing, the sound of dozens of footsteps filled the cavernous space and echoed off the stone walls and floors.

Walker recognized the familiar sounds. The explosion was a flashbang, a device used to incapacitate a subject with a bright light and loud explosion, and the many footsteps belonged to men with aimed rifles and padded armor. A SWAT team had just breached the room.

Meredith was abruptly driven to the ground by the two lead officers and her hands were cuffed behind her back with zip ties. Two other agents grabbed Walker's chair, severed the twine which bound his hands behind it, and gently leaned it back onto the ground. Walker laid on his back, still tied to the chair, his legs dangling above him. The SWAT officers leaned in and took hold of the knife, still protruding from his stomach, as they applied a field dressing around the wound and administered multiple shots to stabilize him as he had already gone into shock.

Two more officers moved past Meredith — now face down on the ground — and approached Amanda, who was now bobbing her head slightly, jolted from her drug-induced state by the explosion from the flashbang. They quickly removed her restraints and laid her carefully on the floor to begin a cursory examination of her injuries, which consisted of minor lacerations and bruises, but nothing that appeared to be life-threatening. The remainder of the SWAT team fanned out across the chamber, rifles raised and flashlights beaming streams of light around the underground cavern.

Walker lay there — still unable to move — as the medicine started to take effect, and he was gently imbued with an extraordinary sense of euphoria. But it was more than the medication. He had been just been saved by his colleagues, rescued by the people he still called his friends. Although his descent had been complete, both literally and figuratively, he was being pulled back to life by the very people he so admired. And this, he told himself, would be the first step in the long road back.

Another officer knelt down next to Walker, but he wasn't dressed in a SWAT uniform. He wore only a blue flak vest with the yellow letters 'FBI' emblazoned on the front. The agent placed his hand tenderly on Walker's shoulder and smiled.

Walker could not help but return the smile before breaking into tears. It was his longtime friend and partner, Mark Lewis.

CHAPTER 55

The bright morning sun blinded Walker as he emerged from the faculty residence strapped to a gurney that was being loaded into a waiting ambulance. Two FBI agents led Meredith out shortly after, her arms still handcuffed behind her back. She was placed in the back seat of an unmarked sedan with government license plates, flanked on both sides by police cruisers. The collection of emergency vehicles, lights flashing, looked out of place on the serene school campus, but that was only half the story.

The other half of the story was buried several yards below the trimmed lawns and sculpted walkways of the prestigious campus. That half had survived for over two centuries and would remain so, but most people would never get to see it, and the legend of Mosby's tunnels would soon pass into history. After the investigative work was finished, the Board of Trustees made the decision to seal off all access to the underground labyrinth, lest it became a kind of tourist attraction and detract from the famed reputation and academic excellence of Washington Academy.

The fantastic story of the abducted girl and the secret society eventually faded from public attention as the academy went to great lengths to rewrite the narrative as a massive hoax on the part of some students to bring notoriety to the school. As a stringent requirement for their continued attendance at WA, all of the boys involved in the *Sons of Liberty* were required by the Board of Trustees to sign a non-disclosure agreement or face expulsion. All of the boys agreed to the reprieve.

Josh Easterly — through intense consultation with his mother's attorneys and the Board of Trustees as well as the local authorities — was transferred to another private school in Virginia, a stipulation which allowed him to avoid criminal prosecution for his leadership role in the *Sons of Liberty*. Rumors of preferential treatment and a behind-the-scenes deal for the Congresswoman's son swirled around the case, but nothing was ever proven.

On a related note, Heather Yates miraculously passed all of her classes during the fall semester, spent the spring semester in Italy on a study abroad scholarship, and was accepted to an Ivy League school the following year. Her academic records from Washington Academy remained under seal, and no news reports of her involvement in the events during that September would ever surface.

Walker was in George Washington University Hospital for nearly a month, healing from his wounds suffered in the tunnels below the immaculate campus. There was nothing immaculate, however, about the physical therapy he endured afterward, but he liked the strenuous activity. He hadn't felt this alive in a long time, and so he took full advantage of it, achieving a level of fitness he hadn't experienced since his time with the FBI. Walker was so committed to his complete recovery that the therapy worked its magic in even less time than his doctors could have predicted. In essence, the hospital stay had actually been a blessing for Walker as there was no alcohol, and he refused any pain medication. It made him stronger, both physically and mentally.

Mark Lewis had stopped in to see him every few days, sharing with him the most recent revelations from the ongoing investigation. The two bonded again as they worked out together in the training rooms, rekindling the friendship that had been lost. As the difficult recovery ebbed and flowed, Lewis also kept Walker laser-focused on the ultimate goal: getting back to his family. He was given a second chance, and he was not going to waste it.

In an ironic twist of fate, he actually owed his life to Dr. Ellis. After his revelatory conversation with the dean and the sprint to Meredith's residence, Walker had convinced Ellis that his career was effectively over and the circumstances surrounding Amanda's disappearance were odd enough to warrant a call to the FBI. It seemed Ellis had feared for Walker's safety, and so the FBI operator, knowing Mark Lewis was working the Washington Academy case, forwarded the call directly to him. Since Lewis was already in the final stages of a raid on the school, it was easy for Lewis to mobilize an elite strike team on short notice. They arrived at the campus quickly, and Ellis immediately confessed the details of his conversation with Walker. With Ellis able to direct Lewis to Meredith's residence, the SWAT team simply followed Walker's trail until they found him. An unlikely ending to a tragic story.

Meredith Thomas was charged with multiple counts of kidnapping, child endangerment, and attempted murder, but to avoid a lengthy and sensational public trial, federal prosecutors offered her a reduced sentence in exchange for being a confidential informant in prison. She pled guilty to lesser charges and began serving a sixteen-year sentence in the low-security female federal correctional facility in Alameda County, California. She would be eligible for parole in seven.

But there was more. The FBI raid was still on the schedule, so the next morning — as Walker was taken into his first of three surgeries and agents were still gathering evidence from the tunnels below campus — Lewis returned with over 100 agents. They seized all documents, databases, and video feeds related to their investigation of numerous illegal activities.

Not wanting to serve time in federal prison on multiple felony charges, Robert Ellis became the Northern Virginia Attorney General's Office star witness and took prosecutors through the complex money laundering, racketeering schemes, and organized crime elements of Washington Academy. Ellis retired from Washington Academy two weeks later, issuing a statement that assured the public his decision was a personal one, and not at all related to the embarrassing hoax that had been perpetrated on the school. His retirement package was sealed from public view by the Board of Trustees, in the interest of not poisoning the well in finding a suitable replacement, but included no severance pay nor retirement benefits.

An older couple moved into a 2,000 square feet rancher in Duluth, Minnesota the next day, and the paperwork for Mr. and Mrs. Kleckner's relocation as part of the Witness Protection Program was completed in the FBI's Minneapolis Field Office that afternoon.

CHAPTER 56

Lorenzo Arcuri's mansion on the Potomac was still breathtaking to Walker even though it was his second visit there. This time, however, Walker had requested the meeting with Arcuri to discuss his retirement. Amanda had been returned safely to her father, and after a planned three-month hiatus from school to recuperate from her trauma and attend counseling, she would return for the start of the second semester.

Walker was again led into the study and sat on the same sofa as before, but Arcuri entered from behind him instead and insisted he not get up. The two men exchanged the usual pleasantries, and Arcuri seemed genuinely concerned about Walker's condition, knowing full well that he had nearly given his life for his daughter. Arcuri was extremely grateful.

He handed Walker a slip of paper with a series of numbers on it. "I have arranged for an account to be established for you, my friend, offshore and untraceable, and payment for your services was wired there this morning. I know it's hard for men like us to walk away from what we do for a living, what we do best. But trust me, if you choose to leave this line of work, there's a substantial amount of money in that account, quite possibly all the money you will ever need. I can never thank you enough for what you did for my daughter and my family, so please accept this as a token of my eternal gratitude."

"Thank you, Lorenzo. I sincerely appreciate your generosity."

"Believe me, Ryan, it is the least I can do for you. You have brought my daughter back to me, against all odds and in perfect health. The emotional scars will take longer to heal, but she is doing quite well and is excited to return to school very soon. I could not have asked for anything more."

"Thank you," Walker said sincerely.

Arcuri leaned back on the sofa and simpered. "There's just one more thing. I am forever indebted to you, and so for as long as you walk this earth, my friend, please know that you will always be protected by the Arcuri family. I have already spoken to the leaders of the other families, and they understand as well. From this point forward, you are untouchable. Whatever you've done in the past, whomever you owe, all is forgiven. You are a free man."

Pausing for a long moment and staring at the huge smile on Arcuri's face, Walker knew the crime lord could easily back up his grandiose offer of protection, and from the sound of it, he already had. Walker leaned forward, "I don't know what to say, Lorenzo, I'm..."

Lorenzo interrupted. "No need, my friend. It's not often I can do things that I truly feel good about, but this is one of them, so no refusals. It's already done. You have my word."

"Thank you again, Lorenzo."

Satisfied the conversation had ended, Arcuri started to rise from the sofa, but Walker spoke again, "There's just one more thing I have to do."

Surprised by the statement, Arcuri — still standing — squinted at Walker.

Walker stayed seated, looked up at the crime boss, and spoke slowly. "When the FBI raided Washington Academy, they discovered droves of documents and digital files proving the existence of an extensive money-laundering operation involving an assortment of your shell companies and the tuition and fees flowing through the academy. On top of that, they found direct evidence of racketeering and fraud because the dean wasn't as good as you guys at covering your tracks. Ellis took a plea deal with the attorney general's office and walked agents through the myriad of transactions going back years."

Arcuri stood frozen, running through the potential scenarios in his mind, but finally making the realization there was simply too much evidence against him, remembering his various business dealings with the academy. Lorenzo had never liked the idea of conducting business through the private school, but his father and Ellis had been old friends, and so the arrangements remained even after Lorenzo had taken over the family business. His father had complete faith that the government would never go after the school because it was simply too high profile with its elite class of wealthy families, but he was wrong. And now, Lorenzo's least favorite business partner had become his Achilles heel.

"So what happens now?" Arcuri said softly, resigned to the fact that he was currently in the crosshairs of the United States Department of Justice. There was no easy escape from that fate, so he knew he had to accept it and determine a way out later. There was always a way out.

"Well, there are about 200 armed agents from the FBI, ATF, and DEA outside the walls of your compound right now. They are prepared to launch an assault if you decide to not go quietly. Or if you decide to kill me. We have a sniper in a helicopter over the river watching us right now."

Walker pulled an earpiece from his ear, and Arcuri could hear the crackling of radio traffic through the small device. Arcuri lowered his head as Walker pulled a packet of folded papers from his jacket pocket and slid the arrest warrant across the table toward him. "However, if you go quietly, ask your men to drop their weapons and surrender, it will go a long way with the prosecutors. You have my word on it." Walker paused, then added, "There's no reason for any bloodshed today."

Arcuri glanced down at the folded papers on the glass coffee table, glared at Walker to determine if he was bluffing, then looked out the window at the sprawling estate, his army of men with their weapons at the ready. He paused for several moments, the tension slowly strangling the room until Arcuri finally loosened the noose by smiling at Walker.

"I must say, Mr. Walker, you continue to impress me. Your perseverance is admirable, and you just won't stop until you've made it right, where everything is concerned. I hired you to find my little girl because deep down I knew you needed it, but whether or not you were looking for atonement, I think you may have found it."

Walker nodded as Arcuri held out his hands and Walker pulled a pair of handcuffs from his jeans. As the former FBI agent latched the metal clasps around Arcuri's wrists, the crime boss grinned again and said, "And please understand this does nothing to change our previous arrangement. You're still free. Take advantage of it."

Minutes later, Ryan Walker exited the front doors of the Arcuri family mansion as the main gates to the compound opened and dozens of federal agents — clad in SWAT gear or lettered windbreakers — swarmed onto the grounds of the estate, followed by unmarked vehicles, armored cars, and police cruisers. Walker moved confidently in the opposite direction as the phalanx of agents descended on the home. Arcuri's armed guards placed their rifles on the ground and raised their hands as law enforcement officers immediately surrounded them.

Walker exited through the open gates of the compound, and for the first time in as long as he could remember, he was proud of what he had done.

CHAPTER 57

The cherry trees that surrounded the Tidal Basin, just south of the National Mall in Washington, D.C., would not blossom for another five months. Their leaves were presently a dark orange color, loosened from their branches by a cool breeze swirling over the circular reservoir, a yellow hue cast over the glassy water by the rising sun from behind the trees.

Ryan Walker sat alone on a bench facing the basin, one of many on the wide sidewalks which encircled the D.C. landmark. He looked at the Jefferson Memorial across the expanse of water and breathed in the crisp November air. His hair was trimmed, his face was clean-shaven, and he wore a new dress shirt just for the occasion.

As he glanced to his left, two females approached, their arms locked, moving slowly toward his position. The woman on the left was slightly taller, her auburn hair radiated in the morning light. The second female was significantly younger, a teenager, but walked with a self-assured confidence built up over the many years of living without a father, he assumed.

Walker almost didn't recognize them — they had changed so much — but as they neared, their familiar faces were unmistakable.

As his wife and daughter took their final steps toward him, Walker could not help but smile at the possibility of a new beginning, his second chance to make it right with the two people he loved most in the world. But now, he was much stronger than before and his journey to start again would begin today.

AUTHOR'S NOTE

Thank you for reading *The Gilded Sanctum*. I sincerely hope you enjoyed my novel. If you have time to write a review, please know that it will be greatly appreciated.

Also, if you enjoyed *The Gilded Sanctum*, please visit my **website** and join my email list. You'll receive access to exclusive content, discounted offers, and sneak peeks of new releases ... including a FREE copy of ...

THE HOSTAGE: A Ryan Walker Short Story

Experience the dramatic, life-changing episode that started it all: the high-profile case referenced in *The Gilded Sanctum*. A congressman's son is kidnapped and a nation is captivated as a tense standoff unfolds in the western mountains of Virginia. Read the pulse-pounding prelude to *The Gilded Sanctum*.

Thanks again!

Keith

www.keithveverka.com

ABOUT THE AUTHOR

A social studies supervisor for a school district in Bucks County, Pennsylvania, Keith Veverka loves writing, history, and education; all of which came together for his first novel, *The Gilded Sanctum*.

Keith began his teaching career twenty-one years ago at a public school in Virginia, not far from the imagined location of the fictional academy in this story. Having lived and worked in the area for several years, he was intimately familiar with the state's rich Civil War history, which provided the perfect backdrop for this mystery thriller.

He lives in Warrington, Pennsylvania with his wife and children.

Learn more at www.keithveverka.com

Made in the USA
Coppell, TX
06 April 2021